Kyrenica

The Opal Mountains

Galandria

KORYNTH ★

ROWAN'S ROCK

Eleanor River

. Tyran

Tulan.
Versan,
GOSSAMER FALLS

Lyrisia• ★ ALLEGRIA

The Weeping Forest

Azarlin

The Lonesome Sea

D0446917

To Logan and Chloe.

The world is a better place because you two are in it.

Books published by Running Press are available at special discounts for bulk purchases in
the United States by corporations, institutions, and other organizations. For more information, please contact the Special Markets Department at the Perseus Books Group,
2300 Chestnut Street, Suite 200, Philadelphia, PA 19103, or call (800) 810-4145, ext.
5000, or e-mail special.markets@perseusbooks.com.

ISBN 978-0-7624-5422-8
Library of Congress Control Number: 2014946596

E-book ISBN 978-0-7624-5552-2

9   8   7   6   5   4   3   2   1
Digit on the right indicates the number of this printing

Cover and interior design by T.L. Bonaddio
Edited by Marlo Scrimizzi
Typography: Berling, Lavanderia, and Trade Gothic

Published by Running Press Teens
An Imprint of Running Press Book Publishers
A Member of the Perseus Books Group
2300 Chestnut Street
Philadelphia, PA 19103–4371

Visit us on the web!
www.runningpress.com/kids

The Opal Crown

JENNY LUNDQUIST

RP | TEENS
PHILADELPHIA · LONDON

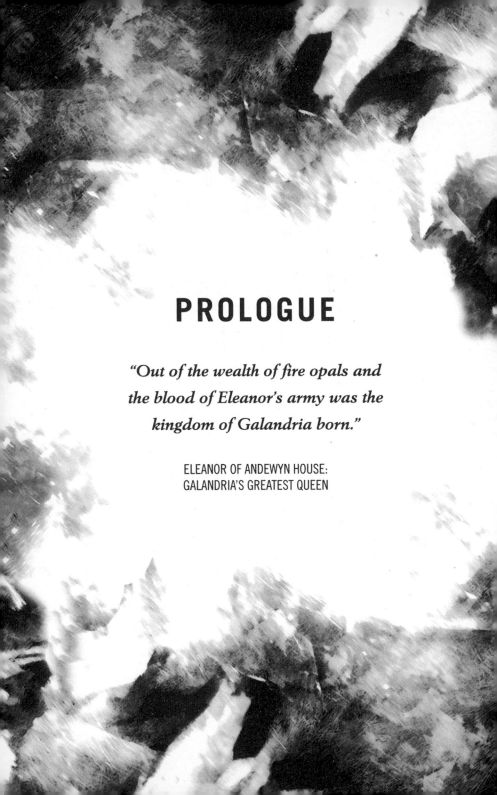

PROLOGUE

"Out of the wealth of fire opals and the blood of Eleanor's army was the kingdom of Galandria born."

ELEANOR OF ANDEWYN HOUSE:
GALANDRIA'S GREATEST QUEEN

*K*ing Fennrick lies in his bed, cursing the spoiled meat that has rendered him bedridden. He has never cared for being alone and has always loved the glittering thrum of the royal court. Solitude gives a man too much time to think, and if there is one thing King Fennrick tries not to do, it is think too deeply. For when he does, the shadows he keeps at bay through forced gaiety slip past his guard and creep toward him.

One day, he supposes, those shadows will strangle him.

Fennrick hollers for more ale and leans back on his silken pillows, dreaming of the amber liquid and the oblivion it will grant him. Oblivion is not the same thing as absolution, but on dark nights like these, it is close enough.

His golden bed curtains are swept aside. It is not his cup-bearer who appears, but his son. He carries a steaming mug of foul-smelling muck, and Fennrick is sorely tempted to throw the boy out.

"I asked for ale," the king says through gritted teeth.

"Tea is better for your stomach, Father," Andrei Andewyn replies.

Fennrick stares at the boy. This is his son. Has he ever loved him? Is it possible to love someone who never should have been born? Fennrick forced his wife—a woman whom he truly *did* love—to conceive a child, when her soul was already broken. He is responsible for her death, though he suspects the boy blames himself.

Andrei stares back at the man who has broken his heart every day of his life. This is his father. Has he ever loved him? Is it possible to love someone who looks right through you, as though a ghost has always stood behind? Andrei looks down at his hands—hands that will one day rule a kingdom—and wonders how he is supposed to become a king when his father won't even teach him how to be a man.

Grudgingly, Fennrick sips the tea and bitter warmth floods his stomach. But he is clumsy and thick-fingered. The mug drops and the tea spills; a dark, spreading stain recedes into the shadows.

Perhaps the tea is slowly working through his stupor; or perhaps King Fennrick has just had a clear thought, all on his very own: It will not just be the crown Andrei inherits, but Fennrick's sins as well.

He beckons his son forward, and begins whispering of the night that shattered his own soul.

A frigid draft creeps into the room. Candles flicker; bed curtains flutter. Andrei's shocked stare locks with Fennrick's weary one.

"Twins?" Andrei whispers.

Fennrick, for once looking his son directly in his eyes, nods.

And the shadows, released from their bindings, come slithering toward them both.

PART ONE

*"As she established the laws of her kingdom,
Eleanor gathered together her Guardians,
and decreed that the opal crown should always
pass to the firstborn of the reigning monarch.
And so it has ever been."*

ELEANOR OF ANDEWYN HOUSE:
GALANDRIA'S GREATEST QUEEN

CHAPTER 1

WILHA

*E*very day I tell myself I should be happy with the life I have chosen. I have fled the gilded walls of my former existence. A life filled with everything anyone could ever want, save for true friendship and love. I walked away from all of it—me, the girl so many others always believed to be fearful and incompetent—and built another life.

As I wrap my thick winter cloak about me, I look around the small bedroom I rent above the Sleeping Dragon. I remind myself that it is paid for by the fruits of my own labor. That I am free to come and go as I please. Free to show my face to the world. Perhaps more than most people, I understand these things are riches beyond measure.

I grab a handful of klarents off my writing desk and count them. It is not much, but it should be enough to pay Marko tonight.

I lock the door to my room and head for the staircase. Downstairs the inn is full, even on such a gelid night—just as I hoped. A group of weather-beaten fishermen hunch over the bar, trying to chase away winter's chill with mugs of ale. Musicians play near the fireplace while the towns-people dance. Victor, the owner, patrols the length of the inn, making sure the festivities do not get out of hand. James is serving a table of men and women, all of whom are wearing costume masks.

Victor scowls when he sees me. "You know I can't spare James tonight. Do you have to visit the castle gates again?"

"I have been living in Korynth for nearly six months now," I remind him. "I think I can manage the streets just fine by myself."

Victor crosses his arms over his massive chest. "One would think you purposely choose our busiest nights to watch the Masked Princess appear on the balcony."

I pause, for he is right. I choose the nights James cannot possibly accompany me. "I will not be too late, Victor, I promise."

I turn away, but stop at James's voice. "Willie, can you wait a moment?"

"Yes?" I turn around, hoping my frustration does not show. I had hoped to slip outside without him noticing.

He shifts uneasily. "I wanted to ask you something."

I force myself to smile. "Ask away."

My heart trumpets an anxious tune. All week, James has been working himself up to ask me something. I am quite sure I know exactly what it is.

I glance around the crowded inn. Surely he would not ask me here, in front of everyone?

"Stay and have dinner with me?" he says. "We've barely seen each other all week."

"I told a few girls from the dress shop I would meet them at the castle gates," I say, hating myself for the lie. "I have to go—I am late as it is."

"If you insist on going, then let me talk to Victor. Maybe he can spare me for an hour or so."

"I already spoke with Victor," I say quickly. "He said he could not. Just let me go see the Masked Princess, and when I return we can have dinner together."

James sighs. "I just don't understand why you feel the need to watch the barbarian princess wave from her balcony so often."

"She is not a *barbarian*, James. She's a Galandrian. You know I do not like it when you use that slur."

"You're right. I'm sorry, Willie." James leans in for a kiss, but I turn away. "People are watching," I say.

James turns back, and the fishermen at the bar raise their mugs in mock salute. "That wouldn't have bothered you last summer," he says, frowning.

"I will be back soon," I say, ignoring his unspoken question. I head for the door and with one last wave, step outside and start up the street.

The sky is mottled with patches of deepening gray. Icicles hang from the rooftops. Men and women hunch forward in thick cloaks, propelled up the street by a frigid wind. Many of them wear costume masks and carry candles. My breath plumes white smoke as I blow on my hands, trying to keep my fingers from going numb. I could go back to the Sleeping Dragon and retrieve my forgotten gloves, but I do not want to face James again.

Because in his words lurks the truth. Last summer, after walking away from a life behind walls, nothing bothered me. Colors seemed brighter, music seemed sweeter, and my heart thrummed from the knowledge that James wanted to be with *me*, and not the Masked Princess. I wanted nothing more than to dance the nights away in the inn and pass the days at Galina's dress shop, talking with my friend Kyra.

But all too soon, the days grew shorter. Summer faded, and after a brief autumn, winter set in. Kyra met a boy named Damek and married him a few weeks later. They live in the countryside now, in his home village. In her last letter, Kyra told me she suspected she was with child.

As the cold has deepened, something within me has changed. So many small things put me in a bad temper, and I cannot share my thoughts with anyone. None save Elara, but during our carefully planned visits she is usually in too much of a frenzy to listen.

When the crowd reaches the west side of the city, I turn up the street heading away from the castle. The street deadends, and I turn once again into a back alley that is ripe with the stench of rotting fish. On an overturned crate sits a glowing lantern, the candle within flickering in the blustery night. A man waits nearby. Upon seeing me, he unsheathes his sword. He steps forward, a grim look on his face—and offers me the hilt.

"You're late," Marko says as I take the sword from him. "If you insist on meeting in secret, at least have the decency to show up on time."

"I am only five minutes late."

"That's still late." He holds out his hand and wiggles his fingers.

I remove the klarents from my cloak and hand them to him. While he counts the coins, I warm up with the sword; the blade makes a satisfying *whoosh* as it cuts the night air. A loud cheer erupts in the distance; Elara must be making her appearance on the balcony. After Marko stuffs the klarents away, he produces a sword of his own.

"Difficult to train in the dark," he says. "Don't know why we can't meet during the day."

"I work during the day." I take my position and wait. He raises his sword, attacks, and we begin to spar.

It was not easy, locating a sword master who was willing to secretly train me. Yet some of the regulars at the Sleeping Dragon have proven more than willing to introduce me to their friends.

Marko is retired, but said to be one of the best sword masters in Korynth. For months I have been continuing the lessons I began with Patric in Allegria. I may have fled my life as the Masked Princess, but my memories remain.

For weeks after the masquerade, I dreamed of Lord Murcendor. Dreamed of him unsheathing his sword and offering me a choice: marriage or death.

Until I decided I needed to do something to stem the tide of fear that threatened to overwhelm me on those nights when I awoke in a panic. I train with Marko a few nights a week. And late at night in my room, while a choir of drunken carousing rises from downstairs, I practice with the wooden sword I keep hidden under my bed. It keeps my nightmares at bay, while reminding me to never forget that Lord Murcendor is still out in the world somewhere, living in exile.

While Marko and I train, my heart thrums and my breathing becomes labored. The night no longer seems cold and biting, but alive with anticipation and promise as Marko and I whirl and spin.

"You're growing stronger," Marko says when we stop to take a break. "Bolder. And that is good. Now I want to show you a new guard. To start, take your sword in front of your body and point it downward. See"—he moves into position, the hilt pressing near his belly, and the tip pointing at the muddy ground—"this will invite your opponent to attack your upper quarters. But when he does, you will lift up"—he demonstrates with a quick, upward drive—"and knock his sword away from him. He will then be open, and you are to go on the offensive."

He invites me to attack. I do, and Marko quickly thrusts

upward, knocking my blade away. His sword is now poised at my shoulder, in perfect position to deliver a crippling cut.

"As you can see, it is a deceptive position."

Marko has me practice until he grudgingly tells me I am not half bad.

"That is high praise indeed, coming from you." I smile.

"Don't get used to it. This is not a game. When an actual opponent comes for you, he is not jousting. He means to kill you."

My smile vanishes. "Believe me," I say. "I shall remember."

*M*arko leaves after our lesson has concluded. Light snow begins to fall as I walk through the silent alley. I should get back to the inn, back to James and my promise of a late dinner, but instead I am drawn to the Kyrenican Castle. A few townspeople still linger at the gates, stamping their feet against the cold and speculating over King Ezebo's health. I see a window glowing with soft, buttery candlelight, and wonder what Elara is doing right this very minute.

A few weeks have passed since our last meeting. It did not go well. The request she made of me still sits in my stomach like a bitter tonic.

I move on to the Broken Statue. It is aptly named, for it is a white stone statue of my own great-great-grandmother Queen Rowan, and it is indeed broken. Her head lies in front of her feet, as though she was beheaded. "When you escaped from the Kyrenican Castle, did it ever occur to you not to go back to Galandria?" I say, crouching down to look into her stone gaze. Yet even as I speak, I realize it is a ridiculous question. Rowan the Brave was a strong queen. Not a terrified princess who ran away from her own life.

The storm begins in earnest and soon snow frosts my cloak. But still I stay, all too aware I am purposefully avoiding returning to James.

When I can no longer stand the cold, I rise and walk slowly back to the inn, reminding myself that I am free, and this is the life I have chosen.

CHAPTER 2

ELARA

Masks are useful when you have things to hide.

This was something I didn't understand when I first donned Wilha's opal-encrusted mask. I saw it only as a confining, stifling thing, and overlooked its benefits entirely. It has taken me some time to understand that the jeweled masks are a powerful, impenetrable weapon. A glittering guard that never drops.

One that will keep my secrets.

Now, I purposely select the most ornate mask from Wilha's collection for my midnight engagement. It's painted gold and crimson, with multihued opals swirling along the cheeks and forehead, matching my golden brocade dress.

It is my hope that by covering myself with so much gilt, Stefan will not notice the anguish I can no longer keep from showing in my eyes.

All is silent as I step out of my chambers and into the corridor. I cross my arms against the bitter chill that seeps through the walls of the castle and hurry through the dimly lit halls, unconcerned about being spotted by a passing servant or guard.

This is what months of lying has bought me: the ability to move freely about the castle at my own leisure.

In the kitchen, Stefan is seated in our usual spot by the fire. Two crystal goblets and a plate filled with slices of spice cake sit on the small wooden table in front of him.

I watch him silently. Shadows cast by the firelight dance along his face; his eyes are troubled and tired as he looks into the flames. Stefan used to serve with the Kyrenican navy, and after so many nights of being lulled to sleep by the sea, he no longer sleeps well on dry ground. Many nights he walks the halls of the castle until dawn. Lately I've been joining him in the kitchen, as I've also found it increasingly difficult to sleep.

My secrets will not allow me rest.

"How long are you going to stand there before announcing yourself?" he says, not looking away from the flames.

I detach myself from the shadows and cross the room. He leans into me, his fingers wrap around my waist, and he rests his forehead against my stomach.

"How is the king?" I ask, putting my arms around him.

Stefan's voice is muffled. "His physician is hopeful the worst is over. Though of course, that is exactly what he said last month."

Ezebo, the king of Kyrenica and Stefan's father, was thrown from his horse a few months ago. It was a nasty fall. Ezebo has not recovered well; he has spent most of the winter bedridden and weak. The duties of running the kingdom have gradually fallen to Stefan. While we all await Ezebo's fate, the fearful thought has crossed my mind: Will I marry a prince this summer? Or a king?

"He'll be all right." I knead Stefan's tense shoulders. "We'll *all* be all right. Winter will end and spring will come. And we'll be all right."

"I am better already now that you are here." He pulls back and looks up at me. "Would you take your mask off, just for a minute?"

"A servant could see," I say quickly. "And your father has always wished for me to wear it." It's a dirty trick, mentioning Ezebo, but a necessary one.

Stefan sighs. "You are right, of course. But when I am king I will not—" He breaks off as the implication of what he's just said dawns on him. "Anyway . . . mask or not, I'm glad you came." He flashes a weak smile. "I love you."

My stomach tightens, and I know he wishes I would return his words. But I won't. I can't. I'm not sure if I love Stefan; I'm not sure I even know what real love looks like. And this, at least, is one lie I will not tell.

"You should try to get some sleep," I say.

Stefan's face falls slightly, but his disappointment is quickly replaced by wearied concern. "These are for you." He gestures to the slices of spice cake. "You hardly touched your dinner tonight—all week, in fact. Are you unwell?"

A lump rises in my throat. Stefan notices so many details. Too many. "I'm fine." I pick up a slice of cake and force myself to choke down a bite.

"What do you know about horses?" he asks suddenly, rubbing his temples.

Such a simple question. And yet it's one I could easily answer wrong. What *does* Wilhamina Andewyn, the famous Masked Princess, know about horses?

"Horses?" I ask, stalling for time.

"Yes. Father was going to purchase one for Ruby's birthday next month. He has asked me to take care of it. I seem to recall being told you had a stable full of your own horses in Allegria, did you not?"

This is new information to me, and I make a mental note to ask Wilha about her horses the next time I see her. I take a large bite of cake—ignoring my stomach's queasy protests—in order to prevent having to answer right away.

Why don't you just tell him the truth?

The voice comes from somewhere deep inside; it's one I've had to stuff away more and more often. I quickly remind myself why the truth isn't an option: Stefan would never forgive me, I'll be hanged as a traitor, and the entire world would come looking for Wilha. So I will have ruined her life, as well as forfeited my own.

"I'm afraid I don't personally know a lot about horses. My father purchased them without consulting me," I say, hoping this is close to the truth.

Stefan leans back in his chair and nods, seemingly too

tired to pursue the matter further.

"Do you have a story for me tonight?" I ask, hoping to change the subject. "Tell me more about your time with the Kyrenican navy."

Stefan shakes his head and grins. "Nope, I've shared enough about my travels. Tell me one of your stories about Tulan."

During our nights by the fire, we pass the time telling tales. He tells me of his adventures on the Lonesome Sea. In return, I tell him of my own life in Tulan. Of course, I pretend they're just ramblings I heard from a maid who served me in the Opal Palace.

Tonight I tell him of a day when I was still quite young, and Cordon and I came upon a tree that had fallen across the Eleanor River.

"And then he dared Elara to walk across the tree and cross over, despite the fact that the rapids were fierce. . . ." Stefan's eyes have closed, his hand is propped under his chin, and I wonder if tonight he'll finally get the rest he deserves.

I know it's dangerous using my own name, but it slipped out one night. The night Stefan first said *I love you*. Not, *I intend to love you*, but simply, *I love you*. In return, though he will never know it, I offered him my own name, and my own life, disguised as a story.

Stefan's eyes pop open. "And did she do it? Did she cross?"

"Of course. She was quite spirited and never one to refuse a dare."

"Sounds like someone else I know." He grins.

I pause, and wonder if he's becoming suspicious. But I see only a weary playfulness in his eyes and continue. "Halfway across she fell in. Her foot became wedged between some stones, and Cordon had to jump in to save her. Her dress had torn, though, and when she returned to the lady of the manor, she was crying and said, *'I'm sorry, Mama. . . .'*" My throat swells as I remember. "And . . . and the lady replied, *'Mama? I'm not your mama, you filthy brat. I'm your mistress.'*"

I stop there. I don't want to finish the story; it ends with a beating and a warning to never, ever call Mistress *Mama* ever again. Up until then, I had always believed I was her daughter. A less-loved, harder-worked daughter than her precious Serena. But a daughter, nevertheless.

A sleepy page enters the kitchen and startles us both. He hands Stefan a small roll of parchment. "I'm sorry, Your Highness. We have just received an important message for the king. But when I brought it to His Highness's chambers he was sleeping. The queen was at his bedside and asked that I deliver it to you."

"Thank you." Stefan begins reading. "It's from Sir Reinhold."

"It would be nice if it was good news for a change," I say, turning to the fire. Ever since Sir Reinhold, Kyrenica's ambassador to Galandria, returned to Allegria, he's sent several messages of the growing unrest in the capitol. I bear little love for my homeland, but I still can't fathom how the glimmering, opal-flecked city of Allegria can be declining so fast.

"Wilha?"

I look away from the flames. Stefan's face is ashen.

"What's wrong? It's more bad news?"

"It seems the whole world is going mad." He turns and addresses the page. "Please rouse my father's advisors and tell them I wish to meet in the great hall. Tell them it's urgent."

"Of course, Your Highness."

After the boy bows himself from the room, Stefan reaches for my hand and reads the letter aloud.

And I understand that the news I've just heard has the power to change everything.

CHAPTER 3

ELARA

"*S*he's in shock," Milly says.

"Wilha." Stefan raises his voice slightly, as though I'm a child. "Come and sit by the fire."

I let him lead me to an armchair. I'm only vaguely aware that Stefan has brought me back to my chambers and awoken Milly, my maid, who promptly burst into tears upon hearing the news.

"I'll see to the princess," Milly is saying to Stefan.

Stefan kneels before me. "I have to meet with my father's advisors." He takes my hands in his. "But as soon as I can, I will return." He frowns and turns away. I hear Milly telling him that I'm mute with grief.

In truth, I am not in shock, nor do I feel any grief. I feel . . . nothing. My mind is racing ahead, calculating what's required of me.

I arrive at this conclusion: Wilha must be told. As soon as possible.

❧

*T*he next morning, Stefan is still in meetings. After a solitary breakfast, I hasten back to my room and remove a crimson-colored gown with silver embroidery from my wardrobe. I take my dagger and dig at the shiny stitches until they tear and unravel.

"Milly," I call. "Please have a carriage prepared. I want to visit the city."

Milly appears in the doorway. "It's freezing outside."

I command my chin to tremble and my eyes to water as I hold out my dress. "I've been needing to get this fixed. Rather than having a maid attend to it I thought . . ." I let my tears spill onto my cheeks. "I thought I would take care of it myself."

Sad kindness fills Milly's eyes—and shame tugs at my belly, but I quickly push it away. The lie is necessary. Wilha must be told.

"A jaunt into the city may do you well," she says, and leaves.

When Milly returns with word that the carriage is ready, I leave my chambers. I pass a scullery maid, who looks at me with knowing eyes. A guard offers me his deepest regrets. Word has already gotten out, then. I pick up my pace; I want Wilha to hear the news firsthand, before the servants' chatter spreads through the city.

I tell the driver where I wish to go, and he urges the horses onward. The streets are mostly deserted and covered in an icy slush from the snow last night, making it difficult for the carriage to move forward over the slippery cobblestones. The tall wooden buildings in Korynth bottleneck into a chimney; smoke spirals from each one we pass. Between the woodsmoke and the morning fog blanketing the city it's difficult to see more than a few feet ahead.

The carriage comes to a halt outside the dress shop. The guards alert the staff to our arrival. The seamstresses walk outside and curtsy in my direction, but not before I see their expressions, irritated that I'm forcing them to stand outside in the bitter cold. It's necessary, though. Wilha and I have both agreed that we cannot be seen standing next to each other, even though I'm wearing the mask. It's too much of a risk, and we need time to speak privately, without fear of being overheard.

"Tell the guards I wish to treat the women to a hot meal." I hand the driver a fistful of klarents. "I may require more time than usual today."

Wilha waits inside, her face wary as she curtsies, and I wonder if she's thinking of our earlier disagreement. I hand her the dress and she paints a smile on her face as she accepts it. This too is necessary, in case any of the guards are watching through the windows.

"I have news."

Instantly, she tenses up. "What is it? Has someone discovered—"

"No, it's not that. But we must come away from the window."

Wilha nods and sweeps her hand wide, as though she's inviting me deeper into the room. I look around at the full-length mirror, the overstuffed couch, and the shelves that are tightly packed with rolls of fabric, spools of thread, and dresses in various stages of alteration. I try to think of the best way to tell her.

I decide it's best to be direct. "I came here," I say, "because King Fennrick is dead."

CHAPTER 4

WILHA

"*D*ead?" The panic that someone has finally discovered our deception leaks away, and is replaced by shock. "Our father is dead?"

"*Your* father is dead." Elara wears a tailored black cloak over a dark purple gown embroidered with black stitching. Her mask is black, with milky lavender opals dripping down the cheeks. Dressed this way, she almost looks to be in mourning. Yet Elara's feelings about our father are quite clear. For all I know, underneath her painted mask she rejoices at his death.

"What happened?" I say, sinking down on a couch.

"What do you mean?" She frowns. "He's dead."

"*How* did he die, Elara? Was there an accident? Did he fall ill? Or did someone . . ." I imagine last year inside the Galandria Courthouse, watching him writhe in pain, an arrow lodged in his cheek.

"Oh," Elara says. "It was bad meat. According to the message Stefan received, several fell ill in the Opal Palace. Fennrick seemed to be getting better, but took a turn for the worse. The cook has been hanged."

I lean back against the couch and close my eyes. I said good-bye to my father—in my heart, if not in person—when

I left Galandria last year. Yet still, that is a vastly different good-bye than death.

"What is the protocol for when a Galandrian king dies?" Elara asks.

"A new king will immediately be proclaimed—Andrei," I say slowly. "He will be under the protection of the Guardian Council until he comes of age." My heart lurches at the thought of Andrei alone, with no one to guide him except our father's advisors. "Plans will be made for his coronation. It will be in the summer most likely, when the weather is better."

"Will I be required to attend?"

I read the anxiety in Elara's eyes and finally understand the true purpose of her visit. She cares not that the man who gave her life is dead. First and foremost she wants to understand what these events will mean for *her*.

"I think not." I blink hard at the pressure building behind my eyes. I pick up a needle and set about repairing the stitches in her dress, trying to calm myself. "Andrei and I were mostly kept separate as children; we are strangers more than siblings, so I do not think he will extend an invitation. But you will want to send a message offering him your support."

Elara exhales loudly. "I had wondered if Andrei would be able to tell the difference if I went back to Galandria." She looks into the mirror as she speaks, gazing at her own masked reflection, and I have to tamp down a flood of irritation. Does she spare no thought whatsoever for our father?

Elara glances at me in the mirror and our gazes hold. "All he was to me," she says sharply, as though she has read my mind, "was the man who sentenced me to life with the Ogdens."

"He could just as easily had you slaughtered in your cradle," I burst out, tears spilling down my cheeks. "Many men would have and not spared it a second thought. His efforts were—"

"His efforts were far from sufficient," she says. "So wipe the disgust off your face."

"But do you not feel any—"

"There's nothing wrong with how I feel! And who are you to lecture me? Fennrick was dead to you the moment you decided you no longer wished to be Wilhamina Andewyn. That was a choice *you* made, not me."

My tears continue to fall and I nod miserably, for I know she's right.

Elara sighs, picks up a small embroidered handkerchief, and hands it to me. "Here."

While I wipe my eyes, she reaches out and touches my shoulder awkwardly, and I know she's trying to be a sister—something that doesn't come easily to either of us.

"Thank you," I say.

She smiles sadly, and I wonder if she's thinking, as I am, what it would have been like if we'd been allowed a whole childhood of small moments like these.

I return to my stitching, repairing the damage Elara has done to her own dress.

"Apparently you had a stable full of your own horses," Elara says, breaking the silence. "What breeds of horses did you own? And what was the name of your favorite horse?"

"Thoroughbreds, mostly. And her name was Hadley." I yank out a stitch that looks a bit crooked. I had hoped we could avoid this part of our visit today.

It galls me that Elara—while staunchly refusing to claim any kinship with the Andewyns—simultaneously feels she has a right to every detail of my life in Galandria, and has quizzed me exhaustively on my likes and dislikes, my memories, and what occurred on the days I attended court. She's asked me many questions about Andrei (though since we were raised separately, I can rarely answer them). Once she even went so far as to inquire about Patric and the exact nature of our relationship.

It was the only time I refused her an answer.

"What about the last time you saw Andrei?" she says. "When I pretended to be you, that last night in the Opal Palace, he did not attend your farewell dinner or come to say good-bye. If I need to write him a letter, I want to know how you parted."

A memory surfaces of the last time I saw Andrei. The impassive look on his face as he watched our father writhe in pain. *"If Father dies, does that mean I get to be king?"*

"I do not remember the last time I spoke to him," I say, concentrating on my stitching. "The memory escapes me."

"Have you given any thought to our last conversation?"

"Must we speak of this now?" I finish stitching and thrust the dress back at her. "Here."

"You didn't want to speak of it a few weeks ago. You know we can't both continue living in Korynth. It's dangerous, and if we're not careful, we'll get caught. One of us needs to leave the city."

"Fine, then. Why don't *you* leave?"

"That's impossible and you know it. The Masked Princess—and soon-to-be member of the Kyrenican royal family—belongs here in the city. You, on the other hand, are free to settle wherever you like."

"I have a life here." I force myself to add, "A life I am happy with."

"As do I—a life you *asked me* to assume. But I can't live it, not the way I want to, with you still here in the city. One day I shall have to take this mask off. And when I do, don't you think someone is bound to notice that I look exactly like the local seamstress? What then? Stefan keeps asking me to take it off." She sighs. "I refuse him only because of you."

"Does it matter to him at all that you are a Galandrian and he is a Kyrenican?" I ask, thinking of James and the horrible things he sometimes says about the people of my homeland.

"Of course not." She looks at me sympathetically. "How is James?"

I shrug. "Sometimes when I am with him I feel so horrible. It feels as though I am just . . ."—I search for the right words, and remember something Elara herself once said—"as though I am just playing a role."

"Everyone plays a role," Elara retorts. "Your job is to figure out which one is yours."

"But we *lie*, Elara. Every day we lie. To James. To Stefan. Does it not bother you?"

Her face hardens. "Leave the city. Then I can build a future with Stefan free of lies."

"But you shall always come to him claiming *my* past. That in itself is a lie. Does it not bother you?"

In answer, Elara picks up her dress and leaves.

I do not sidestep James's hug that evening when I return to the inn. I lean into him, savoring the feel of his arms around me.

"I've missed this," he murmurs into my hair. "I've missed *you*."

"I know," I say, hugging him tightly. "Me, too."

After he releases me, he resumes filling the mugs and pushes them across the bar to the fishermen waiting.

"Tonight we celebrate!" says a man, and they all raise their glasses and drink.

James pours another round and hands me a mug. I slide onto an empty stool. Instead of practicing alone in my room tonight, I think I would rather be here, where it is festive.

"What are we celebrating?" I ask.

"Didn't you hear?" James says. "King Fennrick is dead."

I put my mug down quickly, fighting the urge to be sick.

"What's wrong?" James asks.

"You are celebrating a man's death."

"King Fennrick wasn't a man. He was—"

"He had a *family*," I interrupt, not wanting to hear whatever insult James was about to hurl. "He had people who cared for him, people who would have liked to see him one last—" I break off, aware that my voice is rising and people are looking.

Pressure is building again behind my eyes—tears I will not be able to explain. I push back my stool and head for the stairs. "I'm not feeling that well. I'll see you tomorrow, okay?"

"Willie, I'm sorry," James calls. "Please don't go."

Don't call me Willie! I want to scream as he follows me up the stairs. When I reach my door, James grabs my hand and pulls me back to him. "Willie, wait. Tell me what's wrong. I know it's not just the death of a foreign king. Something's been bothering you for weeks. Whatever it is, you can tell me."

"I—" The words are on the tip of my tongue. *I am Wilhamina Andewyn, the daughter of the barbarian king you despised.* "I have just had a long day at the dress shop." I open my door. "I'm sure I will feel better in the morning."

"If you say so." James frowns. "But I wish you would just talk to me. You can tell me anything. You know that, right?"

After he has gone I lock my door behind me and lie down on my bed. I release the tears I have been holding in and cry. I cry for the father who was not cruel, but who was also not kind. For the man I wanted to know, but who never wanted to know me in return.

Finally, I cry for all the lies I have told.

CHAPTER 5

ELARA

Wilha has tied my hands.

She can't simply walk away from her life—tell me to take it instead—then continue living in the city, only a few miles from the castle. Does she expect me to wear the mask forever? Will I have to hide my face from my own children one day, for fear that they may glimpse Wilha on the streets of Korynth?

Doesn't she realize that the role I play every day is what allows her to go on with her new, nonroyal life? Yet it's obvious she resents me asking her questions about her life— questions whose answers I desperately need—if I am to maintain the charade and keep us both safe.

She barely contained her annoyance when I asked about Andrei. Aren't I entitled to know at least *a little* about my own brother? While it's impossible to accept Astrid and Fennrick as my parents, not after the choice they made, Andrei is innocent; my existence has been kept secret from him. I can't help but have questions about him—questions Wilha seems disinclined to ever answer.

Somehow, I must make her see reason, and I resolve to visit her again soon.

But the opportunity doesn't present itself. One snowstorm

after another pummels the city, and business in Korynth nearly comes to a halt. Finally, the snow gives way to a month of pounding, sleeting rain and frigid winds. Tempers in the castle run short, and I think I might go mad from so many days of being trapped inside.

When Ruby's birthday party arrives, fires are lit in every room, the floors are scrubbed, the rugs beaten, and every noble family in Korynth is invited to the castle to celebrate, not just Ruby's birthday, but the passing of winter.

Ruby is delighted by the thoroughbred Stefan purchased for her, and laughs gaily when she finds a klarent hidden in her slice of cake—a Kyrenican tradition, which is a sign of good things to come. While cake is served to the rest of the guests, I hurry to my room for my gift to Ruby.

On the way back, I run into Stefan's mother, Genevieve, who has just returned from a quick visit to Ezebo's chambers.

"How is he?" I say.

"A little stronger today." Genevieve smiles wanly. She's an elegant-looking woman and a kind queen, but today deep circles line her eyes.

I hug her briefly. "He'll be better soon."

"He will. And I'm so sorry, Wilha. With all that's been going on I feel I have not comforted you well over your father's death."

"That's quite all right," I say, and for the briefest of moments, feel I might start crying. Not out of grief for

Fennrick, but over the kindness Genevieve has always offered me—and the fact that I don't deserve any of it.

"Is that it?" she asks, gesturing to the silken bundle in my hands. After I nod, she says, "Are you sure you want to give it to her?"

"Yes, absolutely. Ruby eyes it every time she visits my chambers."

"That is truly generous of you, Wilha. Ruby will be delighted by your gift."

I smile back at her, but it requires effort. Every time she calls me Wilha, it feels as though someone's punched a hole in my chest.

Genevieve puts her arm around my waist, and together we enter the great hall. Stefan is surrounded by a circle of Ezebo's advisors—as he often is these days—and looks annoyed. The rest of the guests watch Ruby unwrap her birthday presents. Genevieve and I join Leandra and Eudora, the dowager queen. Genevieve winks when she takes her place in between me and Eudora, as she knows the two of us rarely get along.

"Wilha," Leandra whispers as Ruby unwraps a new saddle. "What did you say was the name of your horse in Galandria?"

"Um . . ." What did Wilha say when I asked her? I step away and offer Ruby my present.

"Well?" Leandra says when I return.

"It was . . . Adley," I say, remembering just in time.

Ruby gives an excited squeal. "Look!" She holds up one of my jeweled masks and presses it to her face. "Now I look like Wilha!"

"In a few years it will fit better," I say. "Perhaps one day your parents will throw a masquerade ball for you."

I glance over at Stefan and see he's glowering back at me.

"What's wrong?" I ask as Ruby continues unwrapping more presents.

"Of all the things in the world, you had to give her a mask? It is not a toy, Wilha." He glances at Ruby. "I would never speak an ill word about your parents, but I would never sentence our child to such a fate as to wear a mask."

Stefan has been in a foul mood for days and has not been pleasant to be around. "I just thought—"

"Prince Stefan?" says a page who has just materialized, "Forgive me, but a messenger has just arrived from Galandria and asks to speak to you, as well as the king and queen."

"No doubt he brings word of Allegria's continued decline," Eudora cackles joyfully, making it a point to look at me as she speaks.

"Eudora, please," Genevieve says, casting a worried glance my way.

I dig my hands into my palms, determined to keep my mouth shut and not ruin Ruby's day. Eudora—shrew that she is—never misses an opportunity to mention her hatred of Galandrians in my presence.

"We shall come immediately," Genevieve answers. "Stefan, it is not unusual for a new king to send greetings to foreign rulers. We should . . ." Their voices trail off as they leave the great hall.

After Ruby finishes opening presents, she announces she'd like to play a game of hide-and-seek and asks me to join in.

"Of course," I say, glad for an excuse to get away from Eudora.

I leave the great hall and climb a staircase. After some twists and turns down the corridors, I hear footsteps behind me. I look back and see Leandra.

"Do you want to hide together?" I'm fond of both of Stefan's younger sisters. But I haven't grown as close to Leandra, as her formal manner is slightly off-putting.

"No," she answers, frowning. "I only wanted to ask you something."

"Yes?"

"Well . . ." Leandra squints as though she's thinking very hard. "It is just that you said your horse's name was Adley."

"And?" We enter Ezebo's study, and I look around for a suitable hiding spot.

"But a few days ago you told Mother your horse's name was *Hadley*. With an H."

"It *was* Hadley," I say, realizing that of course she's right. "You just misunderstood me."

"No, I do not think I did. You seem to do these types of things quite often."

I stop and look at her, the game of hide-and-seek forgotten. "What types of things?"

"You constantly forget things. Sometimes you answer a question one way, and then another way the next time. Or you answer the question incorrectly."

"Incorrectly," I repeat, feeling my heart spiral downward. I pull the door closed behind us and gesture for Leandra to join me behind a thick wall hanging, as though I don't want us to be found, which is true enough.

"What do you mean 'incorrectly,' Leandra?"

"Well, for example, last month you mentioned to Stefan that you had never walked in a maze garden, but that can't be right because there is a maze garden on the grounds of the Opal Palace. And the month before that when Ruby's tutor inquired about your education, she came back and said you were surprisingly foggy on the details of Galandrian history. But everyone knows you have a deep reverence for your ancestors. It's almost as though . . ." She pauses again, as though she's searching for just the right words. "It's almost as though I know more about the Masked Princess than you do."

Our gazes hold for a moment; a strange look crosses her face and she says, "I almost think—"

Just then the door bursts open and Ruby's chirpy voice calls out, "Is someone in here?" Skipping footsteps, and then:

"Leandra—come out! I can see the side of your dress!"

"We'll talk later," I mouth at Leandra, falling back deeper behind the tapestry. I put a finger to my lips and smile playfully, as though I merely want to continue playing the game.

Leandra nods solemnly and slips out from behind the tapestry, saying nothing as Ruby exclaims there are only a handful of people she still needs to find. When I'm certain they're gone, I reach behind me and press the embedded opal, thankful to be near an entrance to one of the hidden passageways that curve through the castle. The wall slides back and I hurry through the darkness. After I've entered my chambers and closed the wall behind me, I blow out several breaths. Clearly Leandra has been watching me much more closely than I ever imagined.

I thought I had been so careful these past months. *"It's almost as though I know more about the Masked Princess than you do."* Was she realizing there may be a distinction between Wilhamina Andewyn and the person who stood before her?

A quick lie won't account for all the mistakes she's caught me in. So what will? Should I plead illness? *"My memory is beginning to fail me. Perhaps I should see a physician?"* I imagine the worried, shadowed look on Stefan's face if I told such a lie. My stomach lurches violently, and I make it to the fireplace just in time to deposit the contents of my stomach.

Footsteps sound outside the door. Has Ruby come to find me? Hurriedly, I snatch a cup of cold scarlet tea, swish it around my mouth, and take a few steadying breaths. I cross the room and open the door. Stefan is on the other side.

"I've been searching all over for you," he says, looking as though he's in no better of a mood than when I last saw him.

"I've been playing hide-and-seek with Ruby," I say lightly. "That does actually require hiding." I smile at him, a smile that usually earns me one in return. Yet now Stefan just glares back at me. A chill slides down my back, and I can't help but asking, "Have you spoken to Leandra?"

"No, why? Is she all right?"

"Yes, yes, she's fine. She just seemed . . . tired, I guess, from all the festivities, and a bit out of sorts. I thought perhaps she should have an early night." As I say the words, I hate myself for it.

Stefan nods. "I will see that she is looked after. May I come in?"

I step aside so he can enter. Stefan pours wine into two crystal goblets. He hands me one and settles himself in an armchair, while I continue standing. "I had thought you were coming here to steal a moment alone to grieve for your father."

"Grieve?"

"Yes." Stefan sips from his goblet. "He is dead, after all, and you have not shown the slightest bit of grief. No tears. No mourning at all. Why is that?"

"I mourn Fennrick, just as surely as any Galandrian," I say, and immediately realize how inadequate that sounds.

"Yet Fennrick was not just your king. He was your father."

"He was also the man who forced me to wear the mask. As a father, I barely knew him."

"So you say. Yet you spent a lifetime living as his daughter."

"People grieve in different ways, Stefan. Not everyone wears their heart on their sleeve." After my conversation with Leandra, my nerves are in no mood to continue putting up with his foul temper. "I'm growing tired, and think I'd like to retire for the evening. If you could tell Ruby and your mother—"

"I had the most interesting message from your brother Andrei," he says, as though I haven't spoken. "Accompanied by the most interesting messenger. Do you want to hear it?"

Stefan's eyes are watchful, and all at once, I feel like I'm on a stage. "What is it?" I arrange my features into innocent concern, and imagine myself stuffing the panic rising in my chest into a small box. But something in his eyes tells me I'm right to worry.

"Your brother sent word that shortly before King Fennrick's death he became aware of a plot to send a look-alike to Kyrenica—to *me*—instead of Princess Wilhamina Andewyn herself."

The air is sucked from my lungs. He knows.

"Stefan, I—"

"Not a word," he says, a dangerous edge to his voice. "Not one more lying word from that poisonous tongue of yours."

He stands and advances toward me, and for the first time ever, I feel afraid of him. I step backward and the mantel of the fireplace digs into my shoulder blade. I can smell the stink from my own vomit.

"Is the message true?"

My mind is racing ahead, calculating. Stefan said *look-alike*—not *twin*. "It's true that the king discussed sending someone—"

"And was that someone you? Tell me truly, are you or are you not Wilhamina Andewyn?" His face is a mixture of fury and agony.

As much as I want to find the golden words to smooth this over, it's impossible. All he has to do to determine if I'm truly Wilha is question me extensively. A test Leandra has already proven I will fail.

"I'm not her. I'm not Wilhamina," I say, and the pallid horror that spreads across his face is almost too much to bear. "But I swear I'm royal. I'm not just a look-alike. I'm Wilha's—"

"I don't care who you are!" He hurls his goblet and crystal shatters against the stone wall. "You have done nothing but lie from the very moment you arrived!"

"Stefan, I can explain—"

"Explain? I was falling in love with you," he says, and his voice breaks. "I would have married you and spent my life trying to win your love in return. How can you be so charming? How can you have won our hearts so completely—not just mine, but Ruby's and my mother's as well—and be so wretchedly evil?"

If I ever doubted I love him, I know now that I do. Because the hatred burning in his eyes sears my heart, and I just want to make it stop.

"Stefan, I'm sorry. I do love—"

"Don't say it!" He advances another step toward me. "Not now. Don't add another lie to your long list of offenses!"

"I swear I never meant to hurt you. Please. Please hear me out."

"There's nothing to hear." He turns and calls, "Guards!"

The door opens and soldiers rush into the room.

"What's going on?"

"King Andrei has left your fate in my hands," Stefan says. "Although, he did say that if I sent you back to Galandria he would see to your immediate execution."

The room sways and I have to fight to stay standing. "Where will your guards take me?"

"To a cell until I can decide what I should do with you." He squares his shoulders and holds out his hand. "I'll be needing the bracelet back."

Our gazes lock. I run my hand over the thick rope of pearls and the ruby set in the center. It was the present from Stefan during our betrothal ceremony. On that day we meant nothing to each other. Now, as I slip it from my wrist and hold it out to him, it feels like I'm losing everything.

"I'll also need you to remove the mask." He stretches out his hand again.

Slowly I untie it, and Stefan flinches when he sees my face.

"Please listen." I hand him the mask and get down on my knees, preparing to beg for mercy. "I'm—"

The door bursts open. Ruby comes bounding into the room and throws her arms around my neck. "I've found you, Wilha! And you're not wearing your mask, how lovely!" Her bottom lip puffs out when she pulls away. "But you cheated! I already looked in here. You're not supposed to change hiding spots."

"I know." I hug her tightly, understanding this may be the last chance I ever have to speak to her. "I *have* cheated, more than you will ever know, and I'm—"

"Ruby—get away from her," Stefan says.

Ruby looks over, now noticing the guards. Her arms tighten around me. "What's happened? Is it Father?"

"Father is fine," Stefan says. "Now do what I say and step away from her."

Ruby's eyes fill with tears as she looks at me questioningly.

"Stefan doesn't mean to be cross with you. It's me he's—"

"Don't speak to my sister! Don't speak to any member of my family, ever again! Ruby—get over here. Now!"

"Ruby," I say, noting the wild look in Stefan's eyes, "I think it's best if we just do what he says." I detach her arms from around my neck and push her away.

"But I don't understand." Ruby reluctantly joins her brother.

"I'm sure Stefan will explain it to you." I pause. "Although, whatever explanation he offers you will only be half the truth, since he never asked for one himself."

Stefan looks at me for a moment. "Take her away," he says quietly.

As the guards force me to my feet, all I see are the hard eyes of a man who no longer wishes to know me.

CHAPTER 6

ELARA

I'm taken to a small room with stone walls, a cot in the corner, a wooden stool, a chamber pot, and nothing else. After the guards leave and lock the door behind them, I set about pushing at the stones, hoping to find an opal. But after several hours of searching, I have to concede it's hopeless.

I sink onto the bed. The only sound in the cell is the muffled gulping of my own quiet sobs. It feels as though something unlocks in my heart and the girl I once was—the girl who cried and craved another's love—rises up, screaming and calling me a fool.

I had love. All these months, I had someone who loved me—someone who I loved in return. But I was too blind to see it. Too ignorant to understand that love isn't something that *just happens* to you one day. It sneaks up on you in the dailiness of life, until you can no longer imagine that same life without the person you love.

I wish I could erase the pain I saw in Stefan's eyes. I wish he would have let me explain. But mostly, I wish I had just told him the truth months ago. I wish I had valued him more than I valued my own safety. But I did not. Whether I'm sentenced to execution, or shown mercy, I've lost him. All he'll ever believe is that I was a traitor, bent on deceiving him.

At this thought, my sobs turn to full-blown shrieks, until many hours later, when I finally fall asleep.

⊷⊶

*I*n the morning, the door opens and a guard appears with a plate of bread and cheese. I sit up and rub my swollen eyes. The guard motions to someone standing just outside the door, and my heart begins pounding—hoping that Stefan has come to hear me out.

Instead, Lord Royce strides into the room.

"What are you doing here?" I say, then answer my own question. "You're the messenger Andrei sent, aren't you?"

Lord Royce ignores me and turns to the guard; the distinct clink of coins changing hands echoes through the cell.

"Ten minutes," says the guard as he exits the room.

Lord Royce settles himself on the wooden stool. He's wearing his emerald robe identifying him as a member of Galandria's Guardian Council. "Are you being treated well here?"

"Better than I ever was in the Opal Palace, but that's not saying much. You and your friends never knew anything about hospitality."

"Lord Murcendor and Lord Quinlan were never my friends."

As we look at each other, I'm determined not to beg for his help, not to ask him about Stefan, though everything within me clamors to do so.

"I imagine these are not the circumstances under which you wished to see me again," he says finally. "Just before he died, your father told Andrei of your existence. He told him, too, how both you and your sister were sent to Korynth. Your brother was quite outraged, and shortly after being proclaimed king, dispatched me to collect the both of you."

"*Collect me?*" I say. "Is this how the Andewyns will always treat me? As a possession, to be used or disposed of at will?"

"Your brother is a king now. This means he can treat you—or anyone else in his kingdom—however he pleases."

"But how did he—how did *you*—know that I'm Elara and not Wilha?"

"I didn't *know*; I merely suspected. I suggested to the crown prince that the easiest way to tell if the girl living in his castle was Wilhamina Andewyn was to question her."

"How is he?" I ask, unable to help myself. "How is Stefan?"

"Heartbroken and outraged. You should be thankful he hasn't paid you a visit."

"Thankful? You do realize your actions may have just ruined whatever peace existed between Kyrenica and Galandria. Ezebo could easily declare war over something like this, couldn't he?"

"He could, but he will not. Your brother is bending over backward to appear a diplomatic ruler, sincerely sickened by the deceptions of his father. He has offered to let the Strassburgs keep as many of Wilha's masks as they should like, and has invited Ezebo to be his special guest in Allegria for a series of upcoming events celebrating his coronation. However, he has ordered me to bring you back to the Opal Palace."

"But Stefan told me Andrei had left my fate in his hands?"

"Yes, that is what I told Stefan. Now I'm telling *you* that Andrei has absolutely no intention of leaving you with the Strassburgs. You shall be returning to Allegria with me."

"And how do you propose to do that? Do you think Stefan will just allow you to take me back?"

"I will not be asking the crown prince or King Ezebo for permission, as I am sure it is just a matter of time before they see the folly of allowing you to return to Galandria." He shifts in his seat. "Your absence from public life will inevitably be noticed. The official word the Strassburgs will circulate is that you have fallen ill and are being kept in quarantine to avoid spreading contamination. But privately, you should know that the dowager queen is calling for your immediate execution. She is not a big fan of yours, is she?"

A loud rap sounds at the door. "Five minutes!"

"How do you expect to get me out of here?" I say, flicking my gaze from the door and back to Lord Royce.

"I have many friends in Kyrenica. It takes less money than you might imagine bribing a guard to leave a door unlocked in the middle of the night. I will be leaving Korynth tomorrow—or so the Strassburgs will think. The day after that, one of my men will come for you. And it is here that I can offer you a deal, as I assume you will not want to face your brother."

"A deal?" I laugh mirthlessly. "Every time the palace has offered me a deal, it's always been for their own good—unless you're planning to just let me walk away, never to be found again?"

"Of course not. You will accompany me back to Allegria, but I will see that you do not reach the Opal Palace. Instead, I will provide you with lodgings in the city."

"Why? What do you need me for?" I search his face for clues, but as always, Lord Royce's blue eyes are impassive.

"There's something I want to discuss with you. Something I will not speak of in Kyrenica."

"And what if I prefer to take my chances with Andrei?"

"Would you? Andrei believes you may be a threat to the crown. To *his* crown. Lord Quinlan told him all about Lord Finley's plan to put you on the throne last year. Think carefully, Elara. Do you really want to be handed over to a brother who believes you may want to overthrow him?"

I look away from his gaze and imagine myself stuffing away the disappointment lodging in my chest. I suppose I had held out a line of hope, however thin, that Andrei may be curious about me—may actually want to *know* me. But it seems he's just like his dead father: he's decided I'm a threat before he's even spoken a word to me.

"If I agree to this, what do you want in return?"

Another rap on the door. "One minute!"

"In exchange, you will willingly accompany me back to Galandria. You will agree to have a discussion with me about a matter close to my heart . . . and you will give me Wilhamina's location. Andrei wants her returned to the Opal Palace, and I intend to make good on my king's wishes."

"I have no idea where Wilha is," I say, careful to keep my face blank. "She fled the castle—for all I know she's dead. And I told you once before that—"

He holds up a hand. "Please save your protestations for someone ignorant enough to entertain them. I have made you an offer. You can either accept it or reject it." He stands. "I'll give you a day to think it over. But one way or another, one of you is going back to the Opal Palace. So it's up to you to decide, will it be you, or will it be Wilhamina?"

❧

That night, as I shiver on my cot, I ask myself why I didn't immediately tell Lord Royce where Wilha is hiding. While I rot in a cell—not for the first time—Wilha is provided for.

Anger pierces my insides. King Fennrick sent me to live with the Ogdens. Wilha walked away from her own life and expected me to pick up the pieces. Now Andrei has ordered me back to Galandria. How many lives will the Andewyns take from me? How much more must I give them before I can work myself free from their grasp?

In the morning, after the guard shows Lord Royce into my room, he doesn't waste time. "What have you decided?"

I think of Wilha in the dress shop, telling me she's happy. "She doesn't want to be found," I say, mostly to myself.

"Your brother wants her. Even if you do not disclose her location, men will still be sent to search for her. But if you cooperate with me, I will spare you from Andrei."

"Spare me? Is he really so terrible?"

"I do not think you will want to find out. And once I have you safely hidden away in Allegria, I have a proposition to share with you."

He isn't asking for a lot, I tell myself. Just a few words. Just one sentence.

If I go back to the palace, I have little hope of receiving a warm welcome. But the same can't be said for Wilha. She's the famous Masked Princess, and the sister Andrei grew up with.

I close my eyes. "There's an inn near the docks called the Sleeping Dragon—she rents a room above it."

By the time I open my eyes, Lord Royce is gone. I wonder if, along with giving up Wilha's location, I haven't also just surrendered a piece of my soul.

CHAPTER 7

WILHA

"*Y*our countenance is all wrong," Marko says as we practice in the alley.

"What do you mean?" I lower my sword and stamp my feet to stay warm. Though spring is finally making an appearance, the nights are still chilly.

"It's obvious from the look on your face your heart isn't in it tonight. By revealing yourself like that you send a clear message to your opponent that you are easily beatable."

I nod and blink rapidly, trying to clear away thoughts of James and how his face fell when I said I would not have dinner with him again tonight. As Elara is not currently appearing on the balcony—exactly what illness has befallen her?—I had to tell him I was meeting a few girls from the dress shop for some late-night sewing to catch up on orders. Somehow, this lie felt worse than all the others.

"You will be easily disarmed, if you go into a fight with such a distracted mind," Marko says. "So perhaps we should practice some other moves tonight—clearly you'll be needing them."

"Now then," he says after I've laid aside my sword. "If you are disarmed or you are attacked while walking down the street, your objective is to first free yourself—and then run for help. Turn around."

I do, and Marko wraps his arms around me. "If he grabs you from behind, you will want to throw him off-balance. The key is to act quickly before he can secure his position. You could step backward and stomp on his toes."

I practice for a minute, leaning back into him before stomping on his boots.

"Good," Marko says, with his arms still around me. "Now if he tries to turn you toward him"—he spins me, until we're face-to-face—"then you will want to deliver a kick to his private—"

He breaks off at a shuffling sound behind us. "Who's there?"

Silence.

"Find out if someone is back there," he commands.

"Me?" I say, blinking.

"Yes. Take up your weapon and arm yourself." He gives me a pointed look. "Perhaps facing a real threat will cause your mind not to wander. If you require assistance, I will be here."

Quietly, I pick up my sword and creep down the alley, wishing the night wasn't so dark. My hand grips the hilt so tightly the metal digs into my skin. Blade raised, I swing around the corner.

No one is there.

But in the slick of mud covering the ground is the unmistakable impression of footprints leading away into the street.

"No one's there," I say, coming back to Marko. "But some-one was definitely watching us."

"Probably a beggar trying to find a warm place for the night," he says, sheathing his sword. "Blast this weather. If you are too addled to properly concentrate, then I'm not going to stand out here any longer."

Amid much grumbling, Marko takes his leave. I wander through the city, well aware that with the lie I told James I cannot immediately return to the inn.

The gates outside the castle are deserted save for the guards standing watch, who look sleepy with boredom. Looking up at the castle, I'm only vaguely wondering about Elara's illness. I am much more aware that when I found no one hiding in the alley I felt an emotion cascade through me, and it was not relief.

It was disappointment.

For the briefest of moments, I *wanted* an opponent to face. I wanted someone to vent all my grief and frustration upon. Many men have toasted my father's death at the Sleeping Dragon over the last month, and it has killed me to simply stand by silently, as though the news meant nothing to me. As though *he* meant nothing to me.

I turn and head back to the Sleeping Dragon. At the inn, musicians play while the townspeople dance around them. I move to a seat in front of the fire. My fingers have just begun to thaw when James drops into the seat next to me.

"Who is he?" he says in a tight voice.

"What?"

"Who is he? The man I saw you with in the alley."

I open my mouth in surprise, but no sound comes out.

"I knew something wasn't right, Willie, so I decided to follow you tonight. How long have you been seeing him? You looked quite enthralled as he held you in his arms."

I imagine Marko's arms wrapped around me as he muttered instructions into my ear, and I'm sickened as I realize just how that image must have looked to James.

"You misunderstand," I say. "It is not like that."

"No?" James raises an eyebrow. "Then tell me what it *is* like, Willie. Help me understand."

"Marko is . . ." I stop. How can I explain?

"Is he the reason you've been avoiding me? If you've met someone else you could've had the decency to *say* something Willie, rather than making a fool of me." He leans back in his chair and takes a deep breath. "I think you know I've been trying to ask you something."

I nod, and look away.

I know what he wants to ask. Indeed, it is to be expected. I stare about the inn, at the couples twirling around the musicians. Everyone around me seems so reconciled to their destiny. It all seems so natural for them. If I have chosen this life, why can I not make myself fit into it?

"After Victor retires, he plans to turn over the running of the inn to me," James continues. "I could provide a good life for you, Willie. For *us*. So I will ask you this only once: Will you marry me?"

I look into James's sad eyes. There is nothing wrong with living life as the wife of an innkeeper. None whatsoever. Yet something inside me feels certain this is not what I am meant to do. And if I truly love James, should I not want to say yes, no matter the circumstances?

It seemed enough in the summer's golden light that James chose me. But now in the dim days of winter I think I'm coming to understand that true love doesn't mean you unquestioningly settle with someone who has chosen you. You have to choose them back.

"James, you know I care for you, but—" I am interrupted when the door to the inn opens, and a man with a hooked nose and high forehead walks in. His eyes lock with mine and he does a double take, as though he recognizes me, though I am certain we have never met.

He heads straight for me and holds out his hand as though he is inviting me to dance. "It's time to go," he says in a distinct Galandrian accent.

Immediately, James is on his feet. "Who are you?" He turns back to me. "Willie, do you know this man?"

"Your brother requires your return," the man says, ignoring James. "We must leave now."

I clutch the edge of my chair as realization sets in. His accent. His words.

I have been found.

A fog has descended over my eyes and ears. I only

vaguely hear James arguing with the man, calling him a barbarian and threatening harm if he does not leave us alone. Everything comes back into sharp focus, though, when the door to the inn opens again and Lord Royce enters. "I have more men waiting outside," he says as he nears. He glances at James. "I will send them in if I have to. Rolf," he addresses the man with the hooked nose, "wait by the door."

"This is madness," James says. "You cannot just barge in here and take her against her will—I don't care *what* her family says."

The music and dancing have stopped; everyone watches as James and Lord Royce face each other. Victor arrives, carrying a wooden club—the same one he uses to threaten men who get out of hand in the inn. "What's going on?"

Lord Royce ignores him and looks to me. "Go quietly. You know this is the best possible outcome for everyone involved."

"She's not going anywhere," Victor growls, and takes a step toward Lord Royce, the club raised.

Lord Royce puts a hand up to stop Rolf from rushing over. "I recognize you," he says to Victor. "You were the king's general and once acted in his stead when a dispute broke out near the border over a contested trade route."

"Yes," Victor answers, clearly surprised. His eyes widen and he lowers the club. "You were there, too. You were the Guardian of—" He stops short. His eyes widen and he glances around at the silent inn.

Lord Royce leans in close to him. "If you care for her, you'll let me take her now, before the crowd realizes there's a valuable Galandrian in their midst."

"Galandrian?" James says, going pale.

Victor's eyes flick to me and then back to Lord Royce. "Who is she?"

"You would not believe me, even if I was at liberty to tell you."

Victor turns to me. Gruffly, he pulls me into a hug—the first he has ever offered. "It doesn't matter to me where you come from," he says in my ear. "If these men don't treat you well, send word, and I shall hunt them down."

James is looking at me glassy-eyed. "Tell me it isn't true. You never talk about your family—I just assumed you'd had a falling out."

"My family is from Galandria," I say quietly, dropping the accent I have carefully cultivated. "As am I." I reach out to touch him, but he steps back.

"Stay away from me, Willie—if that's even your real name." He pauses. "Is it?"

I shake my head. "No, but—"

"*No?*" A look of hurt and revulsion twists his features before he turns and pushes through the crowd.

"James, wait—" I go after him, but Lord Royce grabs my arm. "I have to go after him. I have to make this right."

"There's no way to make something like this right. You've

done enough as it is." He steers me toward the door. "Now let's go."

I wait until we're outside before the tears I have been holding back begin falling. Lord Royce leads me across the street to a line of carriages guarded by men who he says are in his service. He opens the door of a carriage. "After you."

Elara sits inside, looking out the opposite window. Her face is blank. Her eyes are swollen and bloodshot.

Lord Royce settles himself next to me. "Do the Strassburgs know of this?" I say.

"Not yet," he answers. "We have been clever. Nevertheless"—he turns and calls out to the driver—"go now, and do not stop until it is absolutely necessary."

As the carriage starts forward, the music inside the inn resumes, as though I was never there at all.

CHAPTER 8

ELARA

I feel nothing.

Not the rattling of the carriage as it bumps its way over the roads leading to Allegria. Not the blustery Kyrenican wind, nor the less frigid Galandrian breeze after we cross the border. Not Wilha's hand on my arm when she asks me if I'm all right and urges me to eat.

I spend most of the journey looking out the window of the carriage. When Rolf came for me in my cell, it was tempting to flee to the kitchen, where I was sure Stefan was spending another sleepless night. It was only the knowledge that he wouldn't welcome me as his love, but revile me as a traitor, that kept me on course.

We pass a road leading to Tulan, and I wonder often about Cordon and the Ogdens. The last time I saw him, Cordon was coming for me in Eleanor Square—just before a palace guard struck me and took me to the Opal Palace. In the year since then, how have they all fared?

We make camp for the night a few hours away from Allegria. One of Lord Royce's men hands me a note, and the haze I've been in finally seems to dissipate. I read the message, glance up to see Lord Royce looking at me, and nod.

For better or worse, I made a deal. Now it's time to pay up.

*E*arly the next morning, I slide out from beneath the blanket Wilha and I sleep under. Wilha stirs, but she turns over and is silent once more.

Outside our tent the sky has lightened; a faint orange glimmer marks the eastern horizon. The noises of the night, the hooting of an owl, the chirping of crickets have given way to a predawn silence. Rolf is making a campfire; woodsmoke spirals through the air in soft curls.

I meet Lord Royce at the edge of the clearing, just as his note instructed.

"What's the plan?" I ask.

"I will tell Wilha I think it's best if you travel in separate carriages. She lacks your propensity for deception; it will go better for her if your escape truly takes her by surprise."

I nod, though I'm tempted to ask him more about Andrei. Exactly who—and what—are we sending Wilha back to?

"Andrei will likely have his men watching for us at the gates, so it is imperative they see that I have two girls with me. We will not make our move until after we have crossed into the city."

"And then what?"

"You are to travel in the last carriage, behind the others. Once we are waved through the gates, we will continue on toward the palace. Rolf will make contact not too long afterward and escort you to a place I have prepared for you."

"How do I know your men can be trusted?"

"They can be trusted. It is *you* who needs to prove your trust. But be warned. Rolf will see you to your new location, whether or not that is where you wish to go."

I don't have anywhere else to go, I want to tell him. *You and the Guardians made sure of that.* I remember again that day in Eleanor Square, and Cordon calling after me. "Do you know what has become of the Ogdens?" I ask.

"They're being watched."

"Watched?" I say sharply. "What do you mean?"

"Remember, up until recently, it was thought you were lost in the world somewhere. The palace has watched over them in the hope that you would return one day. Their daughter, Serena, married a village boy a few months ago— Cordon is his name, I believe—and they continue on, much as they have before, though Lady Ogden's health has been declining. Food has been scarce in Tulan, as it has been in many villages." His features harden. "You have your brother's new tax policies to thank for that."

I imagine Cordon and Serena slowly taking on the demands of life at Ogden Manor. It's hard to picture Mistress, always so fierce, as anything other than healthy and cruel. Last winter, food in Tulan was scarce as well, and I remember there were days when I felt so light-headed from hunger I thought I might pass out. Are things even worse this year?

"I don't suppose we could send worthings to—"

"No." Lord Royce is firm. "I will have enough trouble explaining your disappearance to the palace. I will not add arranging charity to your peasant family on my list of things to do this day."

"The Ogdens are *not* my family."

"Then we are in agreement." He brusquely turns and walks away.

A bird begins chirping, the sound of a new day arriving. Wilha emerges from the tent and wanders over to the campfire. I look out toward the east and the dawning sunlight. The sun rises, the sun sets, and life goes on. I'm happy for Cordon, or at least, I *want* to be happy for him. But I miss him; I miss having a friend. With one last look at the horizon I turn to join Wilha by the fire.

"What were you and Lord Royce talking about?" she asks.

I try to find the strength—and the stomach—to summon my next words. It's only one more lie. Only one more, when I've already told a thousand. "We were discussing plans to enter the city. He wants me to sit in the carriage in the back. I guess he doesn't want to draw attention to the fact that there are two girls."

"And so it begins." Wilha sighs. "It might not be so bad, going back to the palace. At least this time we will be together. . . . Have you ever seen the Opal Palace's gardens? They are quite beautiful. There is one in particular, the

Queen's Garden, that I visit often. I shall have to take you there."

Seeing Wilha's tentative smile makes me question what it is I think I'm doing. For so many years I wanted to find my family. Now I have a sister—a sister I'm beginning to believe I could love if given half a chance. And I'm going to just leave her?

"I wish I had your optimism," I say. "I wish Andrei would simply welcome us back, and we *could* visit the gardens together. But the last time I was brought to the palace, I was thrown into a dungeon and nearly starved to death. And it doesn't sound as though Andrei is eager to embrace me as his sister."

Wilha's smile slips; her brow creases. "Whatever anger Andrei is feeling right now is *my* fault, Elara, not yours. Running away and asking you to step in and live the life I could not was wrong, and I'm truly sorry. It was more than anyone could ever ask, and yet you did it. Where I was a coward, you acted with courage. I shall do my best to let Andrei know that whatever blame he wishes to assign, all of it lies with me, not you."

The guards—all of whom, I now realize, must know Lord Royce's plan—pretend not to look at us while I simply stand there speechless. *Thank you* would be an appropriate response to her apology. "I'm sorry" is what I say instead.

"I do not blame you for telling Lord Royce where I was

living. If Andrei has ordered us both back to Galandria, there is little else we can do."

Little else we can do . . . She's right. And although I hate deceiving Wilha, I know I can't allow myself to fall under Andrei's command. Her dream of the two of us walking in the Queen's Garden is just that: a dream, easily destroyed by the reality of a brother who sees me as a threat to his reign.

"We need to keep faith." Wilha reaches out and takes my hand. "This could all work out just fine."

"Of course it can." I swallow thickly, and the lie slides down my throat, where it sits like arsenic in my stomach, poisoning me from the inside out.

CHAPTER 9

WILHA

*E*lara goes back inside the tent, saying she doesn't feel well. I continue to warm my hands over the fire and watch the sunrise. My sister should not blame herself for our circumstances. I do not view Lord Royce and his men as our captors, but as a royal escort. The men who will help me correct something I made wrong several months ago.

As the days have passed, I have thought of Andrei often. I wonder if now, with our father dead and Andrei king, and the secret behind my mask known to both of us, we can finally become more than strangers to each other.

Rolf asks me to meet Lord Royce inside one of the carriages. He is already there, waiting with a velvet box. I breathe deep and turn questioning eyes upon him.

"Andrei wishes you to enter the city wearing a mask," he says without preamble.

I accept the box from him, but do not open it. "Did he say how long he wishes me to wear it?" As we have traveled anonymously, neither Elara nor I wearing a mask, I have nursed the hope that Andrei would abolish our father's decree.

"I did not ask," Lord Royce replies. "There is also a gown inside here." He gestures to the trunk beside him. "He wants you to enter the city in the full regalia of the Masked Princess."

"Is this my brother's wish? Or the commandment of my king?"

He holds out the velvet box. "Both."

The mask inside is gold, yet tinged with crimson at the top, with fire opals trailing down the cheeks. It seems to stare back at me with malevolent eyes, taunting: *Surely you did not think you would get away so easily?* I pick it up; it feels much heavier than I remembered.

I tie it on and try not to notice that, once again, my world has become much smaller.

❧

At the entrance gates to the city, a line of carts and carriages wait while soldiers search for weapons—something I do not remember them doing previously. When our convoy reaches the front, Lord Royce calls out his greetings. The soldiers recognize him and soon the men are conferring. When they seem to reach an agreement, one soldier mounts his horse and speeds off in the direction of the palace.

Lord Royce enters my carriage with a brief nod and settles himself. A guard waves us through the gates and our procession slowly begins moving through the packed street. The carriage jounces over pockmarks—the glittering, opal-flecked roads are in worse condition than I remember. The air is heavy and unmoving, and the scent of too many bodies, horse manure, and roasting meat is overpowering. Did the city always smell this way? Living in Korynth by the docks, I suppose I had grown used to the salty air and briny breeze always blowing up the streets.

Stone buildings with their golden spires still rise up into the sky. Gargoyles still perch from iron lampstands. Yet now, beggars line the streets, calling out to the passersby for a spare worthing. Along a row of storefronts, one shop must have recently caught fire, for the stone is scorched.

Many of the Allegrians who stroll up the street wear costume masks in hues of various colors. Yet it's not just the women, as I remembered.

"Is it now fashionable for men to wear masks as well?" I ask Lord Royce.

"Fashionable, no. Beneficial, yes. Many men find it easier to avoid their creditors when they cover their faces."

A shout rises from up the street, and our carriage slows.

"Stand back, you fool!" shouts a palace guard. "Those opals are the property of King Andrei!"

A man dressed in ragged clothing is kneeling and digging into the street with a small knife. He attempts to yank an opal out of the ground. I look around at the rest of the pockmarked street, and my heart sinks. The opals must have been dug up.

In times past, those small opals were worthless. Nothing more than colorful flecks to adorn the streets. How far has

Galandria fallen, that men will dig for them, in full view of the palace guard?

The guard clubs the man in the face. Blood spurts from his nose and drips to the ground, staining the street scarlet.

Next to me, Lord Royce says, "You have been away a long time, Your Highness. Much has changed in your absence. Bread is scarce, and fear is rampant."

"What is Andrei doing to address this?"

His expression is guarded. "You will see for yourself soon enough."

A thin hand reaches through the carriage window. "Please, can you spare a—" The voice, which belongs to a small, malnourished boy, stops when his eyes take in my mask. "It's her!" he shouts. "It's the Masked Princess! She has come back!"

Lord Royce yanks the curtains closed as men begin shouting. Soon the curtains take the form of shadow serpents—hands trying to push their way inside as my driver yells for everyone to stand back. The carriage jolts heavily as first one man, then another, jump onto the sides. While Lord Royce yells at them I shrink into my cushions.

The carriage is listing to the side—are the people attempting to overturn it?—when I hear the unsheathing of swords and a soldier ordering everyone to stand back.

"Do it now!" he cries. "Or we'll attack!"

The men jump down, and the carriage seems to sigh in relief.

"Go back to your business!" the soldier calls. "The princess has returned. If you wish to see her, you will have to visit the balcony."

The carriage starts up and rolls forward at a good pace. I glance at Lord Royce. He's pale and breathing heavily; for once his cool demeanor seems rattled. We keep the curtains closed, not wanting to be seen, yet from the sound of heavy, marching footsteps outside, I know the guards have surrounded our procession. We continue on, until the carriage comes to a halt. When I emerge outside, Arianne is waiting on the steps of the Opal Palace. A line of guards stand behind her.

"Which one are you?" she whispers in a sharp voice.

"Wilha. Elara is in another carriage."

Arianne merely grunts in reply. To the guards, she says, "There's a person of interest in one of the other carriages. Deal with her." She grabs my arm and begins leading me into the palace. "The king asks you to wait in your chambers until he is ready to see you."

Almost as an afterthought, she adds, "Welcome home, Princess."

CHAPTER 10

ELARA

Not too long after we're waved through the city gates, my carriage at the back of the convoy heaves and shudders. The driver steers the horses to the side of the road, and when we come to a stop, Rolf appears in my window.

"What happened to the carriage?" I ask.

"Busted axle." Rolf grins. "It makes for a very convenient distraction." He glances around and continues, "In a moment, I want you to step out onto the street. I don't think we're being watched, but nevertheless, we must be cautious. We'll walk the rest of the way."

"The rest of the way where?" I ask, but he doesn't reply.

Rolf watches the street intently. After a few more minutes, he opens the door and I exit the carriage, just as a large crush of men and women pass by. We join them and they nod politely.

Behind us, a few of Lord Royce's men begin shouting and I tense up.

"Keep walking," Rolf says quietly. "They're going to act as though you just escaped and ran back in the direction of the gates."

"Can we trust them?"

"Of course. They've sworn an oath of loyalty."

"To Lord Royce?"

Rolf pauses before answering. "Not exactly."

By now, the rest of the carriages have traveled far ahead of us. All at once, it seems that Wilha is finally recognized. A crowd swarms her carriage, pushing and shoving. I start forward toward them, but Rolf places a restraining hand on my shoulder. "Don't even think about it. There's nothing you can do, and help is already on the way." He gestures to a line of palace guards on horseback. The crowd disperses and the carriage moves forward again. "We're going to turn at the next street."

He grabs my arm, but I shrug out of his grasp. "No, I want to make sure she reaches the Opal Palace."

"His Lordship was quite clear I was to escort you straight to your new lodgings. Against your will, if I have to."

"Really? Well, did *His Lordship* also tell you just how loudly I can scream? Loud enough, I'm sure, to draw attention. I assure you, I can be quite convincing."

"So I've been told," Rolf says sourly. He curses. "Fine, we walk to the palace. The place we're going to is in the southern section of the city, anyway. But keep your head down, and your mouth shut."

A crowd, keeping a wary distance from the guards, has surrounded Wilha's carriage, and they continue on as though they've become a part of the royal escort to bring the Masked Princess home. Rolf and I keep a safe distance behind.

We enter Eleanor Square and journey up the hill leading toward the Opal Palace. The entrance gates to the palace grounds are ornate and golden with a swirling letter *A* at the top. Guards wave the carriages inside. Just before Rolf and I turn away, I glance up at the balcony. A boy whom I recognize as Andrei stands looking down upon the crowd, a displeased expression on his face. The opal crown rests atop his head. The doors behind him open and my gaze is drawn to a second figure emerging onto the balcony.

It's only then that I understand the horrible mistake I have just made.

CHAPTER 11

WILHA

I follow Arianne's quick strides into the palace, but stop when I hear excited shouts echoing from the yard. "What's going on?"

Arianne doesn't slow down; she merely grunts that whatever scene Elara is currently causing isn't her problem.

The palace has not changed in my absence. The cream-colored walls, the vaulted ceilings that drip with crystal chandeliers, the ornate gold-leafed doors and gilded furniture are still here. And yet it all seems far grander than I remembered.

When we arrive at my chambers, maids are scurrying around, lighting candles and stoking a fire in the fireplace. A golden teapot and a platter of cakes sit on a table. Once the servants have left, Arianne waits quietly while I explore my rooms. Here, too, nothing has changed; all is as I remember. Yet somehow I cannot help but see it through new eyes. I pick up the golden teapot and think of the man digging in the streets for a single opal.

A thought occurs to me, and I put down the teapot and enter my closet. Far from being empty, as I had expected, several masks sit inside the glass cases. Most of my collection still resides with the Strassburgs in Korynth; these ones must be brand-new.

"Andrei commissioned Master Welkin to begin producing more masks," Arianne says, entering the closet. She steps closer, and I recognize the tinkling, musical sound that accompanies her movements. "More will be arriving soon." She thrusts the necklace of jeweled keys into my hands. "I'll wait outside a moment while you orient yourself."

After she leaves, I run my finger over the necklace. When I find the jeweled key that unlocks the glass cases, I remember all too keenly why I wanted to flee my life last year. It was not solely because I did not wish to marry Stefan Strassburg. It was the mask and everything that goes with it.

Holding the keys, I finally understand something: I am not the same girl who once spent hours staring into the mirror, wondering what was so wrong with her. Nor am I the girl who once hid under a tarp, too afraid to venture into the city of Korynth.

In the months since then, I have become someone else entirely.

I find Arianne in my sitting room, eating a slice of cake. "Right, then," she says when she sees me. "Your brother has planned a series of parties to welcome you back to the city. He will expect you to show him your support." She pauses, and the scorn in her voice is evident. "So there shall be no complaining about all the public appearances you are to make this month. Understood?"

She pauses again. No doubt she is waiting for me to acquiesce.

Quietly I untie my mask, and thrust it into her hands.

"Tell my brother I no longer prefer to wear the mask." Ignoring the shocked look on her face, I add, "Things will not be as they were before, because *I* will not be as I was before."

CHAPTER 12

WILHA

I pull on the thick black cloak Arianne offers and flip the hood up. We leave my chambers and make our way down the corridor. As we walk, we pass no servants, nor any of the nobles who often linger inside the palace, hoping to be received by the king. I wonder if they have been ordered away so as not to see my face.

After Arianne relayed my message, Andrei sent back one of his own, summoning me to the Eleanor Throne Room to meet with him.

"The king is expecting us," Arianne says to the soldier standing guard outside the doors.

He nods, glances quickly at me, and enters the room. When he emerges again, he signals we should go inside.

Arianne and I approach, our footsteps echoing in the hall. Even though he sits on the gilded throne, I can see Andrei has grown several inches taller in the last year. His hair—curling around his face underneath the opal crown—is brown, the same shade as mine and Elara's. His lips are pursed in a frown. His blue eyes stare at me curiously as I sink into a curtsy before him.

"Leave us," he commands his guards in a voice that is deeper than I remembered. After they've gone and the door has shut behind him, he says, "Show yourself, Sister. I wish to see your face."

I reach up and push away my hood.

He looks at me for a long moment. "I have seen portraits of our mother," he says. "You look like her."

I am not certain he has offered this as a compliment. Our mother died immediately after giving birth to Andrei, so I have no idea if he holds fond feelings toward her. There is so much I do not know about Andrei at all.

"I am happy to be back in your presence," I say, straightening up when he bids me to rise.

"Yes, I cannot imagine it was pleasant, hiding out among the scum of Korynth."

"Thank you, Brother, for bringing me home." If he hears any hesitation, any hint that I am less than pleased at being brought back to Allegria, he does not show it.

"If our father had betrothed *me* to a Kyrenican dog, I would have run away also. You can be sure I will not sentence you to such a fate."

I offer him my thanks again, for it is obviously expected.

"There have been many pigeons between Stefan Strassburg and myself. He is aware that you were in hiding last year, though we have been vague regarding the details. The official story among both kingdoms will be that you fell ill and decided to travel back to Galandria to regain your strength in a warmer climate."

"Are they threatening war?" I ask.

"No. My advisors tell me they most likely don't want to publicly admit they were so easily taken in by the deceptions of a weak, deceased king," he says, and I wince, for it is our own father he speaks of with such little regard. "And Galandria is currently in no position to fight a war, in any event. For now the peace seems to be holding, although a new treaty will have to be negotiated. In a few weeks' time, we will announce that your betrothal to the crown prince has been broken. The Strassburgs also believe your decoy escaped from her cell in the middle of the night." His lip curls. "They are currently searching Korynth for her."

I am unsure how to respond, so I say nothing. In the silence that follows, I'm certain I hear the faint sound of cheering, and turn slightly toward the windows.

"Your return to the city has created a stir," Andrei says, following my gaze. "The people love you, you know. Sometimes they even sing songs about you." He frowns. "No one ever sings about me."

He turns to Arianne. "Where is Lord Royce? I want to know exactly how the other girl escaped."

Escaped? Does he mean Elara? I open my mouth to ask, but think better of it.

With a curt nod, Arianne leaves to summon Lord Royce.

"So, it seems you have a twin," Andrei says.

"Yes. It seems I have."

"And you just became aware of this last year?" Andrei crosses his arms. "This was not something you and Father kept from me?"

"It was kept from me just as surely as it was kept from you."

"I knew there had to be a logical explanation for the mask. I was not as stupid as you to believe the rumors." The scorn in his voice and the expression on his face reminds me of Elara. "Speaking of which," he continues, "what's this I hear about you not wishing to wear your mask?"

"I did not see the point of it," I say carefully. "Now that Elara's presence is known to both of us."

"But it is not known to the people. They still believe the rumors, and they will want to see the Masked Princess."

"I had hoped we could let the people know *me*, Wilhamina, without the mask. . . . I had also hoped they could know Elara. Our sister." I watch his face while I speak, but I can't guess what he's thinking.

The double doors open behind me, and I hear Arianne speaking softly. To Lord Royce, I assume.

Andrei leans back in his throne, studying me. "Your face isn't very interesting without the mask," he decides. "Once you are properly settled in you will resume your appearances on the balcony. I shall be joining you, and I will expect you to show your devotion to me as your new king."

"Are you sure that is such a good idea? The people nearly

attacked me in the street. I do not think they love me nearly as much as you believe."

"Your appearances on the balcony will be a nice diversion. Let them stare in wonder at you and your mask and forget, if only for a moment, their own woes." He turns to Arianne. "Escort her back to her room. She is to wear a mask always. I do not fancy seeing the likeness of my dead mother flitting around the palace like a ghost."

"Of course, Sire," Arianne says with a thinly disguised smile. She reaches for me, but I ignore her outstretched arm.

"Andrei, please. Can you not reconsider? Our father—"

"The king has spoken," says a voice from behind. "You have been taught better than to argue with your sovereign."

For a moment my heart stops altogether. I was mistaken; it was not Lord Royce who accompanied Arianne into the hall. Instinctively, my fingers tense, grasping for a sword I do not have. I turn around.

Lord Murcendor stands behind me.

He does not glower or scowl, or appear threatening in any way. Instead, he wears a disapproving frown, as though I am a child who has just disappointed him. In his hand he carries a jeweled mask.

"Your Highness," he says, bowing. "How nice to see you again."

CHAPTER 13

ELARA

*P*erhaps King Fennrick was right about me all along.
When he first looked upon me, he stared into the future and thought he saw another Aislinn Andewyn. A younger twin who would one day betray her sister. I have hated him for this and refused to acknowledge him as my father. And now what have I done? I have abandoned Wilha to the man who tried to assassinate her.

The gates close. I wrap my fingers around the golden bars, wondering how I could have made such a huge mistake.

"We have to go," Rolf says.

"I can't leave her—"

"You've *already* left her." He pries my fingers off the gates.

"But he tried to kill her. He—"

Rolf grabs me by the shoulders. "You're making a scene," he whispers fiercely. "The best thing you can do for her is not get caught right now." He takes my hand and begins pushing through the crowd.

As we make our way down the hill, I whisper a silent apology to the sister I've just betrayed.

*B*ehind the gleaming shops and apartments that line the main roads of Allegria, the streets become much seedier. They are not opal-flecked, nor are they even cobbled. Instead, I tramp through mud and filth as I follow Rolf to our unknown destination. The buildings, many of them made of wood obviously in need of repair, are only two stories, with storefronts opening out to the street.

"Where are we?" I ask.

"The original section of the city. The one the nobles don't care to think of."

We come upon a street where large cuts of meat hang in nearly every window shop. A river of blood runs from one, mixing in with the mud, and my stomach churns from the scent of raw flesh. Thankfully, we soon turn down another street that's lined with bakeries and smells of rosemary and fresh bread.

"That's where we're going," Rolf says, pointing to a shop where a long line of men stand waiting. We turn into a back alley and enter the bakery from behind, where we hear a woman's voice, "We don't have any more bread today. How many times must I tell you this?"

"Perhaps we should come in and see for ourselves!" Shouts erupt, drowning out the protests of the woman.

We pass through the kitchen and Rolf points to the staircase. "Go upstairs and wait for me." As I walk up the stairs I hear him draw his sword "If any of you come inside this shop, you won't be coming back out again!"

The upper story is one large room sparsely furnished with a wooden table and chairs and a few mattresses strewn around the floor. I cross the room and look out the window to the street below. The line outside the shop begins dispersing.

The stairs begin creaking. "Does that happen often?" comes Rolf's voice.

"We close early every day now," the woman replies. "We're running low on flour. Kendrick declared himself in favor of—" They emerge at the top of the staircase, and the woman breaks off sharply. She has Rolf's angular nose and high forehead.

"Elara, this is my sister, Alinda," he says.

Alinda nods curtly at my greeting, examining me with discerning eyes. "I hope you're worth the risk we're taking for you." Rolf shoots her a look, and Alinda sighs, her expression softening. "Forgive me. I shouldn't have spoken so coarsely. It is an honor to have you in our home."

She sinks into a curtsy and adds, "Your Highness."

CHAPTER 14

WILHA

It takes everything within me not to flee the room as Lord Murcendor steps around me and Arianne and joins Andrei on the dais.

"But I thought he was . . ." I look at Andrei helplessly.

"In exile?" he finishes. "He was. Fortunately, he has returned to offer me counsel."

"But . . . but did you not hear of the events in Korynth? How he—"

"How you went to the Kyrenican Castle that night to switch back with your decoy?" Andrei interrupts. "How he attempted to evacuate you from the castle when he became aware of Lord Quinlan's plan to destroy Korynth, and you misunderstood his intentions? How Lord Quinlan was all too eager to capitalize on your confusion and paint Lord Murcendor as the villain, forcing him to flee? Yes, I have heard it all from Lord Murcendor himself."

"Lord Quinlan's plan?" I say faintly.

"Yes." Andrei frowns. "I will forgive you for your error, of course. But now that Lord Murcendor is returned to us I shall expect you to pay him the honor due him."

"Andrei," Lord Murcendor admonishes, "you are being too hard on your sister." He turns a pained look upon me.

"Surely, Wilha, you cannot really believe that I would have ever hurt you?"

"It is difficult not to," I say, forcing myself to look him in the eyes, "given that you put your sword to my throat and told me you would kill me if I did not marry you."

"Wilha, please." He shakes his head. "I was merely trying to get you to leave the castle. I would have said anything to get you away from Lord Quinlan."

Lord Murcendor's eyes are as kind as I have ever seen. Gone is the madman from last year; all I see is the solicitous Guardian who advised me all the years of my life. Yet I am not the same girl who once blindly trusted him; I shall not be caught in his snare ever again. But as I stare at Andrei, sitting on his throne, Lord Murcendor standing closely next to him, my stomach sinks. Even if Andrei granted me the time to tell him every moment of what transpired in Korynth, he would never believe it.

Andrei and I may have been raised separately when we were children, but we have this one thing in common: Lord Murcendor was our closest friend and confidante. My father never understood how great a need a child has to be loved and listened to. A need, I see now, Lord Murcendor has understood all too well.

"How does Lord Quinlan answer these charges?" I say finally.

"He said he was innocent—right up until the moment he was executed," Andrei says.

My stomach churns; I was never close to Lord Quinlan, but in Andrei's words I hear Lord Murcendor's malice. So what am I to do now? My thoughts turn to Elara; she has always known just the right words to speak. If she were standing here in my place, what would she say if she knew Lord Murcendor was here and playing the role of the devoted advisor?

"Everyone plays a role," I hear her harsh voice in my head. *"Your job is to figure out which one is yours."*

Hoping that the sickness I feel in my stomach does not show on my face, I curtsy before Lord Murcendor. "Forgive me, Your Lordship. I never should have doubted you."

The doors are thrown open once again, and Lord Royce appears. He has changed out of his traveling clothes and into his emerald robe. He strides forward, passing me and Arianne without so much as a nod, and drops to his knees before Andrei.

"I have failed you, my king. If you require my immediate dismissal, I offer it to you." He removes his robe and holds it out to Andrei, both arms outstretched, the picture of perfect submission.

Andrei waves his hand impatiently. "Rise, Lord Royce. I have heard how eager you always were to please my father. I expect no less devotion to me."

"You have it." Lord Royce stands and puts his robe back on. "I am sorry for my failure in letting the girl escape."

"How *did* Elara escape?" Lord Murcendor asks, scowling at Lord Royce.

"There is a bit of confusion on that point," Lord Royce says. "A crowd swarmed Wilha's carriage, and in the ensuing melee Elara may have slipped away. Or she may have escaped earlier when a different carriage broke down. I have spoken with the guards posted at the city gates. They did not report seeing a girl matching her description. It is my opinion that she is still in the city."

"And do you have any idea where she may be?" Lord Murcendor asks.

"No," Lord Royce answers. "I do not."

Lord Royce is lying. I know it from the tension in his shoulders. The slight shift of his eyes as he speaks. The muscle that pulses at his jaw. Does anyone else see? I glance around the room. It appears they do not.

"Then you will find her," Andrei says, "and you will bring her to me."

"Of course, Your Majesty." Lord Royce bows.

"There is an easier way," I say, speaking up. "On the road Elara confided that she feared returning to the palace, as she didn't expect to be treated well here. You could easily put her fears to rest, Andrei. Make Elara's existence known to the entire kingdom. Tell the world I have a twin, and you want nothing more than to meet her, and embrace your second sister as an Andewyn. If you do so, and you mean it, Elara may come to you."

I know I am speaking boldly, but I cannot help myself.

Though I haven't wanted to admit it, I have shared my sister's fears. While her existence is kept a secret, Elara is vulnerable. But Andrei is king now, and the succession is secure. So why not shed the secret and welcome her back as the princess she truly is?

"All that time among the Kyrenicans has made you forget you place." Andrei scowls. "I will not announce Elara's existence, when for all we know she means us nothing but harm. If her intentions were true, if she had any interest at all in being a part of this family, then why did she escape?"

"Well said, Your Majesty," Lord Murcendor says, and Andrei seems to glow under his approval.

"We will speak again, Sister. In the meantime, you may go. And you will wear your mask." He frowns. "I am king now, Wilha. You have to do as I command." He turns expectantly to Lord Murcendor as if to say, *Right?*

Lord Murcendor nods. "You are king, Andrei. We all must do your bidding." He holds up the jeweled mask he carries. "Please, Wilha, put it on."

Reminding myself to play my role, I take the mask and tie it on.

In doing so, it feels as if the shadow of the Masked Princess rises and swallows me whole.

CHAPTER 15

ELARA

*L*ong after night falls and Rolf and Alinda and I have settled down onto our mattresses, I lie awake, thinking of Alinda's words, "*It is an honor to have you in our home . . . Your Highness.*"

How many people has Lord Royce told of my identity? Over a meager dinner of cheese and leftover bread, I tried to question Alinda and Rolf about Lord Royce's intentions, but they remained stubbornly silent.

Downstairs comes the sound of a key turning in a lock, followed by the creaking of a door opening.

I reach over and nudge Rolf. "Someone's here," I whisper.

Immediately, Rolf bolts upright and draws a knife from under his mattress. While he creeps over to the staircase, Alinda sits up and rubs her eyes.

"Who's there?" Rolf calls.

"I was able to procure more grain and flour from the palace," comes Lord Royce's voice. "Enough to last the shop for another few weeks, if you ration it. I heard what happened to Kendrick." He emerges at the top of the stairs. "I left the bags by the hearth. I would hide them, if I were you."

"Who is Kendrick?" I ask.

"He was a miller in the city," says Lord Royce. "A few

weeks ago he publicly criticized Andrei. The next day, his home and mill burned down."

"Taking most of our grain along with it," Alinda interjects. She stands up and reaches over to hug Lord Royce. "Thank you for the grain, Uncle."

Uncle?

"I must speak to the girl alone, and I can only stay for a few minutes," Lord Royce says to Alinda and Rolf. "The king's men will be looking for her tomorrow, and I have been tasked with leading the search. Make sure she stays inside. I will try to direct the men over to the northern section of the city, closer to the gates."

After a few more instructions, Alinda and Rolf go downstairs. Lord Royce lights a lantern and gestures for me to join him at the wooden table.

"How have my niece and nephew been treating you?" he asks.

"Did you know?" I say, ignoring his question.

"Did I know what?"

"That Lord Murcendor had returned to Allegria."

He pauses. "Yes, I did."

"How could you? You *know* what happened that night. What he tried to do. What he would have done to her if—"

"Her?" Lord Royce seems genuinely surprised. "I was under the impression it was *you* who was posing as the Masked Princess on the night of the masquerade."

"It was . . . but originally we had planned to switch back that night . . . and Wilha had arrived when . . ." I sigh. "The story is convoluted."

"Clearly."

"But you know what Lord Murcendor is capable of, and you just handed her over to him."

"I did so with your help."

"But I didn't know—"

"And suppose you had? What would you have done then? Would you have taken her place? Would you have returned to the Opal Palace and kept her location a secret?"

I'm silent, for I know the answer to that question all too well.

"I can explain letting one twin escape, but not both. Either way, one of you was going back to the palace; it was unavoidable." He pauses. "In addition to conducting the search for you, I have other matters I must attend to in the city after being absent for so many weeks. In the meantime, you will have to live here. I will keep the search away from this street, but you will need to stay inside at all times."

"And after you return? You said you had something you wanted to ask of me. What is it?"

"We will speak of it when I return. In the meantime, I offer you this." From the folds of his cloak he produces a book and slides it across the table. It's the book from my mother. *Eleanor of Andewyn House: Galandria's Greatest Queen.*

"Where did you get this?"

"In the commotion on the day you were arrested, the castle was in quite an uproar. It was not difficult to have it removed from your room."

I run my finger over the rich leather cover, but the book is little comfort. I have barely glanced at it in the last few months.

"Aren't you going to thank me?" says Lord Royce. "After all, Lord Finley went to great lengths to see that it came into your possession."

My head snaps up. "You know Lord Finley gave it to me?"

"Lord Finley gave it to you," Lord Royce says, "because I first gave it to him."

CHAPTER 16

WILHA

I am clutching the fire poker. Lord Murcendor faces me, and I read the amusement in his eyes. "This is supposed to be your makeshift sword? You're not even holding it correctly. You should have paid more attention during your lessons. . . ." He draws his sword and I am no match for him. I fall to my knees and realize I will die, a princess who has lived a life that is nothing to be proud of. I have failed the Andewyns. I am weak. I am unworthy. . . .

I awake with a cry. My skin is damp with sweat. A silken bedsheet is twisted around my torso like a coiled snake, and early morning sunlight streams through the window. Relief floods my chest and I quickly extricate myself from the sheet, deciding that I know exactly what I need to do.

Lord Murcendor may have returned to the Opal Palace. But I shall not allow him to return to my dreams.

Later that morning, I pass no one as I make my way to the armory. I run a hand over all the weapons, wondering if Andrei will approve when he gets word of what I'm planning.

"May I help you with something?"

With the voice comes an ache, and I turn around to face Patric. His curly black hair is longer than when last I saw him, but his green eyes are as bright as ever.

"I heard you had arrived." When he steps closer, I smell leather oil and mint.

"Yes, just yesterday," I say, feeling slightly light-headed. As we stare at each other, I remember our last meeting. Me, begging him to let me take off my mask. Begging him to look at me. And him, steadfastly refusing.

"How do you find life in Kyrenica?" he asks politely.

"Are we really going to do this? Are we really going to exchange pleasantries, as though we are old friends, glad to see one another again?"

A brief look of hurt crosses his face before he straightens up and assumes a formal air. "My mistake, Your Highness. How may I assist you, then?"

"I wish to resume my training." I remove a blade from the wall. "As soon as possible."

"You would need to request permission from the king, I would think."

"No, I think not. Andrei is preoccupied with other matters, and I will not trouble him with yet another. I mean to continue my lessons—quietly. And if they come to my brother's attention I shall tell him I thought it would be part of resuming my life here in the palace."

"It is not a bad idea, learning to defend yourself," he says, stepping closer and lowering his voice. "There are rumors—" He breaks off at the sound of footsteps. A maid carrying firewood sweeps down the corridor.

"I care not about rumors," I say. "I have lived my whole life with them."

"No, that's not what I was—" Patric stops again as another maid passes in the corridor. She casts a curious look our way. He quickly steps backward and raises his voice, "I will assign someone to train you. When we left off, you were progressing quite nicely."

Something about the tone of his voice calls to mind an adult encouraging a struggling child, and I have to tamp down a flood of irritation. "I will require more advanced training, as I continued my lessons in Korynth."

It is splendidly gratifying watching the surprise cross his face, if only briefly, before he resumes his stiff demeanor. "I am surprised your beloved allowed that. I'd have thought Stefan Strassburg wary of arming his future Galandrian bride."

My lips part in surprise and I realize now what I did not yesterday: Andrei has committed me to an immense course of deception. If the story is that I have merely traveled to Allegria for an extended stay at the palace, then at the moment everyone believes I am still betrothed to Stefan.

"I would prefer not to speak of Stefan," I say.

"Nor would I," Patric says, sounding almost angry. "Indeed, tales of the love you have found in Kyrenica have been carried all over the kingdom."

"I am not sure if it was love I found," I answer carefully, thinking of James. "But it was something. And he did not *allow* me to do anything. I wished to continue my lessons, and so I did."

"Of course." Patric stares at me as though he has never seen me before. "As a matter of fact, I was going to call on you today. There is great concern for your safety, as well as Andrei's. You are to have soldiers accompanying you at all times, and your brother has appointed me as head of your guard."

"I see. Then I should like you to appoint someone to train me." I do not say it out loud, but I think he hears what I mean: *Anyone other than you.*

"I will need to evaluate your skills if I am to know which of my men to assign to you." He grabs a blade from the wall. I follow him to the training room next door, and we take our positions. I keep my sword pointed downward, in the position Marko taught me.

"You are not holding it correctly," Patric says.

"I am holding it just as I please."

"Very well." His fingers wrap around his sword; they are strong and finely crafted, and for an instant I imagine those same hands cupping my chin.

He attacks and I bring my blade up—just as Marko taught me. But it seems Patric expected the move. He falls back and we begin sparring in earnest. As we trade blows, his breathing quickens—something I do not remember from our training sessions last year. Then, it seemed he was merely humoring me. Did he think me a weak princess, too dimwitted to understand the techniques of battle?

We continue until we are both winded. When we finish, Patric wipes at the beads of sweat dotting his brow. "You have improved quite a bit. You have finally mastered the techniques I tried to teach you."

"I have. I think it likely because my trainer in Korynth was much more skilled than you."

I hand him the blade and leave, no longer willing to continue looking at him.

CHAPTER 17

ELARA

Rolf and Alinda don't allow me to help in the bakery while I wait for Lord Royce to return. Alinda in particular seems happiest when I stay away from her. I spend much time upstairs, looking out the window, watching each day as a line forms outside the bakery, and listening to the men shout when Alinda eventually has to turn them away. The storefront across the bakery is abandoned, and ragged-looking individuals flit in and out of it at all hours. I assume it's because they have nowhere else to go.

This is not the Allegria I visited a year ago. True, Mistress Ogden—intent on patronizing only the finest shops—kept Serena and I away from this section of the city, but the grim expressions of the people on the street, the whispered conversations between Alinda and Rolf of the palace's abuses, this is a new thing.

One morning I wake to see smoke huffing into the air over in the direction of Eleanor Square. Has another shop owner lost his business because he dared to criticize Andrei? Fire, as I remember all too well, is Lord Murcendor's preferred method of destruction.

I wonder if I am foolish to stay here and trust Lord Royce, when it's obvious he knows more about my mother and her book than he has ever let on. If he gave Lord Finley my mother's book, does that mean he was working with him last year?

Lord Finley was a former Guardian who grew disillusioned with King Fennrick and decided he wanted to replace him with a monarch of his own choosing. Me. He had one of his own men find me in Tulan and give me the book—but both of them were arrested and eventually executed before they could tell me of their plans. And now Lord Royce says *he* first gave the book to Finley? Yet last year he sat with Lord Quinlan and Lord Murcendor when they questioned me about Lord Finley's activities and acted as though he knew nothing at all. He has shown himself to be immensely deceptive, as well as resourceful; perhaps I should clear out and leave before he returns.

But the fight seems to have left me, and along with it, the will to set out on my own. Even if I managed to escape Rolf's watchful eyes, where would I go? If guards are posted at the city gates, I can't get out of Allegria. And I know no one inside the city. Except for Wilha.

A not-so-small part of me misses her, and the brief talks we had in her dress shop. While I couldn't admit it at the time, questioning Wilha about her life was a small way to know her. More than once I have found myself wishing I could glimpse the Opal Palace and see how she fares. Perhaps the sight of her would ease the guilt that constantly pierces my conscience.

During the long afternoons, I settle down to read my mother's book, and a few days after I've arrived in the city, I come upon pages where thin pinpricks crown some of the letters. I run my hand over them and feel the slight bump of the tiny holes. I remember noticing this before in Korynth, ages ago it seems—and then promptly forgetting about it. But I remember thinking, if only for a slight moment, that the small punctures didn't seem haphazard, but deliberate.

As though someone intentionally took a needle to the pages.

With a sharp intake of breath, my fingers still. Quickly, I stand up from my place at the window and cross to the wooden table, where I find the quill, parchment, and pot of ink Lord Royce left. I write down each letter with a small puncture above; it forms a long string of letters that mean nothing, but when I separate them into words, a shock echoes through my heart. Because the letters form a message:

THIS BOOK HAS A TWIN. FIND IT AND YOU WILL FIND YOUR NAME.

CHAPTER 18

WILHA

I select a painted white mask with lavender opals and a lavender dress to wear for my first appearance on the balcony. After I have finished getting ready, Lord Murcendor pays a visit to my chambers.

"Good afternoon, Your Highness." He bows. "I have come to escort you to your engagement." He extends his hand.

Judging by the extreme deference I have seen the servants pay Lord Murcendor, his grip over Andrei must be ironlike, and I know it is folly to refuse him. I force myself to keep my own hand from shaking as his fingers twine around mine.

"Surely someone of your stature has more important things to do than accompany me to the balcony?" I say, trying hard to affect a light tone.

"There is nothing more important to me than the happiness and well-being of you and your brother," he says, again with the loving tone.

We emerge from my chambers to find Patric and the rest of my guards waiting for me. Patric pales slightly at the sight of Lord Murcendor and I holding hands.

"Have you settled in well enough?" Lord Murcendor asks me as we sweep along the corridor.

"I have."

"And how do you dream?" He lowers his voice. "The maid who started your fire early this morning reported she heard you crying out in your sleep."

My shoulders tense under the realization that he has servants reporting my behavior to him. I dare not admit my nightmares often feature *him*, and so I think quickly. "Snakes," I answer. "I dream snakes are coming for me, all of them wearing masks. I try to fight them off, but I am outnumbered and they overpower me. . . . In an effort to deal with it, I have resumed my training with a sword, thinking that will help calm me." I add this last part in a burst of inspiration, for if servants are reporting to Lord Murcendor, he will have already heard of my lessons.

Revulsion creeps down my spine as he wraps an arm around my shoulders. "Rest assured, Wilha. I would never see any harm come to you."

I cast a look back at my guards. Patric's eyes are grim, and I read the message they tell me: *Be careful.*

When we arrive at the doors leading out to the balcony, Andrei is waiting with his guards. Lord Murcendor issues instructions and takes his leave of us. Everyone else is silent, though we can all hear the people chanting:

Masked Princess!

Masked Princess!

Masked Princess!

"Did we not announce that I would be appearing, too?" Andrei says.

Uneasy glances are exchanged, until the head of Andrei's guard speaks up. "The people can be slow to understand, Your Majesty."

This seems to mollify Andrei and he nods. When the doors to the balcony open out to the courtyard, we're greeted with bright sunlight and cheers erupting from the crowd. Andrei reaches for me and we stroll outside, arm in arm. The guards fan out around us, with Patric standing on my other side.

The courtyard is packed. More than half the people in the crowd wear face masks. It is eerie not being able to see their true expressions as they chant and clap.

"Curtsy to me," Andrei says. "I want the crowd to see you showing me deference."

I obey and sink into a deep curtsy. When I rise, the chanting grows louder:

Masked Princess!

Masked Princess!

Masked Princess!

Andrei's eyes narrow. "They love you more."

"They don't love me," I say as we both wave. "They love the jewels, the masks, and the mystery. But they have never loved *me*."

A man's voice cries out. "The opal crown belongs to the

Masked Princess! Not to the gluttonous usurper!"

A shocked hush descends and the people begin turning to one another. With so many faces covered, it is difficult to know where the voice came from. Palace guards begin threading through the crowd as the man continues shouting.

"While the palace feasts, your people starve! What say you, Andrei the Usurper? Will you show yourself to be a true—" The guards envelope a man wearing a black leather mask. A blow to the back of the head sends him to the ground, and they begin kicking him.

"Stop them!" I say, turning to Andrei. "They're going to kill—" I break off when I read the hatred in his eyes.

"Your Majesty," Patric says, "I think perhaps we should get you and the princess back inside."

With a final withering look, Andrei sweeps through the doors. Patric orders the rest of the guards inside the palace as well. When it's just the two of us on the balcony, he says, "Before we go back inside there's something you need to know. Andrei has not endeared himself to the people in the short time since he became king. A faction has developed in the city, and they are becoming increasingly bold in expressing their views."

"And what are their views?" A knot forms in my stomach.

"They are saying that Andrei is not the true heir to the throne." He pauses. "Wilha, they are saying that the opal crown should have passed to *you*."

CHAPTER 19

ELARA

*I*s it possible that the king and queen secretly named me? There was a time when finding out my true name was what I wanted most in this world. I would have done anything to obtain it and shed the name Mistress Ogden gave me. In doing so, I hoped to put more distance between myself and the woman I wanted to love as a mother, but grew to hate as a mistress instead.

My search ended abruptly last year when Lord Murcendor told me my parents refused to give me a name, but I wonder now why I accepted his words so easily. While I wait for Lord Royce to return, I study my mother's message until it's burned into my brain:

THIS BOOK HAS A TWIN. FIND IT AND YOU WILL FIND YOUR NAME.

What does it mean? It's an interesting play on words, and I decide there must be another copy of the book somewhere, but where?

I conjure an image of Queen Astrid lying in bed embroidering, surrounded by servants. As soon as she's left alone she casts her work aside and picks up a book by her nightstand. Holding her needle in between her fingers, she flips the book open to a random page and begins pinpricking the message she doesn't trust anyone to carry.

Yet I assume she entrusted Lord Royce with the book itself. I remember his words from last year: *"There were things I could have told her. Things your mother wanted her to know, a message she intended Elara to have."* Did he know the book carried a message? But why couldn't he have simply given me the book, as well as my name last year? Why the secrecy?

⁂

That night at dusk, Lord Royce appears at the bakery wearing a black leather mask and hands me a glittering costumed one. "My face is well-known in this city," he says. "Palace guards still hunt for a girl matching your general description, so anonymity is better for both of us."

Rolf, also wearing a black mask, joins us as we step out from the bakery. The sky swirls with deepening pastels, and the air is warm. Spring is in full bloom. But the impending night hasn't erased the suffering I've glimpsed from Alinda's window. Men dressed in torn and dirty clothing mill about, some muttering to themselves, some calling out to us for worthings as we pass by.

"Stop for no one," Lord Royce says as we hurry up the street.

We pass a small family standing under a lantern. The woman clutches a wailing infant to her breast and tries to comfort him. Next to her stands a small boy saying, "Mama, I'm hungry. . . ." As we pass them I wish more than anything I could turn around, go back to the bakery, and offer them some bread.

But then I remember there isn't any. Alinda ran out earlier than usual this afternoon.

We turn down a number of streets, each becoming slightly less seedy. Finally, Lord Royce leads us inside a tavern. Most of the tables are filled; every single patron wears a mask. Lord Royce flags down a bar mistress and whispers in her ear. She nods, and leads us to the back of the tavern and into a private room with a small wooden table and two chairs. Lord Royce hands Rolf several worthings and commands him to order dinner. After he's left, the two of us settle into the chairs.

"I imagine you have many questions for me," Lord Royce says.

"I do." He nods, indicating that I should ask them.

"Did my mother give you the book?"

"Yes. She felt that of the four Guardians who knew of your existence, I was the most likely to be sympathetic to her. She summoned me privately to her chambers just before she went into confinement to give birth to your brother. She was in a sorrowful state. She produced the book and specifically asked that I find a way to get it into your hands when you were brought back to Allegria. She did not believe it was right to hide your true parentage from you indefinitely. She charged me with telling you who you really are, and with giving you the book."

"Did she say why this was so important to her? In Korynth, you said she had a message for me. What was it?"

Lord Royce's face is grave. "She said she wanted you to know that giving you up was the biggest regret of her life."

"That's it?" I lean back, disappointed.

"That's not enough? There are many people in this world who hope for last words from a parent and never get to hear them. Now you know that your mother, for the brief years she survived after your birth, loved you and missed you terribly."

I am not immune to Lord Royce's words, but I had hoped for something else. Something about the message in the book and what it could mean.

"Why did she give me the book in the first place?"

"She said she wanted you to learn from your ancestors. She was a lover of books. Indeed, she had a great many of them in the Opal Palace's library."

Is it possible the second copy of the book is located in the Opal Palace? Either way, it seems likely Lord Royce is telling the truth and doesn't know about the message.

And, I decide suddenly, that's exactly how I want to keep it.

"You knew Lord Finley was looking for me," I say, changing the subject.

"I did."

"Did you know of his plans last year?"

"To put you on the Galandrian throne? No. I suspected, but never sought confirmation of his motives. It had come to my attention that he was secretly trying to find you, and so I gave him your location."

"My location? But how did you know where I was?"

"I make it my business to know most of what goes on in this kingdom. Your father felt it best if only Lord Murcendor knew where you were hidden. That was unacceptable to me, and so I watched Lord Murcendor—or rather—I employed men to watch him for me. When I discovered your location, I employed those same men to watch you. Long before Lord Finley's man appeared in Tulan, I was receiving regular reports about you."

"You had men watching me," I repeat vaguely. "What does that mean?"

The door opens and Rolf appears. Behind him are several men—the guards we traveled with back to Galandria. A few others stand beside them and they all fan out around the table, forming a circle around Lord Royce and me. I let out a small gasp when I see an unshaven man with oily blond hair. A voice from long ago comes back to me: *Back again, sweetheart? What's a pretty thing like you doing in a place like this?*

"You—what—I recognize you," I finally mange to choke out. "You lived in Tulan. You were a regular at the Draughts of Life."

"Elara, this is Nicolai," Lord Royce says.

"It is an honor to meet you," Nicolai says in a crisp voice I've never heard him use before. The leering demeanor I saw so often in the Draughts seems to have vanished as he bows politely before me.

"But," I stare from Nicolai to Lord Royce, "he lived in Tulan for years."

"As I said before, I sent him there to watch you. I wanted to see if you were becoming the person I needed you to be."

"I don't follow," I say, although I think I do, and it makes my stomach churn.

"Questions have arisen regarding the validity of Andrei's claim to the throne," Lord Royce says. "That, combined with the ineptitude he has already displayed as a ruler, has convinced me beyond a shadow of a doubt that he is not worthy to rule. I believe another should rise up and assert their claim. So I'm asking you, do you wish to possess the opal crown and ascend the Galandrian throne? Because if you do, every single man in this room has taken an oath to support you as their queen." Lord Royce stands and joins the men circling me.

One by one, they all sink to their knees.

"Get up!" I say, casting a look at the door. "Get up before someone sees!" The men take it as a command, and quickly stand.

The bar mistress enters carrying platters of bread, cheese, and fruit and places them on the table. She returns with mugs of ale and casts a wary glance at all of us.

"Don't want any trouble in here," she says.

"You will have none," Lord Royce says, and after a flick of his hand, Rolf, Nicolai, and the rest of the men follow her from the room. Lord Royce closes the door behind them and sits back down at the table. "You and I both want something that, as of yet, we have been unable to obtain."

"Oh yeah? And what exactly is it that you think I want?" I ask. "To possess the opal crown?" Has the long winter driven him insane?

"You want freedom from the Andewyns, and the long shadow of their gilded reach."

I say nothing to this, for I'd have to admit he's right. "And you, what is it *you* want?"

"I want a ruler who will put the Galandrian people's welfare before their own pursuits of wealth and pleasure. Your father, as well as your grandfather before him, failed miserably at this. Your brother is showing himself to be no better."

"And you think I can just—*poof!*—become this wonderful ruler you're hoping for?"

"With the right person advising you, yes."

"I'm assuming the 'right person' would be you?"

"Galandrian law states that the opal crown must pass to the firstborn child of the ruling monarch," he says, ignoring my question. "Your father set aside this law when he removed Wilhamina from the line of succession. Back then, no one thought to contest his actions. After all, she was not formally removed until after Andrei was born, and by then rumors about her and the mask had spread. It seemed fitting to allow the crown to pass to Andrei—a healthy boy—rather than risk it on a girl who the whole kingdom feared may be deformed, or cursed, or something worse. But now that Andrei is failing to win over the public, there are more than a few who are suggesting that the true heir to the crown is Wilhamina."

"But if they're calling for Wilhamina's ascension, why have you come to *me* with this?"

"Because if Wilhamina does not wish to rule—as I do not believe she does—then under the established laws of succession the crown should pass to the next eldest child of King Fennrick and Queen Astrid." He pauses. "That would be you."

"What you're suggesting is treason," I say, glancing at the closed door. "Both of us could be executed if anyone hears this."

"No one in this tavern is a friend to Andrei." Lord Royce leans forward. "Think carefully, Elara. All your life you have been a pawn of the Andewyns. And as long as your existence is kept a secret, that's all you'll ever be. But what if instead of being a pawn—a piece to be moved around, subjected always to the will and whims of another—you became a player yourself?"

"A player, for the crown? I know nothing about being a queen."

"You knew nothing about being a princess, yet you lived as one quite convincingly. And this time would be different. You would not be assuming the name or the life of another. Rather, you would be announcing your own intentions to ascend the throne. The rightful heir, with a stronger claim than Andrei."

"This is madness," I say, shaking my head.

"*This* is palace politics. Something Andrei is all too aware of—particularly with Lord Murcendor whispering in his ear."

"But Wilha is in the palace with the two of them now. Are you saying she isn't safe?"

Lord Royce looks at me steadily. "I am saying, Elara, that while Andrei sits on the throne, Wilha—and you—will *never* be safe."

"What if I refuse? Will you allow me to just walk out of here, or will I find myself thrown into a cell again?"

"I have no intention of harming you. If you refuse, you are free to go."

"Free?" I snap my fingers. "Just like that?"

"Yes. In fact, I will have to insist that you leave immediately and not return to Rolf and Alinda's. I have already asked too much of my niece and nephew, and I will not require them to continue harboring you if you are uninterested in pursuing a claim to the crown. I will make arrangements to smuggle you out of the city and send you away with enough worthings to begin a new life."

"A new life?" I laugh. "You just told me you hired men to watch over me in Tulan. Will I spend the rest of this *new life* looking over my shoulder, waiting for the inevitable day you or someone else decides they have need of another Andewyn heir?"

"If you join with me and we are successful, you need never look over your shoulder ever again." Lord Royce sips his mug. "When we walked through the streets just now, what did you see?"

"Poverty and hunger. Nothing I haven't seen a thousand times before."

"In the village you grew up in, yes. But this is Allegria, the very center of the kingdom. Do you want to know what *I* see when I walk the streets? I see a kingdom on the brink of collapse. Unless," he pauses, "someone rises up with a mind to undo the harm your family's rule has done. And as you said yourself, you have seen poverty and hunger countless times. Wilha, on the other hand, has known only the halls of the Opal Palace all her life."

"Not *all* her life," I say, thinking of the year we spent in Korynth. "Don't underestimate my sister—"

I break off, keenly aware that for the first time, I have publicly acknowledged Wilha as my sister. "Why are you doing this?" I say, changing the subject. When he doesn't immediately answer I add, "You expect me to become the figurehead of your treasonous plot. I don't think it's too much that I understand why this is important to you."

"Your brother has inherited your father's lavish tastes. Every night he throws grand parties for the nobles, while resolutely ignoring the plight of the poor. Yet, unlike your father, who acknowledged he needed the wisdom of the Guardian

Council to properly rule, your brother listens to only one voice: Lord Murcendor. There are many who believe he is the true king in everything but name."

"But if I agree to this and we are successful, would *you* become king in everything but name, while I stood in front of you, little more than a puppet queen?"

"I want only what's best for this kingdom, Elara. That no longer includes your brother."

He asks everything of me. And for once, I want a Guardian to do something for me.

"I will consider it." He opens his mouth to protest, but I press on. "That's the most I can offer. You would not want me to make a hasty decision when there is so much at stake. I swear to you, I will give your offer its due consideration. And I promise to give you an answer—after you do something for me."

"And what would that be?"

"I want to see the brother you expect me to depose. I want to see for my own eyes how Wilha fares. I want you to get me inside the Opal Palace," I say.

What I don't say is that I also want to pay a visit to the Opal Palace's library and find my name, and whatever other secrets my mother may have left for me.

CHAPTER 20

ELARA

*A*ndrei's lavish tastes work in our favor, and Lord Royce easily secures an extra invitation to one of the royal court's nightly masquerades. As I put on the purple-and-silver costume mask Lord Royce found for me, I steel myself for a long night ahead. I have two things I must accomplish. I need to find the Opal Palace's library and, just as important, I want to speak to Wilha and hear from her own lips how she's being treated.

I've also decided I need to tell her what Lord Royce is asking of me. Because if I agree to his plan, Wilha will inevitably be affected.

"Who did you tell them I am?" I ask Lord Royce as our carriage rolls through Eleanor Square.

"My niece, Alinda." He pauses and turns to look at me. "I'm taking an awfully big risk for you, Elara. Do not make me regret it."

The Opal Palace shines with golden light, and I can't help but gasp as the carriage rumbles past the gates. Set against the dark, starless night, it glows like a beacon.

"How many candles does it take to light up the palace like that?"

"Thousands," Lord Royce says curtly. From behind the

goblin mask he wears I can't tell if he's irritated by my question or by Andrei's extravagance.

I glance back at the gates, where several beggars have gathered to watch the palace guards admit the guests invited to the masquerade. "How many worthings does it cost?" I ask.

"Cost means very little to Andrei."

The carriage rumbles to a halt in front of the steps leading up to the palace. The royal official posted at the entrance recognizes Lord Royce and greets him.

"This is my niece," Lord Royce says, presenting him with two tickets. "She is a baker in the city."

"Your niece, of course." The official gives Lord Royce a knowing smirk and waves us through. "I have a few nieces myself."

We follow the faint strains of music and a line of guests, all dressed in fashionable clothing and glittering costume masks, streaming down a wide, mirrored hall. A painted door carved with gold leaf opens, and we're inside.

The Grand Ballroom is the largest room I've ever seen. It shimmers with ornate crystal chandeliers and white curtains that billow from arched windows. One whole wall is lined with tables laden with platters of Galandrian delicacies: apple tarts drizzled with cinnamon and honey, spice cakes and bread puddings, and roasted peacocks dressed with iridescent blue feathers. An orchestra plays while masked couples twirl about the dance floor.

On the dais, Wilha and Andrei sit on high-backed thrones. Andrei wears a sullen expression. The opal crown, bristling with jewels, hangs low on his head. Wilha sits ramrod straight. It's only then that I notice Lord Murcendor standing behind them, one hand resting on each throne. A line of guests wait before Wilha and Andrei.

"What is that about?" I ask Lord Royce.

"Members of the court are invited to offer their greetings and well wishes to the king and princess," he says.

"Really?" As I watch, a palace guard gestures to a couple who steps up on the dais. It gives me the opening I need. "What an excellent idea. I want to speak to Wilha, too. But someplace more private—can you arrange that?"

Lord Royce shakes his head. "You wanted to see if she's faring well, and now you have. But speaking directly to her, that's too dangerous."

I snort. "You're asking me to commit treason; isn't *that* dangerous?"

"Keep your voice down!" He pulls me away from a row of palace guards. "Listening ears are everywhere."

"We had a deal," I say after he has led us into a corner. "I want to speak privately to my—to Her Highness. Tell anyone who asks that your *niece* was dying to meet the famous Masked Princess." I cross my arms. "Otherwise, my answer is no."

Lord Royce looks ready to wring my neck, but I don't

back down. I will not have Wilha find out from someone else about his plans.

"All right," he says finally. "I will arrange it—but we'll wait until later, when the guests are drunk on wine and their own importance and their senses are dulled. In the meantime, there's someone I need to speak with who will be of use to our cause. . . . Do you think you can stay out of trouble until then?"

I roll my eyes at his concerned tone. "I won't burn the place down if that's what you're worried about."

He shoots me a murderous look before he stalks away and finds a man wearing a mask in the shape of a lion's head.

I circle the room, and my thoughts turn to the book. I have not asked Lord Royce about the library, as I haven't wanted to arouse his suspicions. If my mother didn't trust him enough to give the message to him directly, then I won't, either. I had considered attempting to sneak away and search the palace myself. Now I realize what a monumental task that would be. The palace is too large, and I would most likely be caught before I found the library.

I pause before a portrait of King Fennrick and Queen Astrid. The inscription says it was commissioned twenty years ago, shortly after they married. I have more of Astrid's looks than Fennrick's. I have her hair color, and her small nose. Yet I have the same green eyes as King Fennrick, and there is something about the set of his jaw that reminds me of myself. Unexpectedly, I feel tears threatening my eyes.

I have hated the two people in this portrait passionately and without ceasing for the last year. At some point I stopped viewing them as human; but rather as cold, bloodless beings, too callous to spare a thought for their daughter—for *me*—simply because I had the misfortune to be born a younger twin. Yet I have to confront the fact that the man and woman in this portrait don't look cruel. The king in particular has a merry smile and a beautiful face. *King Fennrick the Handsome*, I think, and my heart constricts. On the day they sat for this portrait, did they have any inkling of the choice they would be forced to make only a few years later?

I turn and look around the opulent room, at the dais where Wilha and Andrei recline, both of them so used to this kind of wealth and privilege. I visualize myself sitting up there instead.

Surprisingly, the image doesn't seem all that strange.

CHAPTER 21

WILHA

I remember now why I so disliked attending these events. The barbed comments, the backhanded compliments. The stares and the whispers. Yet tonight I read the distrust and tension in everyone's eyes. The rigid way the men carry themselves. The nervous, high-pitched laughter of the women. I see it all easily. But do Andrei and Lord Murcendor? Do they understand what it means?

Andrei and Lord Murcendor never call for me to attend any meetings of importance, but even Lord Murcendor cannot stop the servants' chatter of burnt buildings, raised taxes, and a king who rarely deigns to hear the people's petitions.

When Lord Murcendor excuses himself and steps down from the dais, I lean over to Andrei and whisper, "You need to make a gesture, something to earn the people's goodwill. You are a new king; this is something you must seek."

"The people's goodwill is nothing when you wear a crown," he says, a bored expression on his face.

"Look around you, Andrei. Even the nobles seem nervous tonight. And you cannot keep raising taxes on the villagers, nor declining to hear their petitions."

"Don't tell me what to do, Wilha. Lord Murcendor says the people must wait for the king's good pleasure to be heard."

"But I seem to recall that Father regularly heard petitions," I say, careful not to directly challenge Lord Murcendor's opinion. I do not add that in the times when I attended court I rarely saw my father settle an issue in a manner that was satisfactory.

Lady Ashland, a hearty woman draped in yards of silk and lace, steps up to greet us. "So nice to have you returned to us, Princess." As she speaks her hand flutters at her side, as though she wishes she could cover her eyes, and I remember she never did seem to care for me. "I do hope you are recovered from all the time you spent with those Kyrenicans."

"The Kyrenicans—and the Strassburgs—treated me quite well," I say. After she has left I lean over to Andrei again. "You could arrange for the leftover food from tonight to be delivered to the poor. Even Father did that. If you keep throwing parties like this and refuse to help the people, it will come back to haunt you. If I were you—"

"But you are not me, nor are you the ruler of this kingdom. And you never will be, despite what some of the traitors in this city are saying," Andrei says, his cheeks flushing with color. "Do you understand?"

Under the intensity of his gaze I can do little more than nod.

Andrei signals to let the next guests in line come forward, and I stare blindly out at the crowd as they greet us. I wish again I had a visit with Elara to look forward to. All my life, I wanted a sister. Someone to pass the long nights in the palace with.

Someone to share my secrets. If Elara were here now, this is the secret I would share with her: Andrei is beginning to scare me.

"May I get a bit of air, Your Majesty?" I say to him.

Andrei makes an irritated grunt. "Do not tarry. I want everyone to see you next to me."

"Of course." I stand, and for the benefit of any who may be looking, sink into a deep curtsy. I make my way over to the orchestra, where I listen to the strains of a violin, and do my best to calm the fierce beating of my heart.

"Are you having a good time, Princess?" I recognize the voice of the man wearing the lion's mask who has appeared next to me, yet I cannot place it.

"Yes, I am." I smile tentatively.

"I am glad to hear it." He removes his mask, and my smile becomes genuine.

"Lord Nichols, how are you?" I have always liked Lord Nichols. He never seemed very concerned by the rumors of my mask and is one of the few nobles in Allegria who genuinely seems to like me. "Do you still serve as the Royal Record Keeper?"

"I do," he says. "It is not a very exciting life, I am afraid. I spend most of my days buried amid old books and letters, but it suits me."

"And where is Lady Nichols?"

"I've sent her to her parents' village," he says, a shadow passing over his face. "It is far north, near the Opal Mountains.

I thought it best if she left Allegria for the time being." His gaze slides to Andrei, and then back to me. "There are strange rumors in the city these days, Your Highness."

The orchestra begins a lively piece, and the music pounds in my ears. This is the first time anyone has dared to speak directly to me about the rumors.

"I appreciate your concern," I say, keeping my voice low and looking around. "But those words raise me up upon the edge of a sword—one I could easily fall on."

"They are more than just words," he says, also glancing around the room. "You are, in fact, the firstborn." He lowers his voice even further. "Do you wish to rule at all?"

I am certain Lord Nichols is merely curious, as, I'm sure, are many others in the kingdom. In this very room, even. Behind the masks of the men and women around us, how many listen while pretending not to? How many have pressed themselves into the shadows, intending to carry my words back to Andrei, in an effort to earn his favor?

"It was my father's desire that Andrei rule, and I shall do nothing to overturn his wishes," I say loudly.

"You're a wise girl, Your Highness." He leans closer and whispers, "And you would do well to be cautious."

"Thank you, Lord Nichols."

After he takes his leave I slowly make my way back to the dais, where a line of guests still wait before Andrei. My eyes fall upon a girl at the front in a dark purple gown and a purple-and-silver costume mask. I halt in midstep, recognizing her slight build, the stubborn way she squares her shoulders, and the color of her hair. . . .

The palace guard nods, and Elara steps forward to speak to Andrei.

CHAPTER 22

ELARA

*S*houldn't I at least *meet* the brother Lord Royce expects me to betray?

I drop into a curtsy and affect the breathless voice that has served me well so many times before. "Good evening, Your Majesty."

"Good evening." He does not look me in the eyes; his gaze roams around the room, giving me time to study him. Elements of his face remind me of myself, and I'm tempted to rip off my mask and tell him the search is over. Tell him that, far from being his enemy, I could become his greatest ally, if he would only accept me.

Even though it's not wise, I can't help myself from saying, "Guards searched a shop I visited yesterday. They were looking for a girl." I giggle and lower my voice conspiratorially. "Tell me, who is she?"

His face twists, and he finally looks at me. Have I gone too far?

"I was only wondering if she was someone important?" I add quickly.

"She is merely a criminal," he says. "Rest assured, when she is caught I will deal with her."

Deal with me? Is he even the slightest bit curious about

me? Or am I simply a problem for him to handle, in much the same way I was for my father?

Andrei seems unaware of my distress and has turned his attention back to the party. "Have a good evening," he says, clearly dismissing me.

I slink into a corner of the room where a portrait of Andrei hangs. I resist the urge to rip it off the wall and tear it to shreds.

Lord Royce was right. I have no reason to believe I will ever be allowed to live peacefully. The options are exactly as he said: Go into hiding, or rise up and declare myself a claimant to the crown.

A voice, soft as a whisper, echoes next to me. "What are you *doing* here?" Wilha has sidled up next to me, the nervousness in her demeanor plain to see, even behind her opal mask.

"I need to speak with you," I whisper back. "Is there somewhere private we can go?" I pause, as inspiration strikes. "A library, maybe?"

"A library?" Wilha says, sounding confused. "Why a library?"

"It's private. I have something important to tell you."

"Shall we go now?" she says.

I glance around the room. Lord Murcendor speaks with a noble couple. Andrei is still sitting on his throne. Lord Royce is in a corner, huddling with several men, plotting who knows what.

"I'll go first and wait for you in the hall. A few minutes later, when you're sure no one is watching, I want you to slip away."

Wilha nods and I quickly leave the room. In the corridor, I plant myself in front of a painting hanging from the wall. If questioned, I'm prepared to say I'm interested in the art contained in the palace, far more so than the tediousness of the masquerade itself.

Wilha emerges and signals that I should join her as she hurries down the hall. The library turns out to be not far from the Grand Ballroom. It consists of several rooms lined with wall-to-wall glass cabinets holding leather-bound books. I inhale sharply; the books are similar in quality to the one Queen Astrid gave me. My eyes scan the titles in the cabinet nearest to us, but I don't see another copy of the book.

"What do you need to tell me?" Wilha says.

"I wanted to make sure you were okay," I say, and find there's a lot more truth than I realized in my words. "I know Lord Murcendor is here. Did he . . . ?" My voice catches. "I mean, has he—"

"He has not tried to harm me, though it is difficult to discern his mental state." She pauses. "Is this why you sneaked into the palace, to inquire after my well-being?"

"It's one reason. You need to be careful, Wilha. I don't know how much news reaches you here in the palace—"

"Formally? Not much. Our brother sees to that."

"Andrei would not have so much power over either of us if he didn't wear the crown," I say, trying to think of the best way to tell her what Lord Royce is asking of me.

Her eyes narrow. "What do you mean? I don't know what you have heard in the city, but I have absolutely no intention of trying to overthrow my own brother. *Our* brother."

"I know that. I wasn't saying—"

I'm interrupted by footsteps in the corridor and the voice of a man calling out, "Wilha?"

"Who is that?" I mouth.

Wilha's lips barely move, but I make out her words: "It's Patric."

CHAPTER 23

WILHA

"*S*tay here," I whisper to Elara. I wait until Patric has walked several yards past the library before stepping into the corridor.

"Patric?"

He turns, relief spreading across his face, before his expression regains its sternness. "You should not be wandering around the palace unescorted. If you wished to leave, you should have informed me or one of your other guards."

"I am not a child, Patric. Nor do I take orders from you. Besides, I just wanted some fresh air."

"You cannot be so careless. You are a fool, Wilha. And Stefan Strassburg is an even bigger fool to have let you return to Galandria."

"*Let* me return?"

"Write to Stefan," Patric says, a pained look crossing his face. "Tell him you wish to return to Kyrenica. Right now you're safer there than you are here."

Seeing the tender look on Patric's face, I want nothing more than to tell him that Stefan and I are not betrothed. But he is the third person tonight who has shown fear for my safety, and I cannot easily dismiss so many concerns.

"Why should I do this? We were something like friends

once, Patric, so I will ask you to tell me the truth." I lower my voice. "Is it because of Andrei that you think I need to leave the kingdom?"

A look of understanding passes between us and he nods. "Anyone who is caught suggesting you are the rightful heir to the crown has their homes or their businesses burned— though I am convinced that is more Lord Murcendor's doing than Andrei's."

I close my eyes. How many have lost their livelihood— and perhaps their very lives— because they dared to speak of me as a queen?

"I don't want to see you get hurt, Wilha," Patric says softly. "And we were more than just friends."

"No," I say, opening my eyes and thinking of his unkindness the night I last saw him. "No, I don't believe we were."

Patric steps closer. "Wilha, I—"

Several heavy thuds echo from the library and his eyes widen. "Is someone in there?"

"No, Patric, don't," I say, but he's already drawn his sword and dashed inside.

Elara kneels in the corner, candlelight glinting off her costume mask. Cabinets stand open and she is on her knees, furiously picking up books that must have just fallen to the ground.

Patric advances toward her until she's backed up against a cabinet, the tip of his sword pointed at her. "Who are you?"

he demands. Elara shifts her eyes to me. For once she seems at a loss for words.

"Sheathe your sword, Patric," I say quietly.

"If you are the girl I think you are," he says to Elara, "then I will have no problem running this blade straight through you."

"Patric—"

"No, Wilha. I don't know if you realize, but the guards were told to watch out for a girl that means the royal family harm. This could be the girl they were speaking of."

"Yes, I do know that." I look into Elara's eyes. "And, yes. This is that girl."

CHAPTER 24

ELARA

I wait for Patric to advance forward. How will they treat me this time? Will I be delivered to the dungeon and to Lord Murcendor? And after he's through questioning me, will I be taken back to my cell? Or will it be straight to the chopping block?

"Sheathe your sword, Patric," Wilha says again. "She is not a trained fighter; she cannot harm you."

"What are you doing in here?" Patric demands, ignoring her. "Were you going to assassinate the princess and then flee? Back away, Wilha," he says as she steps toward him. "I am under orders to take her to Lord Murcendor."

With a graceful sleight of hand, Wilha grabs at a weapon hanging at Patric's waist and pulls it free. It's a short-bladed sword, and I wonder if she's going to help him escort me to the dungeon.

Instead, she points it directly at Patric. "You will not be taking her anywhere."

CHAPTER 25

WILHA

*P*atric's eyes widen with shock. Instinctively, he shifts position, pointing his sword away from Elara and at me. "What are you doing?"

"I cannot allow you to take her."

"Have you ever trained with a short sword?" he asks, blinking rapidly.

"Not even once. But if you attempt to take her anywhere, I shall have to consider this my first lesson."

"Wilha, you have become much more skilled, but you could never best me in a real fight."

"Probably not, but I may give her just enough time to escape. And then you will have to fight me. I wonder how you will explain to everyone why you attacked the Masked Princess?"

I read the calculation in his eyes. He's assessing, trying to understand the scenario before him, finally reaching the conclusion that he simply cannot.

"Lord Murcendor has lied about who she is, then?" he says, lowering his sword.

"Would that surprise you?"

"No," he says after hesitating. "I suppose it would not." He glances over at Elara. "So who is she?"

Patric waits while I consider my answer. He has lowered

his weapon, but only temporarily. He will not allow a suspected assassin to walk away if he is not satisfied by my explanation—even if that means taking up a sword against me.

"Wilha—*don't*," Elara says, seeming to read my mind.

"I believe we can trust him. The secret cannot hold forever. Surely you must have come to this conclusion yourself?" I send her a silent message, and for once, Elara understands. After a slight hesitation, she unties her costume mask and removes it.

Still holding Patric's short sword, I clumsily reach behind my head and fumble to remove my own mask.

"Wilha, stop!" Patric has raised his sword again. "You know it is forbidden."

"Forbidden? By whom? My dead father? Or by my brother and the madman who controls him? I am an Andewyn and I am commanding you—with a sword in my hand—to *look* at me."

Without waiting for an answer, I finish untying my mask and let it fall to the floor with a heavy *thunk*.

Patric pales and glances frantically between me and Elara. He points his sword downward, appearing to lean on it for support.

"She's a look-alike?"

"Not a look-alike," I say. "My twin."

"Your twin?" Patric turns his full attention on me. "That is not possible."

"Think about what you know of our kingdom, of the Andewyns and our history. Ask yourself what would be done if another set of twins were ever born to the reigning king and queen of Galandria."

Patric's eyes stray to the mask at my feet. When he glances up, they're filled with horror. "For the love of Eleanor."

Echoing footsteps sound down the corridor, and the three of us turn.

"We have been gone too long," Patric says. "The other guards will have noticed your absence."

I turn to Elara. "At the back of the last room, you'll find a wall covered by a tapestry of the Opal Mountains. Behind it, three feet up from the right corner, is an opal. Do you understand what I am saying?" Elara blinks and nods slowly, as though she is clearing cobwebs from her mind.

"Good. Press on it and—"

"Wilha," Patric says, "don't tell her about the—"

"She already knows!" I turn back to Elara. "Open the passageway and follow it all the way to the end. It's a direct route that will take you past the armory and the Queen's Library and will—"

"The Queen's Library?" Elara interrupts. "You mean this isn't the only library in the palace?"

"There are many collections of books in the palace. I'd be happy to give you a tour the *next time* you decide to make a fool of yourself and sneak in here, but as I said, the passageway is a direct route and will let out in a cottage behind the palace where our landscapers store their tools. You'll have to circle around to the front, and it shouldn't be a problem for you to exit through the gates. The guards are much more concerned about who wants in, rather than who is leaving." I point to a nearby candelabrum. "Go now, and take a candle with you."

Elara quietly ties on her mask. As usual, her eyes are unreadable. "Thank you," she says, and leaves.

"Are you certain that was wise?" Patric says. "Are you certain she is not a threat to you?"

I toss Patric's sword onto the ground, and pick up my mask and retie it just in time. "Your Highness?" one of my guards calls out.

"The only thing I am certain of," I tell Patric, "is that right now I would like to be alone."

CHAPTER 26

ELARA

As I inch along the tunnel, the dim light from my candle bouncing off the stone walls, the same thought goes through my head: Wilha spared me. When she had the opportunity to turn me over to the guards—something that might have earned her favor, at a time when it sounds like she could desperately use some—she chose to let me go.

If I had been in her position, would I have done the same thing?

Who am I kidding? I *was* in her position—and I handed her right over to Lord Royce, and in turn, to Andrei and Lord Murcendor.

I watched her calm resolve as she raised her blade. I have no doubt she would have attempted to fight Patric while I escaped. She is stronger than I have ever given her credit for. But I am a wretched fool. Did I really think it would be so easy, that I would simply sail into the library and find the book?

The walls of the tunnel are smooth and I run my hand along the stone, hoping my fingertips will brush an embedded opal. Is it possible, that just on the other side where I stand is the Queen's Library? Wilha said the tunnel was a direct route to the garden. Does that mean there are no other entrances into the palace from here?

I spend hours holding my candle up and kneading the walls. Candle wax drips down my hand, burning my flesh, but it's nothing compared to the burning in my own heart. If my mother had any last words for me—even if it's just the name I've always hoped to find—I want it like I have never wanted anything else.

But the walls won't yield to my prodding, and soon the tunnel slopes downward, before dead-ending abruptly at a stone staircase. Cautiously, I hike up my skirts, which have become dirtied from crouching down examining the walls, and make the short climb up to what appears to be a wooden door. There's an embedded opal winking in the candlelight, but next to it, a handhold. I grasp it and shove at the door. Loud, clattering *thunks* immediately sound on the other side of the door. I pull back, gripping the handhold, prepared to shut the passage and flee back into the tunnel at the first sound of someone disturbed by the racket.

After several minutes of silence, I push open the door and slip from the tunnel. As Wilha said, I'm in a cottage filled with gardening tools. Wooden shelves are attached to the wall I dislodged—the commotion I heard was the sound of tools falling from the shelves. Quickly, I blow out my candle and dispose of it, then exit the cottage. The palace grounds are shadowed in the moonless night, and smell of lavender and hyacinth.

By the time I've circled around to the front, carriages have begun leaving the palace. The guards at the golden gates are busy holding back a group of townspeople, most of them clearly drunk, who've gathered outside the gates, demanding an audience with Andrei. They take one look at my dusty appearance and quickly wave me through the gates.

I creep away from Eleanor Square, slinking from shadow to shadow and doing my best to avoid anyone who still roams the streets. A candle burns in Alinda's window. Lord Royce, who looks swelled with more than a small amount of outrage, meets me at the door.

"I'll do it," I say, cutting him off before he can speak. "I'll agree to everything you ask—on one condition."

Lord Royce's lips thin. "And that is?"

"Get Wilha out of the palace. Before we move against Andrei, I want her removed. I don't want her to suffer for our choices. I refuse to leave my sister behind again, and I can only imagine what Andrei's reaction will be when he hears of our plans."

I will not spend the rest of my life in hiding; nor will I flee. Tonight, I slunk away from my late parents' home like unwanted riffraff. Never again.

The next time I return to the Opal Palace, it will be to take the crown.

PART TWO

"Eleanor's army, overzealous and fierce,
caused much suffering to the Galandrian people.
The young queen's first task after being
crowned was to set about building the alliances
she would need to strengthen her rule."

—ELEANOR OF ANDEWYN HOUSE:
GALANDRIA'S GREATEST QUEEN

CHAPTER 27

ANDREI

*A*ndrei Andewyn sits on his throne in the Grand Ballroom. Masked couples twirl before him, yet the new king is bored. It's another night, another party.

Is this what it means to be a king . . . and a man? To preside over another meaningless event? To lend his signature to decrees he does not write, and to accept responsibility for punishments he does not order?

Though in truth, he is not yet a man. The length of time stretching between now and the day he comes of age—the day he can begin ruling in his own right—fills him with unease, though he cannot say why.

The music plays, the wine flows, and the masquerade carries on.

The new king signals to his steward. "I should like to retire early."

"Your Highness," the man replies, "Lord Murcendor says you must stay until at least midnight."

Andrei bites back the temptation to vent his temper upon the poor man. *He* is king. *He* wears the crown. His wishes will not be countered by a lowly servant.

Although he scarcely realizes it, the new king is slowly stumbling upon a new appreciation for the power of words.

Specifically, three little ones: *Lord Murcendor says* . . .

Andrei searches the room. Near the orchestra, Wilhamina chats politely to a noble couple. Her dress and mask clearly stand out, even among this glittering crowd. As his loneliness has grown, the new king has watched his sister more closely these last few weeks. She does not seem to be the monster that haunted his nightmares as a child. She does, in fact, seem quite friendly.

And for the first time, the new king acknowledges that he may be in need of a friend. Andrei decides he shall seek her out; he shall try to know this sister of his. It is upon this happy thought that he retires for the evening.

But he does, of course, wait until after midnight.

CHAPTER 28

WILHA

After Elara's flight from the palace, I am careful. I pay Andrei much deference, and never mention the food shortages, nor the discontent I hear is growing in the city. The Guardian Council brings me word that the betrothal between me and Stefan Strassburg has been formally broken, and that a new treaty will soon be negotiated between the two kingdoms. Soon the whispers of the servants take on a familiar tone: *I bet the crown prince of Kyrenica decided he didn't want her after all. Perhaps she really is cursed. . . .*

I bear it silently, for I would rather they revert to rumors of the past than speak of a future with me on the throne. I hope Andrei hears these rumors and that they cool whatever jealousy may be growing in his heart.

My diligence pays off when Andrei himself visits my chambers and invites me to join him at an outdoor luncheon he has planned for members of the court the next day.

"It would have been Father's birthday tomorrow," he says. "I thought we should spend it together." His haughty manner drops, and in that moment, I do not see a jealous king, but an orphaned boy.

The luncheon is held in a large gazebo surrounded by tulips. It is attended by ladies dripping with sparkling jewels and men dressed in riding gear, many of whom participated in a hunt earlier in the morning. Andrei and Lord Murcendor take their places at either end of the long table. Andrei asks me to sit next to him. A lunch of herbed quiche, apple tarts, and ripe fruit is served, and the air hums with murmured conversation, clinking silverware, and the giddy laughter of a young court.

"How go the plans for your coronation?" I ask Andrei.

"Lord Murcendor is taking care of all the plans." He frowns. "Lord Murcendor takes care of a lot of things."

Do I detect signs of discontent in his eyes?

"Yes, he does," I say softly. "It seems to be a talent of his."

Andrei falls silent, glancing thoughtfully across the table at Lord Murcendor as he eats. To my right sits a couple too deeply entranced with each other to pay me any mind, and I resist the urge to steal a glance at Patric, who stands behind me along with the rest of my guards.

Patric and I have not spoken of Elara since the night she left the palace. I am certain he will keep her existence a secret, though I am less certain Elara will not do something foolish. She is hiding in the city somewhere, but where? I still believe Lord Royce knows where she is. Yesterday at court I saw him speaking with Patric, and I wonder now if I could find a way to get a message to her.

Yet what good will a message do while she's still in hiding? I glance again at Andrei—the food and the sunlight streaming into the gazebo seemed to have cheered him—and wonder if there's a way to talk him into calling off the search, or, even better, welcoming Elara back to the palace as our sister?

I lean over to Andrei and whisper, "Do you still have guards searching for Elara?"

"Yes," he says quietly through a mouthful of bread. "Though it's difficult to find one girl in a crowded city when half the population cover their faces."

"And if your men find her? What will you do with her?"

"What *can* I do with her? Lord Murcendor says she's a traitor."

"She is not a *traitor*, Andrei. She is our sister."

"And is she as bitter as he says she is?" He seems genuinely curious.

"No more or less so than you or I would be in her place. Can you imagine discovering that the people who should have loved you most in this world deliberately betrayed you?"

"No, I cannot." Andrei sips his goblet. "Is it true she wishes me dead?"

"Of course not! In Korynth she asked me about you often. I think she truly wants to know you—or she did, before you decided to have her brought back to Allegria as your prisoner."

Andrei sets his goblet down deliberately. "But Wilha . . . I never gave such an order." He steals a look around the table before turning back to me. "I know Lord Murcendor told Lord Royce that I did, but it was just too much. Elara's existence, Father's death—I wasn't capable of issuing *any* orders. Then one day Lord Murcendor came to me and said that Lord Royce had been dispatched to Kyrenica."

I lean forward. "Andrei, are you telling me Lord Murcendor issues orders without consulting you?"

"I needed him to," he says, a defensive edge creeping into his voice. "No one else—"

"I think our young royals are forgetting themselves," Lord Murcendor's voice cuts across the table, and Andrei and I quickly look up. "There are guests here who hoped to speak with you today, not watch the two of you whispering."

The table falls silent; and though Lord Murcendor's voice merely sounds perplexed, I'm certain I read malevolence in his eyes.

"Yes, what *are* you two whispering about?" Lady Ashland asks.

"Plans for my coronation, of course," Andrei replies smoothly. "My sister and I are unsure what entertainments to provide for the city. If anyone here has an opinion, I should greatly like to hear it."

The conversation turns to the coronation. When I glance at Andrei again, I see he's paled slightly. I follow his gaze. Lord Murcendor looks at us with a displeased expression.

"What's wrong?" I murmur. "Why is he looking at us that way? He couldn't have heard what we were saying."

"I don't think it matters *what* we were saying," Andrei says. "I get the impression he is not particularly pleased when you and I speak to each other." He begins piling his plate with bread and fruit, carefully not looking at me. "Perhaps we should continue this later."

"Of course," I say, his words filling me with hope. He hasn't agreed to anything regarding Elara, but it's a start.

We eat the rest of our lunch in silence, until Lord Murcendor and Andrei excuse themselves to attend to palace business. While Lord Ashland regales everyone with tales of his hunting prowess earlier in the morning, Patric leans close. "In a few minutes, I'd like you to make your apologies and tell everyone you're tired, and then return to your chambers. Please," he adds, "it's important."

A short time later, I am striding back to the palace; Patric and the rest of my guards follow behind me. My heart pounds as I wonder what he wants to speak to me about. I don't know what I expected when I showed him my face. Truly, I wanted to secure Elara's safety and see Patric grant her safe passage from the palace. But I had also hoped for something else from Patric, some sign that the moment meant something to him. A sign that *I* meant something to him.

I finally have to acknowledge that the feelings I had for him last year have come back in full force. Is it the same for him?

When we reach my chambers, Patric asks the other guards to wait outside while he speaks to me privately.

"Wilha, there's something I need to tell you."

"Yes?" My heart pounds harder. "What is it?"

"I had an interesting conversation with Lord Royce yesterday. It seems he's been harboring Elara somewhere in the city."

I nod, aware of the disappointment curling through my chest. "I suspected as much. I had hoped we might get a message to her."

"We can. But when Lord Royce came to me yesterday he asked me if I thought you held any ambitions to be queen."

I sigh. "I assume you told him I did not? I have been working extremely hard to show everyone I am not a threat to Andrei, or his reign."

"I did, but Wilha . . . the reason he asked was because Elara has decided *she* wants to be queen."

"Elara wishes to be queen?" I blink. "Is that some sort of jest?"

"I am afraid not." Patric grimaces. "Elara and Lord Royce are truly plotting to take the throne from Andrei."

I let his words sink in, and try to understand these new turn of events, but find I cannot. "Why is Elara doing this? Has she suddenly sprouted concern for the well-being of our kingdom?"

"Lord Royce didn't say it outright, but it sounded to me as though he had convinced her it was the best option she had, given the position Andrei and Lord Murcendor have put her in."

"And do neither of them realize the consequences of their actions? I believe Andrei is slowly coming around to see Lord Murcendor for who he really is—but that does not mean he will simply surrender the crown he was raised to believe is his by right. He will rise up against Elara, Lord Murcendor at his side, and between the two of them, my siblings will plunge our kingdom into war."

"I believe they do realize that—which is why Lord Royce and Elara are asking you to leave the palace . . . and join them."

"*Join* them? Have they both lost their senses?"

"I think they're genuinely concerned for your safety." Patric pauses and adds, "As am I."

"Did neither Elara nor Lord Royce consider that I could go to Andrei this very moment and tell him of their treason?"

"I think they are counting on you not choosing that course of action."

"Why not?"

"Because by *not* leaving, you will be essentially allying yourself not just with Andrei, but Lord Murcendor. They do not think you will make that choice."

"*I* do not think they know me nearly so well. And it rather feels like Elara is *ordering* me to leave the palace, not asking."

"I wouldn't say *ordered*, exactly," Patric says, grimacing. "I think they genuinely believe this is the best thing for you."

Despite all the fears my father and Lord Murcendor have held concerning Elara, I have never viewed her as a threat to me, or to our family. Yet now she's set her sights on the opal crown. And she asks the impossible.

How do I choose one sibling over another?

"What do you know of Lord Royce?" I ask.

"He's a difficult one to read, but he seemed quite determined when I spoke to him. I think he is fed up with things as they are in Galandria, and quite truthfully, Wilha, he is far from the only one. If a legitimate claimant like Elara rises up against Andrei, I have no doubt many would follow her."

I study Patric's features. "You think I should do as they say. You think I should join them."

"I think, especially after Lord Royce's plans become known to Andrei and Lord Murcendor, you would be safer elsewhere."

CHAPTER 29

WILHA

My mother's statue in the Queen's Garden is as majestic as ever. I stand before her, hoping that some of her wisdom—and the wisdom of all my ruling female ancestors—will help me with the decision I must make now.

Aside from the palace guards who keep watch along the wall, Patric and the rest of my personal guard wait at the edge of the garden under an apple tree. They stand together, laughing quietly among themselves, and I am thankful they are giving me some small measure of privacy. Or pretending to, at least.

Though I find myself in the middle of an impending war between my siblings for the opal crown, it is not lost on me that I am older than both of them. Why, then, if Lord Royce wanted to rise up against Andrei, did he choose my sister— my *younger* sister—and not me? I fear I know the answer to this question, and it does not sit well in my gut.

My eyes stray to the empty spot next to my mother's statue—the space reserved for the next Queen of Galandria. What statue will stand here one day? One of Elara, or of Andrei's wife?

If Elara and Andrei are going to vie for the crown, then why not you? Why not have your own statue in this garden?

The thought creeps in, but I quickly banish it. To consider such a thing is madness. It is treason, and goes directly against the wishes of my father the king, a fact that may mean nothing to Elara, but still matters to me.

I circle about the garden, regarding each of the statues; from Eleanor the Great to Rowan the Brave to my mother, Astrid the Regal. I imagine each of them coming to life and giving me counsel. Yet even in my imagination, their voices are no more than a breeze or a song sung from too far in the distance to hear the precise words.

Has ever a princess of Galandria had to make a decision such as this?

I bring a hand to my masked cheek and trace my fingertips around the encrusted opals. For nearly all my life, I was forced to cover my face because my parents feared civil war. Now, it seems civil war may be inevitable.

The guards' laughter suddenly ceases. I turn and see Lord Murcendor walking toward me, his emerald Guardian's robe flaring around him. I look in Patric's direction. His shoulders have stiffened and his face is grim.

"Your Highness," Lord Murcendor says, bowing, "it has been a while since we visited in these gardens. I thought I would check up on you."

We settle on a nearby bench, and as we stare at my mother's statue, it feels like a metal band begins squeezing my chest. Surely he does not know of Elara's intentions?

"I also wanted to remind you that tonight Andrei is hosting Azarlin's ambassador for a private dinner."

Relief floods my chest. "Yes, I have already told Andrei I will dine with him and Sir Vanderberg."

"Actually, I think it best if you rest this evening."

"Rest?" I say. What game is he playing now?

"Yes. I think it likely that the schedule Andrei has asked you to keep—all the engagements, as well as the feasts he's asked you to attend—may have become too much for you. I had thought under your father's rule you had been a little too sheltered. Now, I see he was right."

"I think I am fine, Lord Murcendor."

He turns, his dark eyes glittering. "Clearly, Wilha, if you are filling Andrei's head with lies about your sister, you are far from *fine*."

My breath catches. Did Andrei go running straight to Lord Murcendor after our conversation?

"I do not understand your meaning," I say carefully.

"No? Andrei came to me asking if perhaps I haven't been mistaken about Elara—*I*, who watched over her all her life. When I pressed him on where he'd gotten such erroneous notions, he finally confessed you had told him that Elara actually wants to be on friendly terms with him."

"That's not what I said," I say, realizing how wrong my earlier words were, now that I know Elara has no intention of meeting with Andrei. All she wants is to take his crown for herself.

"Then what *did* you say?"

"I . . ." I cannot answer him. I cannot defend Elara, and I don't want to say anything that he might use against Andrei.

"Truly Wilha, this convinces me that your mental state is really quite fragile, and in the meantime, I think it best to curtail your engagements for the time being."

I read suppressed triumph in his eyes, and all at once I think I finally understand. My health and mental state mean nothing to him. What I think he really wants is to keep Andrei and I separate. Divided.

"Is this Andrei's wish? If so, I would like to ask him to recon—"

"They are *my* wishes, and I have made Andrei see their wisdom. Your apologies have already been made to Sir Vanderberg."

"I see. . . . And for how long do you wish me to retire from public life?"

"For as long as I think best. Stefan Strassburg will be arriving in the city for your brother's coronation next month, and for obvious reasons he should not spend time in your presence, so this will come at a good time . . . don't look so troubled, Princess." He traces a knuckle down my cheek, and goose-flesh rises on my arms. "Once there was a time when you looked at me like I was your whole world. So trust me now,

Wilha. In the days to come I will prove to you that I know what's best for you. After all, you are the Glory of Galandria."

My breath quickens. I have not heard him call me that since last year, and I had hoped his obsession with the Masked Princess had waned. But now I think he's just been biding his time, waiting for the moment when he could bring me back under his command.

"Thank you, Lord Murcendor," I say, feeling nauseous. "You can be sure I will do all that is required of me."

He smiles. "I knew you would see reason, Princess."

As soon as he has gone, Patric is at my side, looking angrier than I have ever seen him. "If he ever touches you like that again, he will find himself suddenly short a hand."

"And then you will find *yourself* suddenly short a head," I say, forcing myself to take deep breaths.

I glance over at the guards posted on the wall to see if they've heard Patric. But their backs are to us, more concerned, as always, with threats outside the palace.

I thought I had to choose between Andrei and Elara. Now I see clearly: Andrei, despite wearing the crown, does not hold any sort of power. That rests solely with Lord Murcendor, and his grip on the throne—and on *me*—will only strengthen as time passes. If he can send me into seclusion so easily, if he can have the entire palace guard searching for Elara, what could he do to Andrei? Is my brother any safer in this palace than I am?

"Send word to Lord Royce that I accept his proposal. I need to leave the palace *now*, Patric. Before Lord Murcendor makes it impossible for me to do so."

Maybe by joining Elara and Lord Royce, I can find a way to free us all.

CHAPTER 30

ELARA

I am awoken by the squeaking of Alinda's mattress as she rises to begin baking the day's ration of bread. It's still dark outside, and I lie awake, staring at the ceiling, too nervous to fall back asleep. Lord Royce has deemed it unsafe for Wilha and me to stay in the city once she flees the palace. Later today, after Wilha makes her escape, Lord Royce has arranged to have the two of us smuggled past the city gates.

His ability to coordinate and execute such a plan speaks to his wealth and influence. But what do I know of the man, really? He keeps his own counsel. For all I know, he could be just as power-hungry and twisted as Lord Murcendor. Yet after today, I will be more heavily under his influence than ever before. I don't know how he plans to get Wilha out of the palace, nor where we are being taken after we escape the city.

When sleep will not come, I get up and walk downstairs. The bakery is pleasantly warm. The brick ovens are fired up, and Alinda hums while she hunches over a countertop sculpting the dough.

"At least let me help you, today of all days," I say, stepping up to the counter.

Alinda stops humming. "Do you have much experience baking bread?"

"Yes, I grew up serving a noble family and did most of the cooking."

"Were you any good at it?"

"Well . . . no, actually."

Alinda mashes her lips together, as though trying to suppress a smile. She gestures for me to dip my hands into a bowl filled with flour.

"I suppose I should mark this moment," she says, smacking a round of dough onto the countertop in front of me. "One day I'll be able to say I baked bread with the Queen of Galandria."

A chill shivers down my back as I begin kneading. *The Queen of Galandria . . .*

"Tell me something," I say after we've worked side by side for several minutes. "Why is your uncle doing this? I mean, he is the Guardian of Trade, and it appears he is already quite wealthy and influential. It doesn't seem he has a lot to gain by any of this."

Alinda continues working at the dough. "He wasn't always wealthy," she says finally. "Our family has owned this bakery for generations, but his father, Maxim, had a talent for knowing how to trade, for understanding what people wanted and how to get it for them. He was also a very talented bread maker—your grandfather, the king at that time, used to send his servants here specifically to buy his bread. When he visited the city, he even came here himself to meet the talented baker, and the two of them struck up a friendship. The king used to say Maxim ate better than those in the Opal Palace, so talented was he with trading his bread. Eventually, the king was so pleased by Maxim's wit and cunning that he decided to name him Guardian of Trade and bequeathed him a title and land—although there's not a single drop of noble blood in our family line. But Maxim never forgot where he came from, and he taught Uncle—as well as my father, before he died—to love the nobles and the commoners alike. When Maxim died, your father appointed my uncle Guardian of Trade." She pauses. "I don't think Uncle has ever forgotten where he came from, either. He's one of the few commoners to establish himself in noble circles. I think he would like to see a queen who will open the doors for more commoners to rise."

After she finishes, I quietly work at the dough, sobered by her words. I haven't forgotten where I came from, either. So what can *I* possibly know about being a queen? The only guide I ever had in this world was a woman who practiced deception the way other women practice their cross-stitch. But if my options are exile, or queen, I know what I will choose.

Of course, if we fail today, I'll most likely lose both choices. As well as my head.

Rolf comes downstairs, rubbing his eyes. "Big day today. Are you ready?" he asks me.

"Absolutely," I lie, fighting the urge to vomit.

"Good." He turns to Alinda. "Uncle has arranged everything. We should be able to get them out of the city without incident, and I will return in a few days' time. But if we are caught, you must leave immediately and go to the place we discussed. They won't be able to find you there."

Alinda nods as she hunches over the countertop, and wipes away a tear. "Just be careful," she says, suppressing a sob.

"Thank you," I say, understanding for the first time the depth of the sacrifice she and Rolf have made for me. "Thank you for everything."

Alinda straightens up. "Your brother is a gluttonous tyrant. If you wish to repay me, you can start by being a better ruler and taking a bit more interest in the people of this kingdom."

"I will," I say softly. What I mean is, *I will try.*

"We'll be fine, Alinda," Rolf says. "We'll have a carriage waiting in Eleanor Square near the library for the princess, and then—"

"The library?" I interrupt. My heart speeds up and I try to keep my face impassive. "What library?"

"The Allegrian Historical Library. Your sister will leave the palace and end up there. That's the plan anyway, though I'm not quite sure how."

But I am. A tunnel must connect the Opal Palace to the library. Would Astrid have hidden the second book in the Opal Palace, knowing it would be nearly impossible for me to find a way in? Or would she have traveled the tunnel—the same tunnel Wilha will probably travel today—and left it in the Allegrian Historical Library?

Deep down, I know that's where my mother's message is waiting for me.

CHAPTER 31

WILHA

I enter my closet, preparing to leave my life as the Masked Princess behind once again. Near the entrance to the passageway is a large leather purse filled with a simple dress, a costume mask, and a brown cloak. So Patric has already been here. Hurriedly, I change into my new clothes and stuff my golden gown deep into a trunk, where it may never be found again.

I remove my necklace of keys and open the glass cases containing my masks. Lord Royce made it clear to Patric that I should leave the palace with two of my jeweled masks. What he intends to do with them, I am not sure. After I have removed the masks from the cases, in their place I leave the letter I've written to Andrei:

> *By the time you receive this, I shall be very far away. Whatever you hear, whatever rumors or truths reach your ears, know that it was a truly difficult decision to leave you. Circumstances have forced my hand, and I can no longer stay. Know that I love you as my brother and I always shall.*

The note is brief, but I hope it carries a message that Andrei will hear beyond the anger I know he will feel. And I want to be careful with my words, as Lord Murcendor will undoubtedly see the message.

I stuff the two masks inside the leather purse and leave the necklace of keys on a dresser. I press on the opal and the wall slides back. Not too far into the passageway, Patric holds a torch and waits for me. "I'm here to see you safely to the library. Lord Royce does not think Andrei or Lord Murcendor have any cause for suspicion yet. But in case we come upon anyone in the passageway and it comes to a fight, you shall need an escort."

"Maybe you should give me one of your swords," I say. "I'm capable of defending myself now."

Patric gives me a wary look. "The last time you held my sword you pointed it straight at *me*."

We encounter no one as we descend deeper into the passageway. When we reach the appointed door, Patric lights a nearby torch with his own. He bends down and searches the wall until he finds the embedded opal. "On the other side is a private reading room reserved for members of the royal family."

I nod. "I remember, though it has been a while."

"Good." He stands. "Once the passageway has closed behind you, make your way out of the library and into Eleanor Square. Lord Royce has a carriage waiting for you."

"I will," I say. "Thank you for accompanying me." I turn away to press the opal.

"Aren't you forgetting something?"

I turn back. "What?"

"Your mask. You can hardly enter the library wearing it."

"Of course," I say, slightly surprised. When I changed, I completely forgot to take off my jeweled mask and replace it with the costume one.

I start to untie my mask, but hesitate. "I will remove it after you are gone." I give my leather purse a shake. "There is enough room to stuff it in here. If Lord Royce wanted two masks, three cannot hurt."

Now Patric hesitates. Longing blooms in his eyes. "Please, may I see you? May I see your face?"

"You have already," I remind him. *And it meant nothing to you*, I add silently.

"You are mistaken. The shock of learning about Elara overshadowed everything and suddenly you were ready to fight me over her. What I mean is I have not seen you. Not the way I always wanted to."

Both of us are breathing heavily, and I realize I do want him to see me. With everything in my heart, I want him to see me. My fingers are shaking as I untie the mask. Patric holds his torch as close as he dares and his eyes are wide. The cool air of the tunnel caresses my face as I pull the mask away. His gaze roams over my face, pausing at each feature. "You are beautiful," he says.

"No, I am not," I say, in no mood to be lied to. "I may not be ugly, Patric, but neither am I beautiful."

"You are beautiful to *me*." He presses something soft into my hand. "Be safe, and one day we will see each other again."

With that, he turns around and leaves. In the flickering torchlight, I look down. The golden ribbon I gave him so many nights ago curls in my hand.

It is tattered and worn, as though it has been held often.

CHAPTER 32

ELARA

While we wait for Wilha, I peek out the window of the carriage and wonder how I can get inside the library without being stopped by Nicolai and Rolf, who sit out front in the driver's seat.

I fidget with my costume mask. A cloak of crushed velvet covers my much plainer clothing underneath. We are to wait for Wilha here, then proceed directly north where Lord Royce has another carriage waiting. He has arranged for Wilha and me to be smuggled past the city gates by the same man who ferries the contents of Allegria's chamber pots outside the city, judging that the guards would probably want to keep their distance from that particular cart.

I wonder how Wilha fancies spending a few hours being buried, literally, under a pile of dung?

A guard approaches our carriage. "Your employer has been sitting here for quite some time," he says to Rolf. "What is your business in Eleanor Square?"

Before Rolf can respond, I open the carriage door. "I'm afraid I fell asleep and my driver didn't wish to disturb me. But I am quite awake now, and have business inside the library." I step outside, ignoring Rolf's glowering look, and suppress a smile. I've tied his hands; he can't contradict me now, not in front of a soldier.

Two palace guards are stationed at the entrance to the library, and I nod briskly as I pass them. All is quiet amid the bookshelves and long tables where patrons pore over books. The building is several stories high, and in the very center a staircase spirals up to each floor.

I have little time; there's no possible way I can search each floor. I'm hesitant to draw attention to myself, but I don't see how it can be avoided. I find the librarian—a wheezing, elderly man with papery skin who moves slowly.

"Excuse me, good sir, can you help me? I have purposed to read all I can about our new king's ancestry," I say, the lie sliding easily from my lips. "I am looking for a particular book, *Eleanor of Andewyn House: Galandria's Greatest Queen*. Do you know it?"

Amid all the quiet, it's a wonder no one hears the fierce pounding of my heart in the several seconds it takes him to respond.

"Royal history section . . . top floor . . . near the reading rooms," he says.

I take measured, dignified steps up the spiraling staircase, nothing to indicate that it feels as though I may be ascending to another life, a life where I know my birth name.

Two more palace guards are stationed on the top floor. I move past them with a nod. Patrons bend quietly over long wooden tables. Soon I come upon the royal history section.

Two shelves alone are devoted to Aislinn and Rowan Andewyn, and my breath catches when I realize that one day, books about *me* will become a part of this collection. For better or worse, I have committed myself to Lord Royce's scheme; the only choice I have now is to move forward. What will these books, not yet written, say of me?

I peruse the shelves, moving backward through time, thumbing through volumes of works on all of the rulers of Galandria until—finally!—I find it: *Eleanor of Andewyn House: Galandria's Greatest Queen*.

The book is a match to the copy currently stuffed away in the carriage waiting outside, except that the leather cover is puckered, but overall the pages themselves are in much better condition.

Inside the book is a small message: *Donated by and recovered at the request of Queen Astrid*. I furiously blink back the tears rising to my eyes. I turn the pages, searching for the tiny pinpricks that will tell me I've found the right copy. But that will require searching each page carefully, and time is something I don't have. For all I know, Wilha could be inside the carriage right now, waiting for me. Which means I will have to take the book with me.

Quickly, I slip the book inside my cloak. I turn to see if anyone noticed . . . and glimpse Wilha from across the room. Her lips curve in a dreamy smile. She does not walk so much as slowly drift across the room. She's also not wearing a mask as she should be. She clutches a gold ribbon in one hand . . . and in her other hand she holds her jeweled mask.

No, no, no! I immediately make my way forward, but stop quickly. I'm not the only one who notices Wilha. With a dawning sense of horror, I watch as she heads directly for the spiral staircase—and the two palace guards stationed in front of it. They don't seem to notice the mask in her hands, but they are most definitely interested in her face. They watch her with furrowed brows before turning to each other and sharing a silent look. One of them nods slightly and starts down the staircase, while the other one casually shifts position, cutting off our exit.

Quickly, I stride across the room and place a hand on Wilha's shoulder. "How lovely to see you here . . . Serena," I say the first name that comes to me. "It's been ages."

"Elara?" Wilha asks, the dreamy expression on her face vanishing. "What are—"

"You're not wearing a mask," I hiss in her ear, and tap at my own costumed one. "And our description has been circulated throughout the entire palace guard."

Wilha's eyes fly to the soldier stationed at the staircase. Before she can speak, I take her arm. "I have the most wonderful book I want to show you!" I drag her around a bookshelf where a few people are reading quietly at a table. "Guards are most likely on their way right now—we won't be able to exit down the staircase. Where is the passageway you came from?"

"It's in one of the reading rooms," Wilha answers, understanding at once. "But—"

A chair abruptly scrapes against the floor and a heavyset woman rises.

"I recognize your voice," she says, looking at Wilha as though she's seen a ghost. Her gaze strays to the mask in Wilha's hand.

"Lady Ashland, I'm sorry," Wilha says, going pale. "I can explain—"

"There's no time for that!" I say, shoving her forward. "Move!"

We edge along the side of the room as Lady Ashland's voice peals through the air. "Wilhamina Andewyn walks unmasked among us! Raise your hands and cover your eyes!"

The silence breaks as a low murmuring spreads among the patrons. Marching footsteps echoing up the staircase tell me more guards are arriving. Wilha and I weave through the bookcases, until the reading room comes in sight. We make a mad dash for it.

Pounding footsteps sound behind us, though they're nearly drowned out by the thundering of my own heart. We reach an ornate reading room and Wilha pushes forward to the back corner, where she quickly presses on an opal hidden at the bottom of the wall. It slides away, leaving a gaping black hole yawning before us.

Behind us there's the ring of steel and shouted curses as Wilha and I hurry into the passageway. Wilha finds the opal on the other side and presses it. The wall slides back into place—just as a guard slams into it with a heavy *thud*.

A deep silence settles over the tunnel.

The flickering light of a nearby mounted torch casts shadows. Wilha stands facing the wall, shoulders heaving as she takes one deep breath after another. She whispers something to herself, but I don't catch the words. She turns around and looks into the darkness beyond.

I realize this is the moment when she, too, understands that neither of us can go back to our former lives. The only option we have now is to move forward into wherever the tides of history will carry us.

CHAPTER 33

WILHA

*H*ow can such a small action, a walk between two buildings, change everything I have ever known? I left the Opal Palace as the sister of the king. If I were to return, it could only now be as a traitor.

I lean against the wall in the tunnel and try to compose myself. I cannot hear anything beyond the stone. How long before the guards find the embedded opal? Once my breathing has steadied, I stuff my jeweled mask into my leather purse and tie on the costume mask, cursing myself all the while. If I had not been so foolish, so easily distracted by Patric's ribbon, we would not be in this position.

"What now?" Elara asks as we linger in the passageway.

"Now," I say, turning to face her, "you will tell me why you want to be queen."

"We need to leave," Elara says. "The guards could—"

"I had to choose between you and Andrei, and I chose *you*, Elara. I think I have a right to know why you want this so badly."

"We don't have time for this." She grabs my arm, but I shake myself free of her.

"You did not force me to join you today; I came of my own accord. But if you won't answer my question, then perhaps I have made the wrong choice."

"It was the only way, all right?" she shouts, and for once she drops her guard, and I read the raw fear in her eyes. "I'm tired of being hunted. Ever since the day I was brought to the palace and told I was expected to take arrows meant for you, I've been looking over my shoulder, and I'm tired of it. This way, instead of playing someone else's game; *I* get to make the rules for a change." She pauses and adds in a small voice, "And I could be a good queen, Wilha . . . and thank you for choosing me."

The only sound is the flickering of the torch, until I manage to say, "You're welcome." Feeling like I've lost my equilibrium, I lift the torch from its mount. "There is a fork in the tunnel. My ancestors built it to connect the Opal Palace to both the Galandria Courthouse and the library."

"*Our* ancestors, you mean," Elara says as we set off down the passage.

"Our ancestors," I repeat vaguely, surprised that she so readily embraces her heritage now. Would she still be so quick to do so if she were not trying to steal the crown from Andrei?

The tunnel begins ascending again, and soon we reach the exit and emerge into a small, deserted hallway. Quickly, I extinguish the torch and close the chamber behind us. When we reach the doors, Elara pulls me back. "Wait a minute."

"But—"

"Hush!" She seems to be waiting for something, and when a large party of masked nobles sweeps past us—barely sparing us a second look—she shoves me forward. "Stick close to them," she whispers. "Make it seem as though we're part of their group."

We follow them out of the courthouse where they pause. Business in the square seems to have come to a halt. Dozens of palace guards wait outside the library. Lady Ashland stands among a group of guards, gesturing wildly with her hands as she speaks.

"That's where we need to go." Elara points to a carriage parked in the middle of the square, where Rolf and a man I don't recognize sit in the driver's bench. Unlike everyone else, neither of them are watching the palace guards or the library. Their eyes are sweeping across the square. Looking for us, I assume.

We follow the crowd down the steps when they set off again, sticking as close to them as possible. Several yards away from the carriage, they turn abruptly and head toward the Royal Opera House, leaving Elara and I exposed.

"Walk fast!" she says.

Rolf catches sight of us and appears to issue instructions to the other man. He climbs into the carriage, and Elara and I pick up speed.

But we are not fast enough.

"There they are!" comes Lady Ashland's hysterical voice.

"Run!" Elara cries.

Elara sprints into the carriage as it starts up. I have to hurl myself inside in order to avoid getting left behind altogether, and I tumble to the floor of the carriage, my hip striking the side of the wooden seat. I scramble up and Elara closes the door behind me. The carriage takes off from the square.

Above the rattling of the wheels, I hear Rolf shouting, "Change of plans, Nicolai! We won't be leaving the city today. Once we're out of sight of any guards, pull over to the side of the street and run for all you're worth. I'll take care of the girls!"

We continue picking up speed. The carriage shakes and jostles violently. People are scrambling to get out of our way before the horses trample them. A hundred yards behind the carriage, a line of palace guards on horseback chase after us.

We turn one corner and then another. Soon the warm, thick smell of beeswax envelopes us—we're in the candle-makers' section of the city.

All of a sudden, the carriage lurches to a stop, and the three of us are thrown forward. I hear the driver—Nicolai—jump from his seat, and his pounding footsteps as he flees.

"Everyone, out!" Rolf cries.

Elara and I follow him into a shop, where we dodge hundreds of pillar candles. We move straight on through the back door into the alley, where we promptly turn and sweep back into the shop next door. We continue on in this way for several minutes, passing surprised shopkeepers as we emerge into the street, only to turn again into the next shop over and cross through to the alley, thereby staying off the street as much as possible as we make our way through the city.

"You are taking us back toward Eleanor Square," I say to Rolf after some time.

He nods. "There's someone who has quarters nearby who will harbor the two of you until we can figure out how to get you out of the city."

"Who?" I ask, but he does not answer.

We draw close to the square and turn down a quiet street of elegant apartments. Rolf stops at one and raps on the door with two short knocks. After a moment, it opens, and I recognize the face before me.

"Your Highnesses," says Lord Nichols, hastily drawing aside, "please come in."

CHAPTER 34

ELARA

*I*t's dangerous to look out the window of Lord Nichols's bedchamber, but after two weeks of being trapped inside his apartment, I can't help myself. In the windows across the cobblestone street, candlelight glows peacefully. But only a few hours before, palace guards searched the entire building—as well as this one—looking for Wilha and me. Were it not for the hidden chamber in Lord Nichols's pantry, we would have been discovered.

Now that dusk has fallen, the sky is painted lavender and blue, nearly the colors of the Andewyn family. Fitting, since tonight, on the eve of Andrei's coronation, Wilha and I will declare ourselves to the people of Allegria.

All of this waiting has given me ample time to examine my mother's book. And I have found nothing. No pinpricks. No messages. No missing pages. Except for the puckering cover, the book appears to be perfectly preserved. I was so sure I had understood my mother's words. Sure the copy in the Allegrian Historical Library must be where her next message was. It's clear I'm missing something, but I can't figure out what.

"Can you help me with the buttons, Elara?"

I turn to find Wilha, half-dressed in one of the gowns Lord Royce provided for her—for *us*, actually, as we will be dressing identically. Her eyes are fixed on the window, her expression slightly disapproving. But she does not admonish me as I let the curtain fall closed and button her up. After being in hiding for so many days—our only news from the outside world coming from Lord Nichols or Lord Royce—even she is beginning to feel claustrophobic.

According to Lord Nichols, the disruption at the library, followed by the chase through the streets, has set Allegria abuzz, speculating over the Masked Princess's disappearance and the girl whom Andrei wants found so badly, particularly since the palace has made no official comment about the events.

Tonight, we will give them their answers.

"How much do you trust Lord Royce?" Wilha says as I finish with her buttons.

"I trust him more than I trust our fool of a brother." I turn back and peek through the curtain once more, and wish I could see through the apartment building, past Eleanor Square, and up the hill to the Opal Palace. Lord Nichols said Stefan arrived in the city nearly a week ago on behalf of his father to celebrate Andrei's coronation. Does he think of me at all with anything other than hatred?

"I guess what I mean," Wilha says, "is have you thought about what type of queen you'll be?"

"The type who doesn't burn people's homes down just because they don't agree with me."

"There is a lot more to ruling than that," says Wilha. "And all that destruction is Lord Murcendor's doing, not Andrei's."

"If you say so." I see a man turn up the street. He's blond and tall and tanned. My heart begins to pound. It can't be . . . can it? I stand up to take a better look—

The curtain is yanked from my hand. "Don't stare outside so long." Wilha lets the curtain fall closed. "You will only draw suspicion."

"When I am queen, I will do the ordering, and you will do the listening!" I jerk the curtain open. Where is he? My eyes scan the street. . . . There—I spy him again, and my heart sinks. It's definitely not Stefan.

I turn around and face Wilha. "I'm sorry," I say, cursing myself for losing my patience with her. Again. "I'm just jumpy and agitated. If this wasn't our last night in the apartment, I think I would go mad from being cooped up so long."

Wilha sits down in a nearby armchair. "It is difficult being inside all day. But you do realize that when you are queen there will be many days when you may desire to do something, but will be unable to, as kingdom business will require your attention?"

I bite back the tart reply rising to my lips. Must she always be so stoic, so grim all the time? "Yes, I know. . . . Although I doubt kingdom business ever gets in the way of Andrei's pleasures," I can't help but add.

Wilha's eyes are troubled. "Elara, I think we need to talk about—"

The door opens and Rolf enters. "Uncle would like to speak to you." Wilha begins to rise, and he clarifies, "He would like to speak with Elara."

Wilha sits back down. "Of course."

"We'll talk later, okay?" I say to Wilha, and make a promise to myself that I will be more patient with her. I follow Rolf from the room, but turn back and add, "It's amazing when you think about it. By the end of tonight, many people in this kingdom will be calling me queen."

"Yes," Wilha answers slowly. "That truly is amazing."

CHAPTER 35

WILHA

Have I made a mistake?

The thought has been growing like a weed that, once taken root, seems impossible to be rid of. My sister can be angry and impulsive, much like Andrei. Only instead of looking to Lord Murcendor, she looks to Lord Royce as they make their plans—plans they never care to share with me. Whenever I have approached her on the subject, she has preferred to brush me off and stare out the window or thumb through the pages of her book. Whatever preoccupies her so, clearly, it is not the running of the kingdom she wishes to rule.

You would think, given that I grew up in the Opal Palace, Lord Royce and Elara would be a little more eager to solicit my opinion. It was I who suggested to Lord Royce that instead of leaving the city tonight under a pile of excrement, we might simply ask Patric to find out if any of the guards assigned to the city gates are loyal to me instead of Andrei, and wait until the night of their watch, when they could allow us passage out of Allegria.

Lord Royce seemed thoroughly amazed, particularly when Patric was able to accomplish this fairly easily. I suppose he did not believe I possessed the intelligence to propose such a plan.

When we set off from Lord Nichols's apartment, the night is hot and humid. Elara and Lord Royce walk in front of Rolf and me, and I cannot help but look at her as we silently travel up the street.

When I am queen, I will do the ordering, and you will do the listening. . . .

Eleanor Square is packed with masked revelers as they sing and dance and clink ale bottles. Andrei seems to have ceded the night to the people. Along with his coronation tomorrow, a new law shall take effect: No more masks are to be worn in Allegria. It seems the city has decided to celebrate their final night of masked freedom with a public masquerade.

A woman dressed in a gold mask calls, "I am she! I am the Masked Princess!" Her voice is high-pitched with excitement, and, I suspect, a bit too much ale. "Look upon me and meet your doom!" She removes her mask, and amid much cheering, the men around her pretend to fall to the ground, as if dead.

Ever since my disappearance, here and there women have emerged, claiming to be me. The first few times it happened Andrei sent guards after them. According to Lord Royce, the palace has grown weary of such antics and has finally decided to move forward and ban face masks, even though the law is wildly unpopular.

Rolf and I stop to look at the fireworks igniting over the square, spinning, whizzing, and popping in brilliant shades of blue and purple, and pink and gold. Up ahead, Elara and Lord Royce whisper, ignoring the spectacle. No doubt they are going over the plan one last time.

I envision a future of being at Elara's command, as I was so recently at Andrei's. Will she be any better a ruler than he? I see no evidence to believe she will, and I fear all of Galandria will suffer for it.

Unless I surprise everyone, and change the plan.

When the fireworks cease, we resume walking. The Royal Opera House rises up from the southern end of Eleanor Square. Gargoyles perch from the top of the stone building, glaring down at the patrons streaming inside the colonnaded ground floor. They seem to taunt me, *"We know who you are. . . ."*

As we pass through the arched doorway, my stomach lurches at the speech I must shortly give. Lord Royce has invited several nobles whom he knows have grown weary of Andrei and Lord Murcendor to attend tonight, vaguely promising them a show they will not want to miss. He believes many of his guests, who have attended Andrei's parties in the last few weeks, will recognize my voice when I speak. Yet he has not trusted me to find my own words; he has forced me to memorize a speech he and Elara crafted.

The heat from all the candles in the crystal chandeliers is oppressive, and sweat beads my brow. We head up a staircase to the Guardians' box. As planned, Elara and I take seats in the back, where we are hidden in the shadows.

I have always loved the Royal Opera House, with the gilded boxes and red velvet cushions and curtains. I wonder when or if I shall ever visit this place again. The Guardians' box is only slightly less grand than the king's box, which lies directly to my right. I glance over, and see several men seated, their faces hidden under crimson and black costume masks, patiently waiting for the show to start. Andrei himself will be at the coronation ball at the palace, so who is using his box tonight?

Patrons stream up the aisles to take their seats. Lord Royce sits in front of Elara and me, waving to a couple on the ground floor. He is perhaps the only person in the room not wearing a mask. This is by design, not negligence. He is well-known in Allegria and wants our performance tonight to carry the full weight of his presence.

He turns to us and says, "Put the Masked Princess's mask on." With a final glance at each other, Elara and I remove the jeweled metal masks from our cloaks and discreetly begin making the switch with our costume masks.

I run my fingers along my ornate mask. If Elara were to become queen, I would then be in the uncomfortable position of having to ask my sister for permission to remove my mask. Would she grant it? Would she remember how stifling it felt, all those months when she had to cover her own face? Or would she quickly forget, and, when faced with the people's demand to see the Masked Princess, decide I must continue wearing it?

And would she have compassion on our deposed brother? Would she truly understand that Andrei, while not entirely innocent, is not as cruel she believes he is? I want to believe the best about my sister, yet I fear her anger and bitterness would get the best of her.

When I am queen, I will do the ordering, and you will do the listening. . . .

No. I cannot trade one potential tyrant for another. I grip the edges of my seat as my resolve hardens. I can only hope Elara will forgive me for what I am about to do.

Lord Royce leans over to Rolf and whispers, "Go find the first guard you can. Tell him I said he should alert the king that yet another imposter has risen up and is foolishly cavorting inside the opera house. Tell him I will deal with it and there is no need to spare any guards if he cannot."

Rolf nods and leaves. Truly, the Guardian is cunning. With the coming disruption Lord Royce has planned at the palace gates, I doubt Andrei will feel he can spare any guards.

A man appears on the stage. Just as he begins to speak, Lord Royce stands to address the crowd.

And so it begins.

"Ladies and gentlemen, before we enjoy tonight's performance, I bring you a message from the House of Andewyn." Lord Royce's tone is polite, but lacking in the zeal I always heard in my father's voice when he addressed a crowd. Yet everyone quiets down immediately and turns to look at him. "Rumors of the Masked Princess's disappearance have been circulating in the city, yet she is here tonight and wishes to speak."

From the shadows, I see the people turning to one another, as if in disbelief. Lord Royce turns and bows to me.

I stand and remove my velvet cloak, exposing my jeweled gown beneath, and step toward the front of the box. Gasps echo across the room as the people glimpse my dress and mask.

I take a deep breath. "Good evening . . . rumors of my disappearance have circulated these past two weeks." I pause, feeling light-headed under the weight of the stares and the unyielding heat of the theater.

"Yet this is hardly the first time rumors about me have circulated, is it not? I have grown up living with rumors and whispers. Of my ugliness. Of a curse." I pause, still feeling slightly faint. "For years I believed these rumors and considered myself the least of the Andewyns. Yet last year I discovered there was, indeed, a terrible secret behind the mask."

The crowd looks up at me, straining to hear every word. The stage is full of performers who have appeared from behind the curtain to listen to me.

"Most of you know our history. How Aislinn Andewyn betrayed her twin sister, my great-great-grandmother Queen Rowan. Our kingdom and my own family have never truly recovered from these events. For these reasons, my birth was considered a curse, not a blessing. Not because of any defect on my part . . ." I pause. "But simply for the fact that I was not the only daughter born to Queen Astrid that day."

I hear Elara rise and step next to me. Many people remove their masks—their skin pale, their eyes wide—in order to get a better look at Elara and me. Several women look at us through their opera glasses.

Elara's hand finds mine and she squeezes it. "Keep going."

"The girl standing next to me is my twin sister. Hidden away for seventeen years, her existence was known only to a handful of people inside the Opal Palace. My own face was covered to further protect the secret. But tonight, let our own, uncovered faces stand as witnesses that what I say is true."

Elara and I remove our masks. Gasps and shouts erupt. Several people cover their eyes. One man removes a small waxed tablet from his cloak and furiously begins sketching our likeness.

And it is here where I pause. I know exactly what I am supposed to say next; Lord Royce has gone over the speech with me multiple times.

Yet there is one change I must make.

"Convinced my twin sister and I would one day repeat the actions of Aislinn and Rowan, our father removed us from the line of succession. Yet now, after glimpsing what will become of Galandria if Andrei is left to rule, my sister and I have reached a decision."

I turn to Elara. "We have decided we shall rise up, and *we* shall claim our true place as heirs to the opal crown."

CHAPTER 36

ELARA

We? Did I hear that right?

Wilha does not introduce me and invite me to address the crowd, as we agreed. Instead, she continues speaking, pausing and stumbling over her words in a breathy voice as she tells the crowd how *we* will restore our kingdom, how together *we* will begin to repair the damage done.

Behind me, I hear Lord Royce shift. Was he in on this? But a quick glance in his direction tells me no. Lord Royce—for once dropping his impassive gaze—looks just as shocked as I feel.

"In the coming weeks, you shall hear from us. And when you do, I hope you shall rise up and join us." Wilha finishes and the crowd begins to applaud.

And then we're leaving. Lord Royce ushers us from the box and out into the hall, before the spell breaks. Before someone thinks to summon the guards with a message Andrei will not ignore: *The Masked Princess has just declared herself an enemy of the king.*

"We have much to discuss," Lord Royce is saying to Wilha as we travel down the stairs.

"Indeed we do," Wilha says regally, leading the way as we start down a narrow corridor lined with sconced candlelight.

With a pang, I realize Wilha doesn't need Lord Royce to tell her where to turn to find the back entrance where our carriage waits.

Lord Royce drops back, drawing level with me. "Your sister picked a very inconvenient time to suddenly grow a backbone," he says.

"My backbone may be new, but my hearing has always been quite remarkable," Wilha says, turning around. She takes my arm. "And I promise you, Elara, I only did what I thought was best. Let us talk this through tonight after we have left the city."

I nod dazedly and allow Wilha to lead me down the corridor. Are we to *share* the crown now? Is that even possible?

Wilha opens the door at the end of the hall; a blast of heat and acrid smoke greets us as we step into the alley where Rolf and Nicolai are waiting with our carriage. Wilha halts at the sound of screams echoing from atop the hill near the Opal Palace.

"Fire." She turns incredulous eyes upon Lord Royce. "Did you hire men to start a *fire* near the Opal Palace?"

"I merely paid them to create a disturbance at the golden gates," he says, shielding his eyes against the smoke.

"Well, it looks like you've succeeded," Wilha says, her voice edged in steel. "Lord Murcendor himself couldn't have done a better job."

A sharp whistle sounds, and Rolf opens the door of our

carriage. Wilha and Lord Royce enter. I have just handed my jeweled mask to Rolf in exchange for my satchel with my mother's book stuffed inside, when the door to the opera house bursts open.

"Stop!"

I turn. A group of men wearing crimson and black costume masks stand behind me. All of them except for the man in the middle hold a sword. He removes his mask, and my heart both leaps and plummets.

It's Stefan.

His face is gray-tinged. Sweat pours from his brow. "I wanted to enjoy the opera tonight," he says, sounding dazed. "And, and . . ." His eyes flick from me to the carriage, finally landing on me. "Are you . . . ?"

He does not finish his sentence, but I think I understand his question. *Are you the one I knew? The one I loved? The one who betrayed me?*

"Yes," I answer. "I'm the younger twin. I was sent to Kyrenica to serve as Wilhamina's decoy."

Stefan looks like a man in agony. "I don't even know your real name."

"The king and queen never gave me one," I say. "But the family who raised me called me Elara."

"Elara?" The word expels from his mouth in a rush of air, and I see it, the exact moment he understands. "The girl from your stories? That was *you?*"

"Yes."

"But that girl was neglected and abused. She was . . . *you* were . . ." He can't bring himself to finish the thought.

Tears are streaming down both our eyes, whether solely from the smoke, or from something else, I don't know.

Excited screams issue from the front of the building. Behind me I hear the horses whinnying and stamping nervously, and Nicolai's hushed voice as he tries to calm them.

"I could have my men stop you right now," Stefan says hoarsely.

"Look around you, Stefan. This city is on the brink of collapse. You've been in Allegria for nearly a week now. How are your dealings with Andrei and Lord Murcendor?"

His eyes narrow. "Treacherous. I wonder if the truth ever touches their lips."

"That's the conclusion my sister and I have reached as well. Wilhamina and I are daughters of the House of Andewyn— both of us are older than Andrei—and we intend to press our claim to the throne. Whatever the relationship between our two kingdoms, you should wait to discuss a new treaty with Andrei, as it will become null and void if he's deposed."

"I cannot imagine—" The rest of what Stefan says is cut off by shouts within the carriage.

I whirl around and see our carriage rolling forward, quickly gaining speed as it rounds the corner, and vanishes from sight.

CHAPTER 37

WILHA

"Go back!" I pound on the wall, yelling for Nicolai to stop. My cries go unheeded, and we continue on down a backstreet.

"You are only serving to draw attention to us," Lord Royce says.

"But you just—we just . . . *left* her."

"Your sister's loitering with the crown prince did not bode well for any of us," he says calmly. "I am simply ensuring we don't all conclude our evening inside the Opal Palace's dungeon. Besides, we are not leaving her for good." He calls out and orders Nicolai to stop the carriage. He steps outside, and I hear him and Rolf speaking in low tones.

"Go back to Eleanor Square. Do you know what the crown prince's carriage looks like?"

"Yes, Uncle."

"Good. Find her, and take her to the place we discussed. I will send a pigeon when I can."

When Lord Royce is seated once again and the carriage has started up, I say, "Stefan could turn her in. He could take her directly to Andrei."

"I was kept well informed regarding your sister's relationship with the crown prince. He will do no such thing."

"Where are you taking us?"

"Lord Nichols has a manor in Versan where we can hide while we plan. Of course, it seems our plans have now changed, haven't they?" His eyes bore into mine. "I did not realize you held ambitions for the crown, Your Highness."

"Perhaps you should have asked me," I say, forcing myself to match his gaze. "After all, Lord Royce, I am one of Fennrick's heirs."

"But you cannot reasonably expect that both you and your sister will rule jointly as queen. Such a thing has never been done. Why did you not simply state that you alone were making a claim to the crown, and dispense with this *we* business? You are the firstborn, after all."

"I would not do such a thing to my sister. And with that crown comes much power . . . maybe too much for one person."

"In this we agree," Lord Royce says, surprising me. "If we are successful, if you and your sister obtain the throne, I expect us to build a kingdom very different than the one you have grown up in."

"What do you mean?" I ask uneasily.

"The king is advised by the Guardian Council. All ten of the Guardians, save for myself, are of noble birth. And all of us were born in Allegria. Is it any wonder that the villagers have grown to resent the capitol and your family in particular? The *people* are Galandria's greatest resource, not her opals, and if the Andewyns continue choosing not to recognize this, it may one day cost your family not only the crown, but your very lives."

The city gates come into view. We are ordered to halt so the guards can search the carriage. A guard does a double take when he sees the jeweled mask I hold. His eyes linger on my face before asking hesitantly, "Your Highness?" After I nod, he quickly bows. "We were told to expect you tonight. There are many in the palace guard who would serve you over your brother if it came to it."

"One day it *will* come to it," I say with a confidence I do not feel. "And when it does," I add, aware of Lord Royce's probing stare, "I hope I will have your support."

The guard bows again. "With all my heart, Princess, you shall."

He waves us through the gates. Nicolai urges the horses onward, and we start forward, leaving the city, and Elara, far behind.

CHAPTER 38

ELARA

*S*tefan's arms clamp around my shoulders before I can go after the departing carriage. "If you run, you are sure to be discovered." He murmurs instructions to his guards, but I don't hear them.

They've left me. In the space of a moment, I went from being a future queen to being completely expendable.

Stefan jerks me around. "Elara, listen to me. I am merely a guest in this kingdom; there is only so much I can do to protect you."

I nod blindly, still unable to believe that I'm here, in a smoking, screaming city, while Lord Royce and Wilhamina are careening toward the city gates.

"The rest of you," Stefan addresses his guards, "are sworn to secrecy over this. Do you understand?"

"We are loyal to . . . to the princess, just as we were loyal to her when she lived among us in Kyrenica," answers a guard.

I turn back to Stefan and his men. Many of them, I realize now, I recognize as members of the Strassburgs' personal guard.

"Do you have a costume mask you can wear?" Stefan asks.

"Yes." I produce it from the folds of my cloak and put it on.

"Andrei has given me apartments within the city. Once

we're safely away from here, we can figure out what to do," Stefan says.

His guards surround us, and we make for Eleanor Square. We round the corner and stride quickly to the carriage Stefan marks as his own. Once we're settled inside, the guards begin the onerous task of maneuvering through the crowd. The square is still carnival-like with glittering, masked figures cavorting about, despite the smoke issuing from near the palace. Even above the chaos, whispers begin to rise, loud enough to reach inside the carriage.

The Masked Princess has a twin!

They plan to take the throne from Andrei!

I saw her face!

Suddenly, all the carousing comes to a halt as a contingent of Galandrian guards on horseback come tearing through the square. They pass so close the carriage shudders and I feel the heat from the torches they carry.

"They'll be heading for the gates," Stefan murmurs, "guessing—correctly, I assume?—that you and your sister were planning to exit the city as soon as you made your announcement."

I nod, my heart pounding, and tell myself I'm safe. For now, anyway. "Thank you for not turning me in," I say.

"Why didn't you just tell me who you were in Kyrenica?"

Instantly, my gratitude evaporates. "Why didn't I tell you? I seem to recall begging you to spare me a few minutes of your time so I could do exactly that—"

"Only *after* you had already been caught—"

"Instead, you chose to have me thrown into a cell."

Stefan flushes. "You lived among us for nearly a year. You lied—"

"Yes, Stefan, *I lied*. I was dragged back to the Opal Palace, in the most uninspiring welcome home you could imagine, and told I could either impersonate Wilha—or die. There's quite a bit more to it than that, and maybe one day, if I survive all this and you actually give me a smidgen of your valuable time, I shall tell you my whole story."

"Your Highnesses?" A guard steps closer to the carriage window. "The streets are quite lively tonight, but your voices are still carrying."

Stefan and I fall silent. More fireworks explode over the city, and I watch as ribbons of red and gold fizz in the sky. I wonder if Wilha can see them or if she's already gotten past the gates.

"After you left, I had men searching the kingdom for you," Stefan says in a quieter voice. "When no one could find you, I feared the worst . . . I was just hoping you were still alive," he finishes hoarsely.

"I really am sorry for that, Stefan, but what did you expect me to do? Sit in that cell weeping my heart out because you couldn't be bothered to come visit me? The opportunity to save my neck presented itself, and I took it."

We pass a group of drunken revelers singing a song about the Masked Princess. And suddenly, as if the tune conjured him, Rolf appears among them. He walks parallel to the carriage and my heart lightens considerably. They have not left me, after all.

Rolf's eyes meet mine. He nods slightly, then slips from view. A few moments later, the carriage begins rocking and shuddering to a halt.

"What's going on?" Stefan calls out.

"Don't know, Your Highness," says a guard.

Rolf, taking advantage of the guards' momentary confusion, opens the door and extends his hand to me. "I've been sent for you."

"*I* am taking her someplace safe," Stefan says. "Unlike your employer, I will not leave her behind."

"I have no doubt you mean the princess well, Your Highness," Rolf says with a deferential bow. "But your movements are watched by the palace. Can you harbor her without arousing suspicion and devise a plan to see her safely out of the city?"

Stefan hesitates. "I cannot. I assume you can?"

"Yes, but the gates will have closed by now, although Lord Royce and Princess Wilhamina should have already passed through. But he had a safe house prepared in case something like this happened that's well away from Eleanor Square or anyone connected with the court. It will take time to get her out of the city, but I swear to you it can be done. Now call your men off; they're drawing too much attention." Rolf gestures to the guards who have drawn their swords.

Stefan exhales. "Lower your weapons," he commands his guards. "We will look forward to hearing from your employer. Tell Lord Royce to send pigeons to Sir Reinhold when he can."

Stefan turns to me and smiles sadly. "Just when I thought I had finally found you, you leave again."

I look between Rolf and Stefan, knowing I could just choose to stay in the carriage, but knowing, too, that Rolf is right, and I must go. "Can you step away for a moment?" I ask Rolf. After he does, I say, "Why didn't you come visit me in the cell? I would have told you then who I was. If you had just given me the time, I would have told you everything."

"But I *was* going to visit you. On my life, I swear it. I did not want to come until I was myself again and able to truly hear you out."

From the pained look in his eyes, I know he's speaking the truth. "I wish you had. I wish you had come to me before Lord Royce."

Rolf clears his throat. Reluctantly, Stefan gestures toward the door. "Go. But one day, I look forward to hearing your whole story."

As I slip from the carriage and follow Rolf out into the night, I cannot help but wonder how different things would be now, if Stefan had only come for me earlier, or if I had only believed that he would.

CHAPTER 39

WILHA

*L*ord Nichols's manor in Versan is a sprawling country estate with balconies that look out onto sculpted gardens. While we wait for Rolf to smuggle Elara out of the city, Lord Royce and I write messages to every noble we know, asking for their support. They are carried either by pigeon or clandestinely by Nicolai all throughout Galandria. Lord Royce seems to have an endless network of spies and friends, and he has them plant rumors that Elara and I have gone into hiding in a northern village near the Opal Mountains.

One night during dinner a pigeon arrives from Lord Nichols, carrying news of Allegria. "It seems Andrei has dismissed the Guardian Council." Lord Royce looks meaningfully at me over the parchment. "Lord Murcendor has been named the Supreme Guardian of Galandria."

My stomach writhes, and I push away my plate. Officially, that makes Lord Murcendor second in power only to Andrei. Unofficially, I can only imagine what has been going on inside the palace.

"Lord Nichols intends to join us in a few days," Lord Royce continues. "He says with the city sunk in a heat wave, many who have the resources to do so are leaving Allegria in favor of the countryside. He feels now would be a good time to depart without arousing suspicion—"

He breaks off at shouts echoing from the courtyard, followed by the sound of horses galloping.

"You don't think . . ."

Lord Royce shakes his head. "Lord Nichols assured me Andrei has no idea of our whereabouts."

"It's all right," comes Nicolai's voice. "Come and see."

A line of men on horseback wait in the courtyard; it appears to be every member of my personal guard, including Patric. As they dismount, one by one they all sink to their knees in front of me.

"What is the meaning of this?" Lord Royce asks after I've bid them all to rise.

"We had to leave immediately," Patric answers. "I received word that Lord Murcendor intended to have every member of Wilha's guard questioned, and judged it to be safer for all if we fled." He turns to me. "Each of us has pledged our devotion to the twin queens."

"The twin queens?" I say.

"That is what the people have begun calling you."

"Perhaps your men would care to eat?" Lord Royce says. "Then we will get you all settled here."

Lord Royce asks Nicolai to see to the horses, and the men start for the manor. As I turn to leave, Patric stops me. "After everyone else has retired for the evening, meet me in the courtyard."

I look out at Lord Nichols's grounds from my seat at the water fountain. A pale moon hangs in the sapphire-colored sky and the crickets hum their tune. I wind Patric's golden ribbon around my finger while I wait, keenly aware of the hope bubbling in my heart.

"Would you care to take a walk, Princess?" comes Patric's voice.

"Of course." I turn, but his face is unsmiling. "Is everything all right?"

"I think we should take a walk."

I read the tense way he carries himself, the way his eyes constantly shift around, and I hastily tuck away the ribbon. We stroll along and a humid breeze stirs the surrounding willow trees. When we have put some distance between us and the manor, I say, "What is it?"

Patric produces a folded-up parchment and presses it into my hands. "I have a message for you. It's from Andrei."

"From *Andrei*?" Quickly, I unfold the letter and read it:

Wilha,

I feel as though you have deserted me in my hour of need. Dark events conspire at the palace, and I begin to doubt those around me. Can we not lay aside our differences, if only for an hour, and meet alone as brother and sister?

I sit down on a nearby bench. "How did you come into possession of this?"

"It was Andrei himself who tipped us off that Lord Murcendor planned to have me and your other guards questioned. He gave me the note and said he hoped I would flee and take it to you."

"Did you read it?"

Patric hesitates. "No, but I can guess at the contents. Andrei leaves tomorrow to go on summer progress with the court. He made me memorize his itinerary. He seemed eager that I should know exactly when and where he would visit the northern villages, where you and Elara are thought to be in hiding. I'm guessing he wants to meet?"

"He does," I say. "He wants to meet alone, just the two of us."

"No," Patric says firmly. "That is not something you can do."

"Please do not tell me what I can and cannot do, Patric. The first thing we must decide is if his offer is genuine. Tell me the manner of your meeting. Where were you? What was Andrei's countenance? What did his eyes say?"

"What did his eyes say? I don't know, Wilha—do a man's eyes ever say anything?"

"If you have the wisdom to see, they can say quite a bit."

Patric sits on the bench next to me. "It was at night. I was standing guard at the western turret. Andrei appeared to warn me, and then he gave me the note."

"What time at night was it? Was he alone?"

"Not too long after midnight, I think. And yes, he was alone."

"What was he wearing?"

Patric closes his eyes as he thinks. "He was dressed as a stable hand. And he was wearing a cloak; the hood was flipped up."

"Is it possible that Andrei had you followed tonight?"

"Definitely not," Patric says, sounding offended. "We doubled back, we switched trails—it took us twice as long to reach Versan as—"

"I don't doubt your competence, nor do I doubt this offer from Andrei is genuine." Patric begins to protest, but I cut him off. "I had already suspected Andrei may be slowly breaking faith with Lord Murcendor. And from what you said it sounds as though he went to great pains to visit you secretly. He guessed that you knew my location, but he did not allow you to be questioned by Lord Murcendor, nor does it appear that he had you followed here. Both courses of action would have made more sense than writing a letter where he could only *hope* to lure me into a trap, if that was all he was interested in."

"The offer may be genuine, but even so, I still don't think you should meet with him. It's dangerous, for one thing. It will be difficult to catch Andrei alone, even if we know his itinerary. And you shouldn't be alone in his company, anyway."

"What do you mean?"

"People are saying that Andrei . . . that he . . . I don't know how to say this, Wilha, but some are inclined to think that he was responsible for your father's death."

I inhale sharply. "No, that cannot be. Allegria trades in gossip just as surely as it trades in worthings. Andrei is just a boy who's been coddled his whole life. He may be spoiled and petulant, but he is no murderer."

I reach inside my cloak and remove the golden ribbon, unconsciously twining it again around my finger, trying to figure out how to honor Andrei's request. When I glance at Patric, I see him looking at the ribbon. "I held it every day after you left," he says quietly. Then, as though he has just breached protocol, he straightens up quickly. "I was never able to offer you my condolences. I was sorry to hear of your broken betrothal to Stefan Strassburg."

"Sorry?" I ask. "How so?"

"Stories were carried back to the Opal Palace of how you and the crown prince were falling in love," he says, and I read the pain in his eyes. "How those who stood in your presence could see it enveloping you, how you smiled at him."

I take a deep breath. "I was not sorry to see the betrothal broken. For I swear to you, Patric, I have never even *met* the crown prince."

"*Y*ou fled the castle?" Patric asks, dumbfounded. For nearly an hour he has sat silently as I related meeting

Elara, her preparations to begin impersonating me, and our journey to the Kyrenican Castle. "And then what happened?"

"I found lodging in a room above a tavern and employment in the city."

"You got a job?" Patric says the words as though he's speaking a foreign tongue. "Doing what?"

"Working at a seamstress's shop. I am quite talented with a needle, you know."

"Did you make many friends?"

"Yes." And, because I know it would be a lie of omission not to say more, I add, "I met someone, actually."

"I see." Patric shifts and the slightest distance opens between us. "Did you love him?"

"I wanted to. I loved the idea that someone wanted to be with me, but in truth, I did not love him as he loved me. I suppose when it came down to it, what I really wanted was a friend."

"You have always had one, Wilha." He reaches out and our fingers lace together. "I may not like your decision, but I did swear my allegiance to you." He sighs. "If you want to meet with Andrei, I think I know a way to make it happen."

CHAPTER 40

ELARA

*A*linda and I sit quietly at the wooden table eating our lunch of leftover potato stew. We do our best not to look at each other. The "safe house" Lord Royce had prepared is an abandoned butcher's shop. It's similar in layout to Alinda's bakery (or it was, before Andrei's men burned the bakery in retaliation for Lord Royce's betrayal), so the upper apartment consists of only one room, making it difficult for Alinda and I to avoid each other.

But we try, nevertheless. Alinda cries often over the loss of her home, and I know she blames me. It's taken every bit of my willpower not to shout at her, not to remind her that it's her uncle's fault we're both homeless and trapped in the city until Rolf can arrange a means of escape. This is proving difficult to do. Apparently half the city wants to see Wilha and I crowned as joint queens.

The other half wants us executed.

Although rumors circulate that Wilha and I are hiding in a northern village, the palace is taking no chances. Every person, cart, or carriage attempting to either enter or leave Allegria is stopped and thoroughly searched at the city gates by guards known to be loyal to Andrei.

"Are you all finished?" I ask Alinda.

She nods and I take our empty bowls downstairs to clean them, thankful for a little space. When I'm finished, I look outside at the street. Large carcasses of bloody meat dangle from metal hooks in the butchery across the way. The shop is open, but business is light. As the weeks have passed, the heat has grown more and more oppressive. The butchers' section of the city now reeks with the stench of blood and rotting meat, scaring away most potential buyers.

If venturing out into the city was ill-advised while I hid at the bakery, it's next to impossible now. Fliers bearing my and Wilha's likeness circulate the city. After so much time in obscurity, our face is now one of the most recognizable in Allegria.

The door unlocks and Rolf enters the shop carrying bags of apples and potatoes. "How's my sister?" he says, setting the bags on a counter.

"The same. Although she's eating more today, so that's a good sign."

"I'm going to send pigeons to some friends of ours in the villages. I don't think she's in any condition to accompany us to Versan, although I don't know if anyone will take her in."

"Why not?" I stow the bags in the cupboard where we've been hiding our supplies.

"Your brother's new taxes are killing the villages. Many who barely got by last year may not live to see next year if grain or worthings don't start flowing more readily." He heads for the door. "I'm going to go buy bread, if there's any to be had today. Lock the door behind me."

After he's gone, I linger downstairs, wondering, not for the first time, how Cordon and the Ogdens are faring. I wonder if Mistress is still ill, and if so, if they have enough worthings to visit a healer.

Upstairs Alinda has chosen to lie back down on her mattress. This suits me fine, and I try to block out the sound of her whimpering by settling in front of the window and opening my mother's book. Halfheartedly I flip through it, as I have done a hundred times before. I was so certain I'd find a message inside these pages, but clearly I have been wrong. . . . What am I missing?

I blow out a breath and look out the window. As I watch, a woman hurries furtively up the street, a small cake tucked under her arm, as though she's expecting to be robbed of her treasure. I smile as a memory surfaces. Of Ruby digging into her cake at her birthday party, and her delight when she discovered the coin contained inside—

I stop suddenly and push the memory away. I find the librarian's message. . . . *Donated by and recovered at the request of Queen Astrid* . . . I run my finger over the thick, puckered cover. What if Astrid wasn't referring to the pages, themselves, but literally meant *inside* the book?

Or, more specifically, inside the cover?

With growing excitement, I begin digging at the cover, pulling and yanking, until finally, the leather splits. I keep pulling and I remove the pasteboard underneath. I flip it over . . . there's a yellowed piece of parchment clinging to the other side. With shaking hands I smooth it out.

As I read, the entire world dissolves and remakes itself.

CHAPTER 41

ELARA

My Dearest Daughter,

My heart is heavy tonight. My body is swollen with child—your own younger brother or sister. My confinement looms and soon I will depart from the public until the babe I carry is born. I should like to think that one day I will be able to look upon you from afar and see you, the daughter that I long for just as keenly as a drowning man longs for air. But a deep foreboding has taken root in my heart, and caution as well as my own desires demanded I write this by my own hand.

If you have followed my clues and this letter has come into your possession, then I assume you know who I am and who you are. I assume, too, that you hate your father and me for the choice we made. For how could you bear us anything but ill will, when you come to understand the life that was denied to you?

I cannot imagine how this knowledge must sit with you, to know that a crown was valued more than your own life. So many nights I lie awake and think of you and wonder where you are, what you are doing. Who you are becoming. But that knowledge is kept secret even from me, your own mother.

Yet I have a secret of my own.

Your father has decreed you will be brought back to Allegria after your sister is married and sent to a foreign kingdom. This was all decided while I was still weak from childbirth and my grip on consciousness was fleeting. How I wish you could have seen me cry, still weak, still bleeding, the moment he told me of the decision he and the four Guardians reached. A mask for the first-born; an anonymous home for the second.

It was, they said, the best they could do for the both of you. Your father insisted we not name our second daughter. "If she doesn't have a name, she cannot be hunted," he said. And although I did not then, and still do not agree with him, I went along with it.

You must understand, we had no inkling I was carrying twins. Only one cradle—a beautiful, golden one—was crafted. And when a second daughter was born, surprising us all, there simply was not a space prepared for her. And so we placed her in a wooden trunk and kept it next to the cradle.

I lost two babies early on before I became pregnant with you and your sister. But somehow I knew this time would be different. And when I held my baby, my beautiful Wilhamina, I knew I was victorious, for I had accomplished what I had purposed to do, and my heart was full of gratitude. Yet only a few minutes later, pain dragged at my insides and a second daughter was granted to me. Truly, I had the desire of my heart in a double measure!

Though the name Wilhamina had been decided upon ages ago if we were to have a girl, I gave my lovelies, my two beloveds, secret names. I called my oldest Victory and my second Desire.

Even from birth, my two daughters, my two beloveds, were so different. Wilhamina was born with her eyes wide open, ready to embrace life. My younger daughter came into this world crying and fearful. Did she sense, even then, the fate she would be sentenced to? Watching the two of you sleep, a golden cradle next to a wooden trunk, I saw clearly the life my two daughters would lead: the older, golden and royal; the younger, orphaned and unknown. A mother never stops fearing for her child, and so I believed that whatever precautions your father and the four Guardians took would never be enough.

I believe that is why I did what I did that night.

An hour before Lord Murcendor was to arrive to spirit away the younger twin, I picked up both of my beloveds and cradled them. For those precious minutes I knew one of the highest joys of motherhood, one that is often denied to a queen, the feel of my children in my arms as they nursed at my own breasts. And when I put them back down, I placed Wilhamina in the trunk, and the younger twin in the cradle. In doing so, I hoped to give both of my girls a claim to the Andewyn name and heritage. One, a claim by birthright as the firstborn of the king and heir to the crown; and the other, the claim of time, for she would grow up in the Opal Palace.

Do you understand my words, dear daughter? You are the older twin. Your true name, the name given to you at birth, is Wilhamina Andewyn.

Your father has decided to have you brought back to Allegria after your sister leaves, and to give you a new life here. But he feels you should never be told of your true identity. He feels it is best for all.

All save me, for I want to know you, my dear darling. If I am still drawing breath in this world on the day that you read this, I want you to take this letter and come to me. Offer it up as proof to anyone who would oppose you that you are an Andewyn. You are Wilhamina, Fennrick's firstborn, and your true place should have been here, with me.

By the time you receive this letter, your childhood will have passed. Forgive me, please, my darling daughter, for how I've wronged you. You should have grown up in the Opal Palace; you should have been the recognized princess of Galandria. I know not whether my actions will have helped or hurt you and your sister. I know only that on that night I was nearly mad with grief and believed I was helping.

I am Queen Astrid and I write these things by my own hand.

For a few brief moments, I have a peace I have never known. I have a name, and a mother who loved me. A mother who thought of me every day. The knowledge reaches in, touches my heart, and I let myself feel it.

But the feeling is short-lived as the reality of what I've just read sets in. If what she's saying is true, *I* am the oldest of \ the Andewyn children. The one with the strongest claim to the throne. And Astrid has just handed me the evidence to prove it.

CHAPTER 42

WILHA

"What did you tell Lord Royce?" I ask Patric as we set off from the manor on the horses we borrowed from Lord Nichols's stable.

"I told him we wished to go on a picnic," he says. "I assured him we would not journey outside of Lord Nichols's property, and that we would be back at sunset. This, of course, will be impossible, and when we return tomorrow, I will tell him you took a slight fall from your horse and I thought it best if we made camp for the evening before returning."

We continue down the road, our horses keeping a steady pace. I am not happy that this journey requires so many lies, and yet it is necessary. I remind myself that if I am to rule with Elara one day, it shall mean a lifetime of making difficult decisions.

Once the manor has faded from sight, we steer the horses sharply to the east, back toward Allegria. We travel down lesser-used roads, and I am careful to keep my hood flipped up; with so many fliers of my image circulating around the kingdom, I will not chance being recognized on the road. And as Andrei and the whole court believe Elara and I are farther north, Patric and I have judged it safer if I surprise my brother by paying him a visit early on in his summer progress. His first stop is just outside of Allegria at a manor maintained by Lord and Lady Ashland.

Patric and I ride in easy silence, and yet I cannot keep from glancing at him from time to time, and admiring the way the sun glints off his black hair, or the way his deep green eyes continually sweep side to side, always alert for danger. As much as I want to meet with Andrei, much in me wishes Patric and I really could spend the day picnicking together.

"How will we get inside the manor?" I ask after we have journeyed for some time.

"Your father visited the Ashlands on progress every year. Lord Ashland always gave up his own quarters to him, so I have no doubt he will make the same offer to Andrei. Since I attended the king on many of those nights, I am familiar with the manor's layout."

"You attended him?" I say, startled to realize Patric possesses memories of my father that I do not. "How did he seem on those nights?"

Patric gives me a sideways look. "Old and very sad. Once or twice I heard him weeping in the middle of the night."

It is difficult to imagine my father, always so ready for another feast, another ball, weeping in the night like a child waking from a nightmare. Or did he weep because, upon waking, he discovered his nightmares were true? What if those dark nights were the only hours he allowed himself to think of what he had done?

I shake the past from my thoughts, and will myself back to the present. "Do you mean for us to visit Andrei in Lord Ashland's chambers, then? How will we get in?"

"The estate was originally built by your family before being given to the Ashlands as a gift," Patric says. "There's a passageway leading from Lord Ashland's chambers to the back of the manor." He shifts uncomfortably in his saddle. "I have seen your father use it to receive different lady friends in the middle of the night."

I nod silently, choosing not to comment on my father's late-night activities.

"When we arrive we'll wait in the woods at the back of the manor. I think it best if we enter at night, but earlier, when Andrei should still be feasting with the court. I would rather we already be in his chambers when he retires for the evening. When we cross to the manor we'll keep our hoods up and our heads down. Even if someone were to see the two of us entering the passageway, they may assume I'm one of Andrei's guards, and have been ordered to bring you to his room."

Patric's inclinations prove correct, and long after night has fallen, we make it inside the passageway, certain we have not been noticed. Just before he presses on the embedded opal leading to Lord Ashland's chambers, I say, "I want you to wait in here."

"Absolutely not. If there's a problem and you need me, I want to be right—"

"Andrei will not take kindly to the idea that I have brought an armed guard with me. He may misunderstand my intentions."

Patric seems to think about this before reluctantly nodding. "I will stay. But I won't send you in unarmed." He unsheathes a sword and hands it to me. "If you need anything, rap on the wall." He demonstrates with a loud knock. "I will hear it on my side, and I will come to your aid."

I move to press on the opal, but Patric stops me. "Wait a second," he says, his eyes roaming over my face. "Don't go just yet."

"Why not?" I ask, keenly aware of my heart knocking against my rib cage; aware that we're alone in the dark. Patric leans closer and, almost unwillingly, my eyes flutter closed and I can't help but wonder if his lips are as soft as they look.

But I'm not given the chance to find out. Patric plucks several stray threads of grass from my hair. "Okay, you're good to go. Please be safe. And signal me if you need to."

"I will."

I step through the passageway, feeling out of sorts and vaguely wishing I could slash something with my sword.

⚛

*J*ust as Patric predicted, the room is empty. It's also smaller than I expected, and stiflingly hot. In the dim candlelight, I glimpse dark tapestries, a canopied bed, and a flagon of wine on a table next to some plush armchairs. I hide myself behind a tapestry, but I do not have long to wait. The door bursts open, and arguing voices fill the room.

"I don't understand why you needed to execute them," Andrei says. "They were harmless."

"They were flouting the law," Lord Murcendor says. "I decided to make an example of them." My mouth goes dry, and I grip my sword tighter.

Andrei's voice swells with petulance. "But I told you not to do it. And *I* am the king."

"Those Maskrens refused to take off their masks, even when it is now illegal. It was as good as declaring themselves in favor of your sisters."

My stomach turns. The Maskrens, with their brown cloaks and gold-threaded masks, were always loyal to me. Now it seems their devotion will cost them their lives. While I have been away, how many in Allegria are being executed?

"But—" Andrei begins.

"Your Highness, it was for the best. If you reach your maturity and come of age, perhaps you will understand these things better."

From Andrei's silence, I think he hears the threat in Lord Murcendor's words just as I do.

"Of course," Andrei finally replies. "I am sorry, Your Lordship."

"You are always welcome to share your differing views with me. Just . . . not in public," Lord Murcendor says.

I hear the sound of a door opening and closing again. I chance a peek at the edge of the tapestry and see Andrei is now alone and locking the door. He turns and looks into the empty fireplace, as though the weight of the world rests upon his shoulders. Quietly, I slip out from behind the tapestry and step forward.

"Does Lord Murcendor always speak to you so?"

Andrei jumps and screams for the guards before whipping around to face me. "Wilha?"

"I'm sorry," I whisper, as the stone floor thrums with clattering footsteps and guards begin pounding at the locked door. "I should have announced myself properly."

"Your Majesty! Open the door!"

Andrei's eyes stray to the sword in my hand. "Have you come to kill me?"

"I have come as you asked," I murmur, as the guards continue to shout. I grip my sword tighter. "Did you invite me here only to have me arrested?"

"Hardly. Step behind the tapestry and be quiet."

I comply and force myself to take soft, shallow breaths as Andrei turns the lock and guards spill into the room.

"Your Majesty, are you all right? We thought we heard voices."

"I thought I heard something outside the window, but it was just an owl. You are free to go."

Silence. When the guards don't move, Andrei's voice

turns icy. "Leave. That is an order from your king."

"But, Your Majesty," the guard's voice shakes. "Lord Murcendor said—"

"I don't care what Lord Murcendor said. *I* am telling you to leave. If you do not, I shall call for more guards and have you both removed."

"Of course, Your Majesty, forgive us." The guard now sounds eager to leave. "Call for us if you need anything."

After the door closes behind them, I hear the click of the lock turning again. "You may come out now," Andrei says in a hushed voice.

When I step out from behind the tapestry, his eyes search my face.

"Do you know as a young boy I was terrified of you? I actually thought the rumors were true. I spent countless nights imagining your face and the monster I believed you to be. You haunted my dreams and terrified my steps. On the few occasions when I found myself alone in the palace, I was certain you were hiding in the shadows, just waiting for the right moment to curse me."

"Why did you believe the rumors?" I ask.

"Because Lord Murcendor said—" he breaks off, and his eyes search my face again.

"Lord Murcendor is not a true friend, Andrei. I was under the impression you invited me here because you were beginning to see that."

"He is the only friend I have ever had." His eyes stray toward the door, and I wonder if he's regretting his decision to meet with me.

"I thought the same," I say quickly. "All my life I imagined Lord Murcendor was my most trusted friend—right up until the night he held a sword to my throat and offered me a choice: marry him, or die that very night."

"He said you were confused," Andrei insists, though weakly.

"Can you really still believe that? I heard him threaten you just now. If he's as true a friend as he claims, can you make a decree without consulting him? Could you dismiss him from your service and your wishes would be obeyed without question?"

The sigh Andrei heaves seems too deep for a fifteen-year-old. "You know I cannot."

"Meet with Lord Royce," I begin, "and we—"

"Meet with him? Why? So I can hand the crown over to him? To you and our sister?"

"So we can figure something out," I say. "There are more people involved here than you or me or Elara. Than Lord Murcendor or Lord Royce, even."

Andrei frowns. "Who are you speaking of?"

"The Galandrian people, Andrei," I say, burning with the same sense of frustration I often feel around Elara. "They have a right to a ruler who is actually concerned with their well-being."

"I *am* concerned. But there's little I can do when—" he breaks off and takes a deep breath. He pours himself a glass of wine. Cautiously, he sniffs at the goblet before making a face and pouring it out into the empty fireplace.

"Don't you have a taster?" I say.

"Yes, but he is employed by Lord Murcendor." His face turns dark. "And there are ways to get poison past a taster." He sighs. "But your suspicions are correct. The guards and the palace staff—I fear most of them are more loyal to Lord Murcendor than to me."

"Then meet with Elara and me and Lord Royce—"

"Is Lord Royce any more trustworthy than Lord Murcendor?" Andrei interrupts, unconsciously voicing my own suspicions.

"He is not particularly likeable," I say, "but he has never tried to kill me."

At this Andrei gives me a sorrowful look. "Is it not sad, that this is the most we can say about the advisor we are to cast our lots with? How did it come to this, Wilha?"

From his wearied expression, I don't think he expects an answer. And yet I have spent months asking myself nearly this same question. "A long time ago a series of terrible choices were made, and the three of us—you, me, and Elara—are the ones who must pay for them."

"What if just the three of us meet?" Andrei says suddenly. "You, me, and Elara. Without Lord Royce or anyone else whispering their own agendas into our ears. I know nothing of Elara, only what Lord Murcendor has told me—which, I am beginning to accept, is nothing at all like the truth. There are still a handful of guards who remain loyal to me above all others. If you can get Elara to agree to a meeting, I will make arrangements for us to meet alone, and I will guarantee your safety."

Staring at him, with his jaw set in the stubborn way that reminds me of Elara, my heart constricts. "Perhaps Elara and I have underestimated you," I say.

Andrei smiles sadly. "Perhaps all three of us have underestimated each other."

CHAPTER 43

ELARA

My name is Wilhamina Andewyn.

As more days pass in this rotting shop, the peace I initially felt dissolves completely and is replaced by a growing rage—just as the scent of rotting meat grows—until it crawls down my throat, threatening to choke me with its rancid stench.

Did Astrid think her words would bring me comfort? Did she think I would be *happy* to know that for a few shining moments I slept in a golden cradle? Until, by a very deliberate act of her will, she chose to send me away instead of Wilhamina?

Wilhamina, who is really me.

I imagine my life if I had grown up in the Opal Palace. Once I became old enough, I would have refused to wear the mask. I would have taken up a dagger against anyone who tried to force it over my face; or more likely, used any one of the number of techniques Mistress taught me—

But . . . if I had grown up in the Opal Palace, I never would have known Mistress. I never would have known her anger, true. But I never would have learned her tactics, either. How much of who I am today is because she raised me? If I had grown up wearing the mask, if that was all I'd ever known, would I have been more docile, more fearful, more . . . like Wilha?

Something vaguely resembling a grudging thanks creeps into my gut. Astrid's blood flows through me. Astrid, who, by her own admission, was too weak to stand up to my father and the Guardians to prevent them from tearing her own family apart. But it's Mistress who mentored me. She taught me to lie and deceive.

Ultimately, she taught me how to survive.

And so, one night when I'm downstairs—as far away from Alinda's merciless crying as I can possibly get—I decide I'm tired of waiting around for Lord Royce and Rolf to come up with a plan to rescue me from this rotting city. I'll rescue my own self. It shouldn't be a difficult thing to do. Thanks to Mistress, I possess a very special set of skills.

The guards are on the lookout for two girls bearing my likeness.

My eyes fall on a pair of the butcher's abandoned scissors. Two *girls*.

A plan begins to form, and I ask myself if I have what it takes to stare directly into an armed guard's eyes and lie my way to freedom.

I take up the scissors and begin hacking at my hair.

After all, I'm at my best when I'm someone else.

CHAPTER 44

ELARA

The wooden blocks in Rolf's old boots make me taller. The padding in my borrowed clothing makes me broader, and my shorn hair makes me gruffer.

A long line snakes from the city gates; the guards searching each cart and carriage seem no more than small dots from where Rolf and I stand.

"Are you sure you're up for this?" Rolf asks.

"Of course," I say in the coarse, mannish voice I've been practicing for the last week. I point to our carriage where Alinda waits inside. "My wife needs to leave the city, and I intend to see that she does."

"Amazing," Rolf says. "You make a fearsome man."

"I'm going to take a walk and get a little more comfortable in these clothes."

"Are you sure that's wise?" Rolf says, frowning. "The less attention we call to ourselves, the better."

"I know what I'm doing," I say, though of course he's right. But I have no pigeons to send, and if I go back inside the carriage, I won't be able to find someone to carry my note to Tulan.

Rolf makes a face, but says nothing and steps back up to the driver's bench. I stroll up the line, weaving through carriages laden with trunks, carts overflowing with hay, and farmers trying to keep their goats and chickens from wandering off as we wait for the line to inch forward.

I slip my note from my pocket and read it one last time, even though I've memorized it by heart:

> *Cordon,*
>
> *I heard that you and Serena are married now, and while I was unable to properly congratulate you sooner, I do so now. I have heard that life in the villages is tough, and I am concerned for how you are faring. If you are in need of any assistance, send a pigeon to Lord Nichols's estate in Versan, and I will make sure you have all you need. I'm not sure what news has come to you by now from Allegria, but I think you will understand why I could not travel to Tulan personally.*

All I've heard about since returning to Galandria are the food shortages and the suffering in the villages, and though I bear little love for the Ogdens, I can't bring myself to turn my back on them completely. Lord Royce won't like it when I ask him for worthings to give to Cordon, and by extension, the Ogdens. But he's made it clear his wealth is at my disposal, and I intend to hold him to it.

I fold up my message and continue on down the line, until I come upon a man and woman sitting in the driver's bench of a cart. Both of them are dressed in rags. The man sips a bottle of ale while the woman dots her brow with a gray handkerchief. In the back, between a dusty trunk and two dirty children, sit three carrier pigeons in cages.

"Good afternoon," I say in my new voice. "Don't suppose a single worthing would buy me use of one of your pigeons? I have a letter I need to deliver."

The man takes a long pull of ale. "A single worthing won't get you anything in this city."

The woman looks at me strangely. "You look familiar—don't you think he looks familiar, Stan?"

"Yeah." Stan scrutinizes me. "Are you related to the Andewyns?"

"Distantly, according to my mother," I say without missing a beat, for I'd expected something like this. "Fat lot of good it's done me. Tried to get big britches Andrei himself to help me when things got hard. All I got was the golden gates slammed in my face." I spit on the ground. "Should've taken a sledgehammer to those gates."

Stan passes me the bottle of ale and nods. "Should get some men together and show that Andewyn brat how easily he can lose *his* home."

A chill passes over me as I take a sip of ale. He sounds completely sober. And completely serious. "Yes . . . at any rate, I am in need of a carrier pigeon."

I pass the bottle back and Stan surveys my clothing, trying to decide, I think, just how much a distant relative of the Andewyns can cough up. "Ten worthings," he says.

"*Ten* worthings? That's more than my whole life's worth," I say, although I've got twice that amount stashed in my cloak, courtesy of Lord Royce, and the wealth he left hidden in the butcher's shop.

"Fine. Eight, then."

In the end we settle on five. Once I've watched the pigeon clear the city gates, the letter safely strapped to its leg, I take my leave of them.

As I walk back to the carriage, I imagine the look on Cordon's face—on Mistress's face—when they see my letter. I admit a part of me wants Mistress to know I now have access to the wealth she always craved. Didn't I used to dream of walking into Ogden Manor holding a bag of worthings and watch her scramble to please me, just as she always forced me to do on the nights Lord Murcendor visited us?

When I step back inside our carriage, Alinda tries to shrink away from me, but I hold her firm. "I know you don't care for me, but if we do not convince the guards we're man and wife, we'll both suffer for it."

She nods and stares blankly out the carriage window. "I just need you to pretend, just for a little while," I add. "Your uncle's friends have agreed to take you in. As soon as we get past the gates, we'll take you there, and you'll never have to see me again."

The line slowly moves forward, until the sun is high in the sky, punishing us all with its unceasing heat. Finally, Rolf steers us to the front and a guard strides up to my window.

Let the show begin.

"We need you to step out of the carriage, Sir."

"Of course." I stand up awkwardly, but Alinda remains seated. "Get up!" I command her in my new voice. "Or you'll find yourself walking the rest of the way." I grab her arm, haul her to her feet, and practically push her outside.

Guards enter the carriage, presumably to check for hidden compartments.

"What business do you have in the country?" says the first guard.

"Not business, family," I say. "The events of the last couple months have not put my wife in a good mind." I point to Alinda, who looks down at the dirt, tears leaking from her eyes. "I thought her mother—shrew of a woman that she is—would know what to do with her."

The guard nods sympathetically. "You're not the first to leave. Ever since the Masked Princess and her twin declared themselves, more people are leaving Allegria and heading for the countryside. Some are even fleeing to Azarlin." He scowls and gestures to the line of carriages behind us. "It makes watching these gates a tedious business, I can tell you that."

I utter a string of creative curses that would have impressed even Mister Ogden. "If you ever capture those twin traitors, I'll return to the city, just so I can watch them hang."

The guard laughs heartily, and when our carriage has

passed inspection, he waves us through. But I don't release the breath I've been holding until we're well past the gates, and deep into the countryside.

We travel hard down the main road, and don't stop to make camp until after night has fallen. There's no need to make a campfire in this incessant heat, so we share a meal of mushy apples, spread out our cloaks, and sleep on the warm ground.

Or Rolf and Alinda do, at least. I lie awake, unable to sleep. I bring a hand to my pocket, where I've stuffed Astrid's letter. At some point, I'm going to have to decide if I want to show it to Wilha.

Her notion that the two of us can rule jointly is whimsical at best, dim-witted at worst. In the act of producing Astrid's letter, I could effectively extinguish whatever hopes she has for the crown. And if I know anything about my sister, it's that she's dutiful; she will do what's required of her, which in this case, would be to follow the Galandrian laws of succession. The same laws that will proclaim *me* as the true heir to the opal crown.

But what will the cost be to Wilha?

I roll over and look up at the stars. How will she feel when she finds out her entire world has been built on yet another lie? That really, the name she has carried these last seventeen years is essentially mine?

CHAPTER 45

WILHA

*I*t has been two weeks since I returned from my meeting with Andrei. Two weeks of waiting for Elara to slip from Allegria's grip. She and Rolf arrive late one night after everyone has retired for the evening. I hear Lord Nichols show her into the room across from my own. They murmur quietly, and I assume he is informing her of the guest who arrived just a few hours ago.

Once Lord Nichols has excused himself, I open my door cautiously. I should wait to speak to Elara until the morning, but I have stewed for days trying to figure out how to convince her to agree to a meeting with Andrei.

Elara's door is cracked open a couple inches, and it creaks as I step inside the room. "I am sorry to disturb you. I wanted to see how you were—" I bring a hand to my mouth when I see her. Elara sits in an armchair, looking tiredly at a yellowed piece of parchment she holds, but her long tresses . . . they've been sheared off. "Why did you cut your hair?"

"Because the guards were looking for a girl, not a boy," she says shortly, folding up the parchment.

"I see." Truly, my sister is a force to be reckoned with. "Well . . . I wanted to tell you something, but also I . . . I just wanted to say I was sorry. For leaving you behind in the city, I mean. I swear to you I tried to stop Lord Royce, but . . ."

A strange look crosses Elara's face and she glances again at the parchment, before leaning over and deftly sliding it into a writing desk. "It seems our family is filled with women unable to stand up to the men around them."

I open my mouth to protest, but she continues, "You did more than just leave me behind, though, didn't you? You decided you wanted the crown for yourself—or half of it, anyway."

"I wanted—I *do* want—what is best for everyone," I say carefully, realizing I should have expected her anger. "I never meant to wrong you, Elara, but I really believe that right now sharing the crown is best for all."

"So springing that on me while you gave your speech was the best option, then? You don't think you might've found the time to tell me that *before* we walked into the opera house?"

"There *are* no good options right now, Elara. I tried to talk to you numerous times—"

"You should have tried harder. You should have untied that faltering tongue of yours for once and—"

"But that's just it. Next to you, my voice has seemed slight and inconsequential. You are braver than I am, and you always know what to say, and many days I wish I was more like you. But that does *not* mean I will quietly stand by while you and Lord Royce decide my future—as well as the future of this entire kingdom."

"All I expected," Elara says, "was that you—"

"Was that I would be obedient!" I say, my voice rising. "You have ridiculed me for being too obedient, too weak, when I was a child, but the minute you decided you wanted to be queen you required that same obedience. I am sorry for the way things happened, Elara, I truly am. But it is time you finally understood that even if I am different than you, I have my own will, and I shall not always bend it to yours—nor am I convinced that you and Lord Royce alone are the answer to our kingdom's problems. So . . . *yes*! I want the crown—or half of it, like you said."

By the time I finish speaking, I am standing and my fists are clenched. Elara is staring up at me in shock.

"That was remarkably articulate," she says after a moment.

"Thank you." I take a deep breath and try to calm myself. I had intended to apologize to my sister, not start shouting at her. "And I'm sorry—I shouldn't have just barged in on you so late. Perhaps tomorrow we can speak more about what joint rulership"—I break off as her eyes stray again to the writing desk. "What was that letter you were reading? You keep looking at it."

"It's . . . nothing I want to talk about tonight." She leans back in her chair and rubs her temples. "Didn't you come in here because you said you had something you wanted to tell me?"

"We can discuss it later." After all the things I just said, I should probably find another time to talk to her about

Andrei. "It's not that important," I say as I head for the door.

"You're a terrible liar, Wilha—and I'm not saying that to ridicule you. I can tell something's bothering you. What is it?"

Hesitantly, I turn back and sit down. I've come too far not to talk to her now. "I was just thinking . . . what would you say if we could arrange a meeting with Andrei? Just the three of us?"

"I'd say it's an excellent idea."

I pause. "Really?"

"Yes." Her face breaks into a wicked grin. "Then we could capture him and hand him over to the villagers. Let him experience their poverty—and their anger—firsthand."

My stomach curdles at the gleeful tone in her voice. "Elara, I don't think Andrei has very much power these days. He's—"

"He's hunting us!" she bursts out. "He's been hunting *me* since the moment he became king, Wilha—and it feels like you don't care about any of that. You yell at me for not listening to you more . . . but are you at all interested in what *my* life has been like for these last few weeks?" A watery glint appears in her eyes. "While you and Lord Royce were reclining here in the country, I was stuck in the city hoping I wouldn't be found by Andrei—the same brother you expect me to try to understand."

I silently reach out and take her hand. "I do care, Elara. Sometimes you just seem so much tougher than I am, like you could survive anything. I did not mean to be callous."

"Yeah, well"—she casts a quick glance over to the writing desk—"you would've learned how to be tough, too, if you'd grown up with the Ogdens."

"I would love to know what it was like for you growing up in Tulan," I say. "But every time I have asked, you are curt, as though I am a nuisance. And I must confess, sometimes it seems to me as though I disgust you." I swallow nervously. "I am used to people not liking me, Elara. But for my part, I want to be your friend, as well as your sister. I have always wanted that."

Elara looks down at our twined hands. "I haven't had a lot of friends in my life," she says.

"Neither have I. The noblegirls were always afraid I would rip off my mask and curse them."

At that, we both laugh quietly. "Idiots," Elara says. "You should have told them you *would* curse them, if they didn't do what you wanted."

"Maybe I should have," I say, laughing. "But tomorrow, do you think we could spend time together? Without anyone else around? I think we have a lot to talk about."

"I would like that a lot," she says.

"Maybe after we are finished meeting with Stefan tomorrow, we can—"

"Stefan?" Her eyes widen. "He's *here*? In the manor?"

"Yes, he arrived a few hours ago. I had assumed Lord Nichols already told you?"

She shakes her head. "He must have forgotten—but can we talk more tomorrow? I'd like to get something to eat." She stands up to head for the door, all traces of her earlier tiredness seemingly vanished. "Unless"—she turns back quickly—"did you have more you wanted to say?"

I can tell she's trying so hard to be patient, when I know she wants more than anything to see Stefan. And I don't want to ruin this moment with my sister, not even for Andrei. Not when it feels like this is one of the first times we've truly heard each other.

"No," I say. "It can wait until tomorrow."

CHAPTER 46

ELARA

I hurry from the room, feeling hollow and wrung out from my conversation with Wilha. I want to find a way to know my sister and truly become her friend, but how can I do that when it feels as though there's so much that divides us? She couldn't have been serious about meeting with Andrei. Has she forgotten his cunning and cruelty? It's a meeting we'd likely never return from.

But despite all that I'm looking forward to talking with Wilha more; and I resolve to be more patient with her tomorrow.

In the kitchen, Stefan sits cross-legged on a thick rug and faces the fire. The planes of his face are hardened, and sunk in shadow. It's been a while since I was able to truly just look at him, and my insides melt a bit at the brooding look on his face.

"It's a little warm for a fire tonight, isn't it?" I say, stepping closer to him.

Stefan glances over, not looking terribly surprised to see me, before turning back to the flames. "It helps me think," he says. "And I never expected I would be able to sleep tonight."

"Why? What's happened?"

"It's not what *has* happened, it's what has not." He turns to me. "Do you really not remember what day it is?"

At his stricken look, I do.

"Today should have been our wedding," I say, and my heart aches for what we've lost. What I ruined.

"Well . . . not *our* wedding, I suppose. Mine and Wilhamina Andewyn's. But nevertheless." He turns back to the fire. "It should have been a happy day, indeed."

"Stefan, I'm sorry I forgot. I just . . . I've had a lot on my mind and . . ." I flounder about, trying to figure out how to erase the hurt on his face, when my stomach makes a loud, and decidedly unfeminine, grumbling sound.

"Are you hungry?" He picks up a wooden bowl next to him and gestures to the rug. "Sit," he says, handing me the bowl. It's full of warm broth, and hope rises as I settle next to him. Was he hoping I would come to the kitchen tonight? Is that why he had the broth ready?

Stefan's eyes sweep over my face. "I see you favor short hair now."

I bring a hand to my head. "It was the price I had to pay to get out of the city."

"It was well spent." His brows knit together. "I was worried, actually, when I arrived and saw you weren't here yet. If I had known it would take them so long to get you out of the city, I might have demanded you stay with me."

"Maybe I should have," I say, thinking of Alinda's wails, and the rotting stench of the butcher's shop. "Maybe that would have been for the best, after all."

We both sit silently for a while, watching the fire while I sip the broth. The room feels heavy with enough regret to fill the entire kingdom.

"What has been preoccupying you so?" Stefan says when I've put the bowl aside.

"A number of things," I say. "But I don't want to talk about my family or palace politics tonight." I lean back and settle more comfortably onto the rug. "Tulan, the village I grew up in, is only a few hours' ride from here. I sent a letter to Cordon—do you remember me telling you about him?" I say, and he nods. "I offered to send him and the Ogdens wor- things. Lord Royce told me months ago that Mistress was ailing." I shrug. "I guess I just thought I could help somehow."

"That is very kind of you," he says softly. "Kinder, I suspect, than she would have treated you. Mistress is the woman from your stories, is she not?"

"Yes, I was sent to live with her when I was a small child. I loved her once, I think, when I was young—too young to realize how much she hated me."

Stefan's face is guarded. "How many of the stories you told me about her were true?"

I look away. "All of them. Since I could not tell you the truth, the stories were the most I could offer."

"You promised me once you would tell me your whole story. We have a long night ahead of us, and I have little hope for sleep. So tell it to me now. All of it, from the very beginning."

A lump forms in my throat. "Are you sure you want to hear it?"

"Yes," he says quietly. "I really do."

"Okay." I take a deep breath, and know that I will tell him everything—except of the existence of Astrid's letter.

Until I can decide what I want to do, her words are a secret I must keep.

CHAPTER 47

ELARA

My cheeks are wet by the time I finish speaking. Stefan reaches out awkwardly, but then drops his hand. "After you escaped the castle, I wondered every day about you," he says quietly. "Who you truly were, and the life you had led before I met you."

"Can you forgive me, for all my lies?" I say, wiping my eyes.

"Forgiveness is more than just casually speaking a few words. True forgiveness is a concentrated act of the will and the heart." He sighs. "I am doing the best I can, and in some ways, it feels like I have only truly met you tonight."

I nod. "Thank you for listening. I know it's more than I deserve."

Hurried footsteps sound in the hall, and Patric bursts into the kitchen. "Put out the fire!"

Immediately, Stefan is up and dousing the flames. "What is it? What is going on?"

"Men were spotted sneaking onto the grounds," he says, planting himself in front of the window. "I have sent guards to deal with them."

We wait silently, and in the darkness Stefan's hand finds mine. "Don't be afraid," he says. "The guards will take care of it."

"I'm not afraid," I say, louder than I should have, because

Patric turns around and tells me to be quiet.

Stefan laughs quietly and squeezes my hand. We stay in the darkness for a long time, until a guard comes into the kitchen. "They got away. There were three of them, but they didn't appear keen to attack. I'm thinking they were scouts."

Patric nods grimly. "Get everyone up and in here immediately."

The guard leaves, and Patric lights a candle from the smoldering embers of the fire. Minutes later, people begin stumbling into the room, bleary-eyed and bearing expressions of confusion. We crowd around Patric, the candlelight casting shadows on our faces.

"Scouts were spotted at the edge of the property," he announces. "They escaped before we could detain them. Caution demands that we consider the possibility they are allied with Andrei."

"I have been most careful," Lord Nichols says, sounding offended. "I have never given Andrei or anyone else at court cause to believe I am anything less than loyal to them."

Patric turns to Lord Royce. "Have any of your sources in Allegria reported that Andrei has discovered our whereabouts?"

"They have not," he replies.

"And you, Your Highness"—Patric looks at Stefan—"do you have any reason to believe you could have been followed here?"

Stefan shakes his head. "My men and I followed every precaution you asked us to take."

"What about the letters you were writing?" Patric asks Wilha and Lord Royce. "Is it possible you wrote something that could have disclosed our location?"

"Of course not," Wilha says. "Lord Royce and I have been careful."

Dread snakes through me as I remember the letter I sent to Cordon. This can't be *my* doing, can it?

"Well, *something* must have tipped them off." Lord Royce's gaze lands on me. "When you were in the city, did you have contact with anyone?"

"Not . . . exactly," I say.

His eyes narrow. "Then what, *exactly*, did you do?"

Stefan squeezes my hand. "Tell him," he says.

"You told me Mistress was sick, and you refused to send help, so . . . I sent a letter to Tulan."

Silence.

"Oh, Elara," Wilha says. "Please tell me you didn't."

"And in this letter," Lord Royce says, his voice dangerously calm, "did you tell them how to contact you?"

I swallow. "I told them to send a message here."

The guards begin murmuring to themselves and Lord Royce curses. "You ignorant, foolish girl! Did I not *tell* you that the palace had people watching in Tulan, waiting to see if you would try to contact the Ogdens?"

"Yes," I say, my stomach sickening as I remember, "but—"

"*But*, you played right into their hands! It seems I've

pinned all my hopes on a dim-witted—"

"That's enough, Lord Royce," Stefan says. "What's done is done. What are we to do now in response?"

"We have to leave immediately," Patric says. "Those scouts—"

"We don't know they were scouts," I say desperately, hoping he's wrong. Hoping I haven't just ruined everything. "They could have been anyone."

"If I'm wrong," Patric says, "we can return tomorrow. But if I'm right, those scouts could come back with troops in too great a number for us to hold off. We must leave."

"And go where?" Lord Nichols asks. "Who would receive us?"

"There is a place," Lord Royce answers. "I have been in contact with the Lyrisians. Their village is small, but I have been regularly providing them with grain—they would undoubtedly welcome the princesses and all who support them."

Patric raises his voice. "Pack only what you can carry on horseback. We leave in an hour."

The manor becomes a whirl of activity, and I watch as images spin before me: Lord Royce stuffing Wilha's jeweled masks into a saddlebag; Wilha shrugging a cloak over her shoulders; Patric shoving a sword into her hands and saying, "I don't think it will come to it, but if it does . . ."; Rolf and Nicolai raiding the kitchen for supplies; Lord Nichols flying through the rooms, trying to decide which of his possessions he wants to take with him, finally ordering guards to remove a stack of books and scrolls from his library.

All around me they hurry, while I stand silently, keenly aware that other than my mother's letter, I have nothing of value to pack.

And that this is all my fault.

Light is just beginning to appear in the eastern sky when we're saddled up and ready to leave. We ride hard all day, stopping only to water and rest the horses. We don't hear Andrei's men thundering behind us in pursuit. Only the smell of smoke, carried along by an acrid summer breeze chases us, and eventually we see angry black clouds billowing into the sky.

"They've burned the manor," Lord Nichols says during one of our brief stops.

"We don't know that," Wilha says.

"Of course we do," he answers, sounding dazed. "That's what Lord Murcendor does with every traitor. He burns their home."

"When we take the crown from Andrei, we'll make sure they're both held accountable," I say, grateful that Lord Nichols doesn't seem to blame me for the loss of his estate. I catch Wilha looking at me strangely before her gaze quickly shifts away.

Everyone mounts up to ride again, but I hesitate, staring at the blackening sky and dreaming of all the ways I'd like to make Andrei pay for what he's done.

CHAPTER 48

WILHA

The village of Lyrisia is little more than a small collection of dilapidated cottages bordered by a lush hillside to the west, and patches of cornfields and blueberry bushes to the east. The villagers eagerly offer us their homes; one family clears out of their cottage completely and turns it over to Elara and me. Lord Royce sends Nicolai to assess the damage done to Lord Nichols's manor. The rest of us settle in, and life continues on around us. The men tend to the crops while the women weave tapestries they plan to sell at the Allegrian market in the quickly approaching autumn. The children in particular seem taken with Elara and me. They ask us both to cover our hair and sit side by side while they make guesses, trying to tell us apart. All of them, it seems, are eager to see Andrei fall. Many of the men have offered to fight on our behalf, if it comes to it.

I sincerely hope it does not.

But I find I have lost my nerve entirely. Although Elara and I have made efforts to spend time together, I cannot bring myself to ask her about a meeting with Andrei. Her anger toward him for hunting us and for burning Lord Nichols's manor is great, and she will not listen when I try to explain these are Lord Murcendor's doings, not our brother's.

Finally I write a message to Andrei and tell him I need more time. Patric sends it via pigeon to a guard he trusts, instructing him to secretly pass it to the king.

Andrei sends a message almost immediately in return:

> *Please do not desert me now, Sister. There are few in the palace I can trust, and none I can confide in. I am certain it is only because of you and Elara that I am still alive. If I were to die now, the crown would still be expected to pass to you and Elara. But if all three of us were to perish, I fear it would pave the way for Lord Murcendor to have himself crowned king. Please convince Elara to meet with us. Either way, rest assured that I am now prepared to wholly entrust myself to Lord Royce, and all who support you.*

It occurs to me I could bypass Elara completely and simply go to Lord Royce and tell him I've been corresponding with Andrei. But the picture of Elara gleefully smiling and saying we could use a meeting as a way to lure Andrei into a trap has stayed with me. Could I hope for any better a response from Lord Royce? Or would he, too, see my brother not as a person, but as a pawn to be used for his own agenda? I cannot be sure, so I decide to say nothing.

I tuck Andrei's message away, and hope an opportunity to make Elara see reason presents itself.

"*W*hat of Azarlin's ambassador, Sir Vanderberg?" Lord Royce asks one morning when we're all gathered around a wooden table in the cottage he's staying in. "Has he agreed to meet with us?"

"He's waffling," I say, shuffling through the parchments in front of me until I find his reply. "He fears the consequences for Azarlin will be severe if Lord Murcendor gets wind of it."

The responses to the letters Lord Royce and I have been writing have been less than encouraging. Many of the diplomats in Allegria, as well as the noble families, seem too scared to openly declare themselves against Lord Murcendor.

"We need something to force his hand. . . ." Lord Royce leans back in his chair, thinking. "He's a collector of fine things. . . ." He sits up suddenly. "And in our possession we have the masks that Wilhamina Andewyn and her twin were seen wearing at the Royal Opera House on the night they declared their intentions for the throne. Such items are nearly priceless."

"So you want to offer him the masks as a way of forcing a meeting with him?" I ask.

"With your permission, yes."

"You have my permission as well." Elara's voice is like an out-of-turn horn, blasting bitter dissonance. Lord Royce gives her a withering look; the two of them have not gotten along at all since we arrived in Lyrisia.

"Those items belong to the Masked Princess, Wilhamina Andewyn," Lord Royce says. "Not *you*."

Elara leans forward intently and opens her mouth to speak. She seems to think better of it, though, and turns away.

"What about King Ezebo?" I say quickly, eager to avoid another argument between Elara and Lord Royce. "Where does he stand?"

We all turn to Stefan, who has decided to remain with us for the time being. I feel awkward around him, the man I should have married. Judging from the polite way he avoids me, I believe he feels the same.

"You should remember that my father is still king," Stefan begins. "And so I must speak on his behalf."

I nod. "Of course."

"He is not inclined to support either you or Andrei, but to remain neutral. Once the question of Galandria's succession is settled, he will resume talks of a new treaty between our two kingdoms."

The atmosphere in the room changes; Lord Royce and Lord Nichols glance at each other, neither of them quite concealing their distaste. "I know His Majesty is hesitant," Lord Royce begins, "but he must understand that—"

"I was not finished," Stefan says. "I told you my father's position. For *my* part, I have seen enough with my own eyes to understand that Andrei and Lord Murcendor cannot be allowed to remain in power. I intend to return to Kyrenica soon, and I will do everything I can to see that my father comes to the same conclusion."

Lord Royce nods grudgingly at Stefan and turns to Patric. "Have you had any luck with your contacts in the palace guard?"

"Yes. Several now secretly claim allegiance to the twins."

"Good. If Andrei finds himself deeply unpopular in his own kingdom, unable to trust his own palace guard, and surrounded by kings who support the twins, his rule may crumble sooner than we could hope."

The meeting soon ends, and Elara and Stefan leave. Patric and the rest of the men also depart. Lord Royce and I remain, working on more letters.

A short while later Rolf appears. "A message came for you, Uncle." He hands Lord Royce a roll of parchment. "You'll want to read it straightaway. . . . I'll be outside helping in the cornfields if you need me."

Lord Royce opens the letter, his frown deepening as he reads, and I prepare myself for more bad news.

Once he's finished, he clears his throat. "This is from Nicolai. It seems your brother was quite a bit more destructive than we first imagined."

"Whatever my brother has done, it was most likely done under Lord Murcendor's influence," I remind him. "But what is it? What have you learned?"

"Being a queen means more than giving speeches or throwing parties and enjoying the fruits of your ancestors' wealth. An essential part of ruling is possessing the sturdiness of heart to carry bad news." Lord Royce gives me an appraising stare, and I wonder if this is some sort of test.

"You speak to me, Lord Royce, as though I have no idea what it means to bear the responsibility of being a royal. If you have news you wish me to deliver, tell me what it is."

"Very well."

By the time he's finished reading the message, my mouth has gone dry, and my hands are shaking.

"If you find this to be too difficult," Lord Royce begins, as if reading my mind, "then—"

"I will do it," I say. "I will tell her."

"I knew you would," Lord Royce says.

And for the first time, I'm certain I read respect in his eyes.

I find Elara hidden under a cluster of willow trees atop a hill near the outskirts of the village. She smiles tiredly as Stefan speaks to her. I have heard them talking late at night near the fire in the cottage Elara and I share. I know she's having trouble sleeping, and feels responsible for the burning of Lord Nichols's manor.

More than anything I want to turn away and not deliver

my message, for I do not want to burden her further.

"Sometimes the fog is so thick," Stefan is saying, "that you cannot see your hand in front of your face."

"Hello," Elara says when she sees me approach. She rests her head against the trunk of the tree. "Stefan was just telling me about life on the Lonesome Sea."

I nod politely at Stefan. "I have just spoken with Lord Royce. Nicolai wrote to him with his findings now that he has had a chance to visit Lord Nichols's manor . . . as well as the surrounding area." I phrase my words carefully.

"I'm sure Andrei's men were quite thorough," she says. "How is Lord Nichols taking it?"

"I don't know. I believe Lord Royce has gone to inform him, but it seems the men were not content to merely destroy the manor. It seems they moved northeast. To Tulan. It appears they wanted to make a statement that anyone who comes into contact with either of us and does not report it to the king will suffer." I pause. "So . . . they burned Ogden Manor as well. Lord Ogden was away . . . at a tavern, according to Nicolai . . . but the Lady Ogden was inside, and I'm told that she was ill, and would not have been able to get out and—"

"Are you telling me that Mistress burned to death?" Elara says, and I'm surprised to see that she looks stricken. Is this not the woman who abused her all those years?

"Yes, but . . ." I pause, wishing I did not have more grief to add. "It is hard to tell—the remains were unidentifiable—but it also appears as though her daughter, Serena, returned and tried to save her. And then . . . Serena's husband went in after her and . . . he perished, too."

"They're all dead?" Elara's stare is eerily vacant.

"Yes," I say quietly. "They are dead."

Elara slumps against the tree, her eyes unfocused.

"If that is all of your message," Stefan says, "would you mind terribly if you left us alone?"

I hesitate, wanting to comfort my sister. But from the way she grips Stefan's hand I know it's not me she truly needs right now.

"Yes, of course," I say. "I will be in Lord Royce's cottage if you need me."

Soon after I step out of sight, Elara begins screaming.

CHAPTER 49

ELARA

*T*he pain claws its way up my throat and I yield to it. I yield to all the memories it brings, all the words I have ever heard from Mistress Ogden. *Worthless. Unwanted. Unlovable.* . . . Everything I thought I'd stuffed away and forgotten, it bursts forth in a scream that shakes my bones.

Stefan pulls me into his arms and I cling to him. How can they all be dead? Just when I thought I was doing something right, when I thought I was offering help, it turns out I was merely hastening Mistress's death. And not only hers, but Cordon and Serena's as well.

"They're dead because of me," I say, pulling away from Stefan. "Because I was stupid and—"

"No." Stefan cups my chin so he can look into my eyes. "They're dead because Lord Murcendor and Andrei are cruel and vindictive. All you did was try to offer help to someone who needed it. That's an admirable thing, Elara."

But all being admirable has bought me are bodies burnt beyond recognition and the destruction of the only place I have ever been able to truly call home, miserable though it was. And the death of my friend, the only one I ever had as a child.

I push Stefan away and stand up. Then I'm flying down the hill, and Stefan is behind me calling my name. I burst through the door of Lord Royce's cottage where I find Wilha and Patric seated around the wooden table. They look up, startled.

Wilha stands. "Elara, are you all right? I think you should sit—"

"I want Andrei executed the minute we take the crown from him," I say.

"We don't know that Andrei is behind this," Wilha says, going pale. "From all the accounts that I—that *we*—have received, it appears that Lord Murcendor is ultimately in control."

"That is nothing more than an excuse and you know it. *Andrei* wears the crown. He could have Lord Murcendor arrested, or whatever he should like. But he does not."

"He does not because Lord Murcendor has been the closest thing Andrei has ever had to a father. Elara, please, you do not understand what it was like in the palace. Andrei is surrounded by—"

I slam my hands down on the table. "Don't tell me what I don't understand, Wilha! I am fed up with your constant excuses for Andrei. I understand enough to know that he is far from innocent. And when I am queen, I intend to make him pay for his crimes."

A beat, and then Wilha says, "I assume you meant to say when *we* are queen?" Her voice softens. "Please, Elara. You've just received horrible news. Can we not—"

"No! You need to choose, Wilha. Is it going to be Andrei or me?" I ignore Stefan, who has come up behind me and is pulling at my arms. "If you cannot support me on this, then I shall hold you responsible as well."

"What exactly do you mean by that?" Patric stands, his eyes blazing.

"She doesn't mean anything." Stefan's arms wrap around my shoulders. "She's had a shock, that's all."

"That doesn't give her the right to issue threats against Wilha, Your Highness," Patric says. "And I will not—"

"Everyone, please just *stop*!" Wilha places a hand on Patric. "We don't need to make this decision now." She turns to me. "I understand you are upset, Elara. It's only natural that—"

"Don't condescend to me, Wilha," I say, struggling out of Stefan's embrace. "I'm telling you *I want him dead*." The words hiss from my mouth, ugly and twisted, but they do nothing to ease the grief and rage blowing in my veins.

"And I'm telling *you*," Wilha says, "that I will not see our own brother executed. And if ever *we* are queen, I will not support that decision."

I reach into my pocket and take out Astrid's letter. I no longer care what the truth will cost Wilha. It can't be higher than the price Cordon, Serena, and Mistress—and who knows how many others—have already paid.

But before I can say anything, Stefan is tugging at my elbow. "Elara, let's go. Let's go cool off."

"No—"

"Whatever it is you want to say can wait until you've both had time to think."

Wilha and I continue glaring at each other, until I grudgingly admit Stefan is right. I slide the letter back into my pocket. But I know at some point now I'm going to have to show it to her.

Because I think it just became clear to everyone that Wilha and I cannot rule together.

CHAPTER 50

ELARA

As our stay in Lyrisia has dragged on, Wilha has become the favored twin. No one says it, but I see it. I see it in the wide berth Wilha's guards give me, in the way Lord Royce's men—many of whom once bowed before me in a dusty tavern—look at me warily. In the way Wilha and Patric whisper while he trains her to use a sword. In the way Lord Royce seeks out Wilha more often for her opinion. It seems after living her whole life in Allegria, she has accumulated a wealth of knowledge.

Knowledge I don't have.

That night at the opera house, Lord Royce rode safely out of the city and took Wilha with him. Who's to say he won't one day decide Wilha would make a better queen and leave me behind again?

But should Wilha be allowed to rule, even jointly? After all Andrei has done, all the death and destruction he's caused, it's clear she pities him. *Pities him*, when with a snap of his fingers he could begin righting so many of the wrongs in this kingdom. If Wilha became queen, would she hold him accountable for all the evil things he's done, all the ways he's made people suffer? Or would she continue to make excuses for him? Should someone who's sympathetic to Andrei, someone who's never truly seen the suffering of the villagers, be allowed to rule them all?

When I first agreed to Lord Royce's plan, I admit it had more to do with wanting to come out of hiding than any sense of duty I felt to Galandria, or her people. But now I wonder . . . shouldn't someone who actually knows what it is to go hungry, someone who knows firsthand how a decision made in a palace affects the people in the villages, be the one to sit upon the throne? Someone like . . . me.

Me alone—without Wilha.

With all this in mind, for the time being I'm not showing Wilha—or anyone else—Astrid's letter. I fear if I did, it would change nothing. What is my proof, really, but a small slip of parchment? Lord Royce has shown himself to be nothing if not determined. I don't believe he would allow something that could be so easily destroyed to stand between him and his prize.

No, I will have to bide my time and earn back everyone's favor. Then I will show them the letter.

"Promise me you will not do anything rash after I have gone," Stefan says once he's packed and ready to leave. Behind us, his guards wait on horseback for him to say good-bye. His eyes stray to my mouth, and I wonder if he'll try to kiss me. We've spent many nights by the fire. He has held me as I have cried for Cordon; he has listened to me rage. But he has never once tried to kiss me, even when I'm certain he has wanted to.

"I promise."

He nods, and my heart pounds, hoping he'll show some sign that he's truly forgiven me.

"Rest assured, I am thoroughly committed to your cause. I have already sent messages to my father detailing my belief that Andrei cannot retain power for much longer. Now I will return and tell him in person my findings."

He reaches out, as though to hug me, but seems to change his mind at the last second. "Send a pigeon if you need anything." He mounts his horse, and with one last wave, rides away.

I watch until he's out of sight, disappointment threading my insides.

"Excellent job, Your Highness."

I jump, startled at Lord Royce's voice behind me. "How so?"

"Your charms have solidified the sympathies of the future king of Kyrenica. We now have a powerful ally."

"I'm glad my grief could be of service to you, Lord Royce." I brush past him and return to the village, determined to find a way to earn back his favor, so he can help me become queen.

And then once I do, my first official act will be to dismiss him from my service.

⌘

The temptation of the mask proves too much to resist for Sir Vanderberg, and he finally agrees to a meeting.

He asks us to visit him at his old hunting lodge four days from now.

"Tell him no," Lord Royce instructs Lord Nichols after he's finished reading the ambassador's reply. "I will be seeing someone about obtaining more grain for the village that day."

The men gathered around the wooden table all nod, and I see my chance.

"Tell him yes—Wilha and I will meet with him." I look at Lord Royce. "If we wish to secure his support, turning down his first request is hardly the way to do it."

"I need to be there," Lord Royce says.

"Why? It is Wilha and I who hope to rule this kingdom one day, not *you*."

"Sir Vanderberg is quite old and particular. I do not think—"

"I can handle an old man with a predilection for fine things," I say. "And I don't believe either Wilha or I require your permission on this matter. After all, when we are queen, you will merely be advising us; you will not command us." I turn to Wilha. "Don't you agree?"

Wilha smiles tentatively, a hopeful look in her eyes, and nods. And for the first time, I feel the power of being a twin. As Wilha and I stare back at Lord Royce with the same face I say, "Send a pigeon to Sir Vanderberg. Tell him we accept."

The ambassador's hunting lodge is located in the Weeping Forest. We travel in a plain carriage that bumps its way into a forest canopied by drooping willow trees with spindly branches and knotted trunks. We continue through overgrown paths strewn with moss and wild mushrooms, until the carriage shudders to a halt just as the sun is setting. The hunting lodge before us is small and decrepit with a thatch roof and splintering wooden walls.

Patric tells us to sit tight while he and the guards search the area.

"What do you know of the Azarlin ambassador?" I ask Wilha as we wait. I'm thinking ahead, trying to calculate the best way to secure his support. If we return from this meeting without it, Lord Royce will most likely place the blame solely on me.

"He's been in his position since I can remember. He enjoys Galandria, and I think he much prefers to live here rather than in Azarlin. I was once told that he is quite snobbish and cantankerous, and that it's best to appear accommodating when you are negotiating with him."

"Who told you that?"

Wilha pauses. "Lord Murcendor. You remember I told you he once served as my tutor? He told me then."

I slide my hand inside the pocket of my cloak, grip my mother's letter, and wonder if I should just tell Wilha, only

Wilha, of its existence. We have avoided each other since the day I learned of Cordon's death, and our last disagreement still hangs in the air between us.

"Why do you want to be queen?" I ask suddenly. "You asked me once; now I'm asking you."

"What I really want is to find a way to keep the three of us from tearing this kingdom apart." Her answer is immediate, as though she has given the matter much thought.

"Three of us?" I say, my voice hardening. "By that I assume you mean Andrei?"

"He is our brother, however much you wish he were not."

I don't answer. I don't want to start yet another fight over Andrei.

"Elara, I really think your attitude toward Andrei would change if—" She stops when I reach into my leather bag and pull out a jeweled mask. "What are you doing?" she asks as I tie one on.

"What does it look like I'm doing? If the ambassador is interested in the masks, then we should let him see the merchandise." I lift out the second mask and hand it to her. "And what better way to add to the spectacle than to appear masked before him?"

Silently, Wilha ties on the mask, and soon after, Patric tells us it's safe for us to exit the carriage.

"We searched the area and the grounds are secure," Patric says as we head for the front door. "The guards have spread out around the premises. We will dine with the ambassador, but I do not think it wise to accept his offer of lodgings for the night. I would rather that, upon concluding your meeting, you allow us to return to Lyrisia. I would not risk traveling by daylight again if we don't have to. The guards and I are prepared to ride through the night."

Wilha nods. "Then that is what we will do."

I stride ahead, frustrated that neither of them bothered to ask my opinion. When we reach the cottage, I take a steadying breath, and knock on the door.

CHAPTER 51

WILHA

"*I*t is not customary for a queen, nor any other member of the royal family to knock on the door," I call out to Elara.

Elara rounds on me. "I didn't know that!"

"But Sir Vanderberg *does* know that," I say, surprised by her sudden anger. "Let Patric handle the initial greetings. This is how it is done."

Elara steps back from the doorstep, a murderous look in her eyes, and I have to tamp down a flood of irritation, as I have had to do so many times before in her presence. I tell myself again that she has recently suffered a great loss. Yet oftentimes these days my sister reminds me of an untrained horse. Unbroken and wild, easily angered or startled.

The cottage door opens; a young woman appears and identifies herself as Sir Vanderberg's maid. She exchanges greetings with Patric and gestures us inside, her expression remaining carefully blank as we pass her.

Sir Vanderberg's eyes widen as he takes in our jeweled masks. "Ghosts," he whispers. "I've seen you from your balcony numerous times. I always thought you looked like a jeweled ghost."

"I assure you, Sir Vanderberg, we are quite real," Elara says, a lilt in her voice. Yet judging from the expression I read in her eyes she is momentarily taken aback by him. His beard is tangled and dirty; his skin is waxy and wrinkled, and spittle dangles from the corners of his mouth. His teeth are yellowed and decayed. Perhaps I should have thought to tell her of his appearance beforehand.

"Thank you for agreeing to meet with us," I say quickly. "I am Wilhamina Andewyn, and this is my sister . . . Elara Andewyn," I say, although her full name sounds strange to my ears.

He bows before us. "Your Highnesses, it's a pleasure to meet you. Please, come and dine with me."

"How did you know about this place?" Elara asks, quickly regaining her composure as we settle around a small wooden table.

"The lodge is mine. When I was a younger man I used to come here often to hunt." Sir Vanderberg's hands shake greatly as he gestures to his maid to get a fire going. "Use lots of wood," he says. "My bones are old." He turns back to us. "You're certain no one followed you here?"

"My men checked the area; we were not followed," Patric answers.

"How many do your men number?" Sir Vanderberg says.

"Four," says Patric. "They are standing watch outside."

While Patric stands behind us and looks on, Sir Vanderberg's maid pours the three of us glasses of wine and brings out small plates of braised rabbit and stewed pears. "I am afraid this is the most we can manage in the way of hospitality here," he says after she has excused herself from the room. He takes the candle from the table, lights four more, and places them in the window.

"Lord Royce told us you were interested in obtaining the masks," Elara says. "Do you find them to your liking?"

He plucks the spectacles hanging on a chain from around his neck and sets them on the bridge of his nose. He looks first at me, then at Elara. "You're the princess's sister?" he says.

"I am," Elara answers, sounding slightly annoyed. "As Wilhamina just said, my name is Elara."

"Well, you could be anyone under that mask. Take them off."

A red stain appears on Elara's neck, and I read the fury in her eyes at being commanded by a man she finds repulsive.

"Of course, Sir Vanderberg," I say quickly. "We should like nothing better."

We remove our masks, and he looks back and forth between Elara and me, clearly disappointed by our appearance. Perhaps he hoped we were incomparably beautiful. Or hideously ugly.

"You were raised in Tulan, were you not?" he says to Elara. Two thick bands of spittle form between his lips, and his breath is sour, like curdled milk.

"Yes," Elara says, making a soft gagging sound, "I was sent there when I was a child."

"Well, then, what makes you think you could possibly rule?" He bites into his meat. Brown juice runs down his chin, and soaks into his beard.

"I am an Andewyn. It is my birthright."

"That's your brother's position, and look what a mess he's making," Sir Vanderberg says, brandishing his wine glass. "Many men may bend the knee to your sister, but I fail to see how *you*—raised as nothing more than a peasant—could presume to rule this kingdom."

The flush on Elara's neck deepens. She opens her mouth to speak, but I rush to cut her off. "But unlike Andrei, we are committed to searching out and listening to wise counsel. You, of course, would be among that treasured counsel if you were to support us."

Sir Vanderberg does not respond. He stands and hobbles over to the hearth. While he adds more wood to the fire, I shake my head at Elara slightly. "Just let him say whatever he wants. We need him," I whisper.

"I'm aware of that. Stop interrupting me."

I settle back into my chair. I do not understand why Elara is so determined to lead this meeting, but I decide not to argue with her.

When the ambassador has returned to the table, Elara resumes her coquettish air. "Now that you have had time to see the masks, what do you think of them? They are quite beautiful, are they not?"

"Yes, yes." His eyes flit to the window and his shaking resumes. "It is all in hand."

"*What* is all in hand?" she asks, her smile becoming strained.

"Well"—he waves his hand vaguely—"it is difficult to know what the right course of action is, is it not?"

Patric and I share a look. Sir Vanderberg is shaking uncontrollably—has he been afflicted with palsy?

"Oh, I don't know." Elara tilts her head slightly, and her voice takes on a breathy tone. "Sometimes the right course of action is quite obvious. . . ."

Elara makes another attempt to engage him in conversation, and I resist the urge to kick her under the table. Does she honestly think she can *charm* him into supporting us? I look around the room. The maid is in the hallway, watching us. When she catches me looking at her, she quickly turns and hurries away.

"Sir Vanderberg," Elara says. "We are here because we were under the impression that—"

Abruptly, he stands again and ambles over to the hearth.

"Why is he adding more wood to the fire?" Elara whispers. "If those flames get any larger he's likely to burn the place down."

I nod. It *is* stifling in here; sweat has begun trickling down my back.

"At any rate," Elara says when he has sat back down. "We

should like to know that after we leave here tonight you will write to your king and—"

Yet again he stands and moves to the window. He puts his hands out, as if to warm himself over the candle flames, before repositioning them equidistant from each other.

"This is ridiculous," Elara whispers. "I don't see how we'll get anything out of him—he doesn't even seem right in the head." She fans herself. "I need some air before I suffocate. I'm going outside."

CHAPTER 52

ELARA

*A*fter I've excused myself, I stride from the cottage, thankful to be away from the rotting corpse that is Sir Vanderberg. Wilha's guards aren't outside the cottage as they should be. Figures. They're only ever around when *she* needs them.

Is this what being a queen will require of me, smiling prettily while a man with one foot already in the grave insults me? It was tempting to pull out Astrid's letter from where I've hidden it in my pocket and show him I am the firstborn, and that if Sir Vanderberg knows what's good for him he'll keep his putrid mouth shut.

I cross the short courtyard to the forest. The guard who was to be stationed at the carriage seems to have also abandoned his post. I open the door, but pull back when my fingers brush something wet and sticky. And red.

Blood.

A soft scream issues from my throat, and too late, I realize that was exactly the wrong choice. There's a snap of a twig, and a sudden glint of silver. A knife appears near my throat and a hushed voice says, "Don't move."

CHAPTER 53

WILHA

I resist the urge to call Elara back. Better to give her a little space, as I do not want her to lose her temper in front of the ambassador. However, Sir Vanderberg is still looking out the window and doesn't appear to notice her absence.

"Of course," I say, suddenly inspired, "my sister and I were thinking of giving up our claim altogether and joining the royal circus."

"Yes, yes. Of course," Sir Vanderberg says. He's racked by more trembling.

Patric and I glance at each other again and frown. From the way his eyes suddenly widen and he draws his sword, I think we have arrived at the same conclusion. Patric knocks two times on the door and receives no answer.

"Did anyone know we were coming tonight?" I say, pushing my chair away from the table and standing up.

"What?" Sir Vanderberg turns around, startled.

"Did you tell anyone Elara and I were visiting you?"

His shaking increases, and I finally understand. It's not palsy; it's nerves.

"They came a week ago and questioned me," he whispers. "They asked me if you had contacted me. When I showed them the letter Lord Royce wrote, they demanded I contact you and agree to the meeting you requested. I'm sorry," he says, his eyes becoming watery. "My children live in Allegria, and they threatened to do terrible things if I refused. Once you arrived, I was to give the signal."

"What signal?"

"Smoke," Patric says, looking at the roaring fire. "That way they could watch from afar before approaching." He turns about the room, his gaze landing on the line of candles in the window. "Four candles, for four men," he murmurs. "Wilha, he's already given the signal. Andrei's men are most likely on their way right now."

Just as he finishes speaking, the window shatters, and the cottage explodes in flames.

CHAPTER 54

WILHA

*F*laming arrows pour through the broken windows. One strikes Sir Vanderberg's maid squarely in the chest, and she collapses in the hallway. Another lands near my cloak and ignites. I shrug out of it, screaming, and try to stamp out not only the flames, but the panic threatening to overwhelm me.

The curtains and wooden beams are already burning. Patric, Sir Vanderberg, and I flee into the hallway.

"Is there a back entrance?" Patric shouts to be heard over the roaring of the flames.

"There is," Sir Vanderberg says, eerily calm, "but they will have surrounded it."

"Is there any other way out?"

"The wall of the storeroom is decaying. There's a thick hedge beyond—it pokes right through; you may be able to get out that way."

Patric grabs my hand. "Come with us," he says to the ambassador.

Sir Vanderberg shakes his head. "I'm too old to run. I have decades behind me, and most likely only days ahead of me. Besides, the smoke will get me before the flames." And with that, he steps back into the room, his head held high.

Patric begins pulling me toward the back of the lodge.

"No!" I say, struggling against him. "We have to go back for Elara."

"They already have her," he shouts, pulling me forward.

"But—"

"Wilha—they have her. The best thing you can do for your sister is to flee now and try to help her later."

At the back of the storeroom, Patric tosses aside crates of wax candles and begins pulling at the rotted wooden planks. "Look through the supplies and grab anything you think will be helpful! If we can get out, we're going to need to run!"

I try to stem the tide of fear rolling over me, and grab a saddlebag hanging from a peg. The shelves are mostly empty, but I find a tinderbox and a small pot and stuff them inside. Smoke billows; orange flames lick into the room and begin racing along the ceiling.

"Help me!" Patric shouts. "We need to work faster!"

I join him, and work at the planks, crying out when thick splinters from a rotted board pierce my hand.

The smoke stings my eyes, and we're both coughing violently. With a grunt, Patric wrestles another plank from the wall, creating a space large enough for us to push through. "Now!" Patric lunges into the hedge beyond and begins hacking at branches with his sword, cutting a path for us. Gratefully, I drink in gulps of fresh night air. But the storeroom is engulfed in flames, and the heat at my back is unbearable.

"Go! The fire is following us!"

Branches slap at my cheeks and claw at my arms and legs as we push forward. We reach the end of the hedge and Patric peers out. "When I give the word, I want you to run into the cluster of willow trees over there."

Above the roar of the flames I hear the guards shouting at each other. The frame of the lodge heaves and buckles with a loud, splintering *crack*. Patric gives me a push. "Go!"

We sprint for the trees, and a night wind pulls at our clothes as we run, accompanied by the sounds of the lodge burning, small creatures skittering, and the rustling of willow tree branches. We run for what seems like hours, until my lungs are gasping for air and a stitch pierces my side.

Patric slows and takes the saddlebag from me and slings it over his shoulder. "We need to head south," he says.

"South? But that will take us deeper into the forest."

"Exactly. Andrei's guards will most likely expect us to head north, back to Allegria. So we will move south."

CHAPTER 55

ELARA

I look into the eyes of Wolfram, the guard who held me captive last year in the Opal Palace's dungeon. "Tell the others I have one of them," he calls to another guard up ahead.

"Which one are you?" he asks, pointing his knife at me. "The Masked Princess, or the other one?"

In response, I spit in his face.

He wipes his cheek, seemingly unmoved, and smiles.

The blow comes suddenly, bruising pain across my brow and cheek. My head snaps back. My eyes water, and my vision blurs.

"Nice to see you again, too, Elara."

I spit blood and something else from my mouth—a tooth, I think—and laugh dazedly. Now Wilha and I aren't quite so identical.

"You think this is *funny*?" He raises his hand to strike me again when the smell of smoke reaches us both at the same time.

"No!" He lurches to his feet, dragging me along with him. In front of the lodge, palace guards watch silently as fire engulfs the wooden structure. Glass shatters, wood splinters, and orange flames claw the night. My stomach seizes and I sink to the ground as several nearby trees ignite.

No one could survive a fire like this.

The guards' voices come to me in snatches, though they seem very far away.

"You weren't supposed to start the fire until we had them!"

"You *did* say you had them!"

"I said I had *one* of them, you fool!"

While they argue, my gaze is drawn to the thick hedge at the side of the lodge. Is it my imagination, or does it shake slightly? Dim shadows fly like overgrown bats from the hedge to the thick patch of trees beyond. I'm certain I recognized Wilha's outline. I quickly flick my eyes back to the burning inferno that once was the lodge, and go still, hardly daring to breathe. Did anyone else see them?

We watch the lodge burn until ash rains from the sky, coating our clothing like acrid snow. When there's nothing left but a smoldering stain of earth, Wolfram sends a few men to inspect the scene.

"We found the remains of two people," a guard says after they return. "A man and a woman, we think. We also found these." He tosses the two jeweled masks on the ground. The white paint has melted, the jewels have blackened, and smoke rises from the scorched metal.

I lean my face to the ground, thinking. Two remains, but *four* people were in the lodge. Wilha and Patric most likely escaped; I know it was her shadow I saw. Yet it seems to me it's to Wilha's benefit if the guards at least entertain the thought that she's dead, rather than go searching for her.

Uttering a guttural scream, I reach out and grab one of the masks and clutch it, not caring that it sears my hands. Fake tears fall, bathing the mask, washing away some of the ash. The guards don't seem to know what to do with me, but my performance has them squirming.

"If we killed one of the twins," begins one, "then—"

"Then we will have eliminated a serious threat to the king," Wolfram says. "Saddle up the horses." He pulls me to my feet and gives me a shake. "There's someone in Allegria who wants to talk to you."

CHAPTER 56

WILHA

We travel south for hours. Patric finds a small stream and we take turns drinking from the tin pot I found at the lodge. When the sky has turned from black to a deep, steel gray, we come upon a large willow tree with leaves that reach the ground.

"Let's rest under there for a few hours," Patric says.

We settle against the trunk in between two thick roots. For a few minutes I'm keenly aware of Patric's nearness. Then exhaustion closes in and I'm falling, falling. . . .

I am wet and shivering in front of the fireplace in the Kyrenican Castle. There's something I'm supposed to be doing, someone I'm supposed to be saving, but I cannot remember who. The flames in the fireplace morph into the shape of my own face, screaming for help. No, not my face. Elara's.

"Help me!" she screams. "You're the only one who can."

"I'm coming." I reach out for her. My burning sister.

But somehow it's started raining in the castle, and already her image is sizzling and hissing. Dissolving into nothingness.

"Wilha! Wilha, help me!"

"I'm trying!"

"Wilha," comes another voice. "Wilha, wake up."

With a start, I open my eyes. The image of the flames is

replaced by waves of willow tree branches, the sound of pattering rain, and the scent of leather oil and mint. My head rests on Patric's chest; his arm is around my shoulders.

"How long have I been asleep?" I mumble.

"A few hours," he replies. "I didn't want to wake you, and when the rainstorm started I thought we should stay here awhile. You were crying out in your sleep—were you having a nightmare?"

I shift away to look up at him. A throbbing pain shoots up my arm and I groan.

"What is it?" Patric says, sitting up straight. "Are you hurt?"

"No, no. It's nothing," I say, grimacing. "It's just a few splinters." I hold out my hand.

"Those aren't splinters, Wilha. Those are small sticks impaled in your hand. You should have said something earlier."

"I didn't want to stop in case we were being followed."

Patric takes my hand and examines the wounds. "We're going to have to remove these," he says grimly. "It will hurt, and you might want to look away."

He begins gently pulling, trying to ease the splinters from my hand. I grit my teeth against the pain and try to concentrate on the sound of the rain. The willow trees form a parasol around us, keeping us mostly dry. My eyes drift to Patric. He's careful as he works, always stopping if I make even the slightest sound. His expression is intent, and I blush when he catches me staring at him.

When he has finally pulled the last splinter free, he examines my hand one last time. "We'll need to put a poultice on it to prevent infection. I saw some yarrow not too far from here. Do you happen to have any extra strips of fabric with you?"

I check the pockets of my cloak and pull out the golden ribbon.

"We'll find something else," he says, quickly averting his eyes. "Stay here."

I lean back against the trunk and close my eyes; the image of Elara on fire is burned onto the back of my eyelids. I assume if she was caught by the guards she will be taken to the Opal Palace. I can only hope she'll be shown a measure of mercy.

When Patric returns, soaking wet and smelling of earth and rain, he's holding stalks of small spindly green leaves. He fills the tin pot with rainwater and gets a small fire going. Then he drops the yarrow into the pot.

"While we wait for the water to heat, would it be all right if I ripped a small swatch of fabric from the bottom of your dress?"

"Of course." Awkwardly, I straighten out my skirts.

Patric begins tugging until I feel the fabric give. "You never answered my question," he says as he lays a silken strip over a rock. "Were you having a nightmare?"

"I was dreaming of Elara. She was burning and screaming for me to help her. I was trying to, but I couldn't reach her. I couldn't save her." I lean back against the tree, tears threatening my eyes. "We shouldn't have just left her there, Patric."

"We were vastly outnumbered, Wilha. We had no other choice." Patric checks the water's temperature. When he looks up, his eyes are pained. "And I could not have lived with myself if something had happened to you."

The current between Patric and me has always bubbled under the surface, hidden from view of others. But now when I have been branded a traitor and am being hunted by men from my own kingdom, what is to keep us from saying all the words we never could before?

"Do you say this to me as merely a guard, or my friend . . . or someone else?"

"The last one," Patric says, his eyes intent on mine. "I have always been your friend, Wilha . . . but it has also never been enough."

"It has never been enough for me, either."

"You are the daughter of a king, and I am the son of a soldier. It always seemed to me that our paths had been mapped out for us before we even took our first breath. But now . . ." His lips curve into a smile. "Now that the world is spinning out of control, I wonder if we couldn't chart our own course."

He leans close, and his lips meet mine in a kiss that is everything I have ever hoped for.

CHAPTER 57

ELARA

Wolfram finds a horse for me, and bile rises to my throat when I realize it belonged to one of Wilha's assassinated guards. We ride nonstop back to Allegria and reach the city gates a few hours after sunrise. My hands are bound with chains, and I'm escorted to a common cart used to transport criminals. The burnt mask is hastily tied to my face; I wince when the metal presses against my bruised cheek. Wolfram instructs the driver to travel slowly. "Ride ahead," he says to another guard. "Let the people know we've captured one of the twins."

I nearly smile at Wolfram's cunning. They want to create a scene and parade me through the city's streets. They want to put on a show.

And I know how to give them one.

The gates open, and my driver urges the horses onward. I haul myself to my feet, ignoring the burning in my thighs from so many hours on horseback. I refuse to enter the city as a beaten down captive. I force myself to stand straight, bracing my legs against the jostling of the cart. And though my face is throbbing, though the chains are cutting into my skin and my hands are slick with blood, I do not wince or cower. Instead, I lift my chin and keep my eyes fixed forward.

I imagine I am in a grand procession, on my way to my own coronation, the chains no more than bracelets of gold around my wrists. I do not see the people, but I hear their whispers:

Which one is she?

They think the other one might be dead. . . .

What happened to her hair, did the king's men do that to her?

She even looks like a queen. . . .

The Opal Palace nears, the golden gates are unlocked, and I prepare myself to face a madman.

CHAPTER 58

ELARA

I run my hands along my chamber wall, ignoring the pain shooting up my fingers from where the chains rubbed my skin raw. If there's an embedded opal, and a hidden passageway near this room, I intend to find it.

Upon arriving at the Opal Palace, I expected to be led to the dungeon. Instead, a guard showed me to this small, windowless room with creamy gold-leafed walls and armchairs with pastel-colored cushions. I suppose this is what being the publicly recognized sister of the king has bought me: better accommodations than the last time I was held prisoner.

Though this time around, I actually am the traitor they believe me to be.

They let me keep one of the burnt masks; I suppose they intend it to be a reminder of my defeat. I place it on the mantel and think often of Wilha, hoping that wherever she is, she's safe. Meals arrive regularly, and the guards stationed outside my door are polite, if distant.

When I finally acknowledge there's no way to escape, I collapse into an armchair. I had intended to come back to this palace a queen, not a captive. I had planned on walking through every room, exploring every tunnel, and truly getting to know the place that should have been my childhood home. I had wanted to find the golden cradle Astrid spoke of, and take a walk with Wilha in the Queen's Garden. Now I don't know if I'll ever see my sister again. But I refuse to give in to the panic pricking at my heart.

Because I know what's coming. And I know I need to stay alert.

My wait is over the next day when the door unlocks, and Wolfram enters. He holds out an empty brown bag.

"You know the drill," he says flatly. "Put it on." He leads me through a series of twisting halls. Dank air fills my lungs, so oppressive I think I may actually choke on it. My body turns instinctively without much guidance from Wolfram; my legs have trod this path before.

As I walk, I tell myself to be strong. Stronger than I have ever been. I tell myself I survived a childhood with Mistress, I can survive an afternoon (is it the afternoon?) of Lord Murcendor's company.

There's a sharp knock and a door opens. The bag is jerked off my head.

This time, the torches are already lit. The gruesome paintings on the wall are in sharp focus, showing me all the ways Lord Murcendor and Andrei could hurt me. Lord Murcendor himself sits behind the same wooden table, but this time there's no feast. No wine bottles. No jewel-encrusted goblets.

"Your hospitality seems to be lacking this time."

"Sit down," he says. After I'm settled, he gets straight to the point. "Your brother has grown enamored of your cunning and wishes to know you—the sister whose very existence was denied to him all his life. He is not eager to see you die."

I glance at the paintings on the walls, the closest of which features a woman being strangled, and suppress a shudder. "And what will I be required to do in exchange for knowing my brother?"

"We know Lord Royce, Lord Nichols, and many other of your supporters are in hiding. I want to know where they are. Your brother is prepared to pardon you, if you will only cooperate with us."

"Pardon me? And then what? Will we live a happy life, here in this palace, my brother and I?"

"I'm offering you a deal, Elara. I suggest you take it." He glances meaningfully at the paintings. "Your brother doesn't want any harm to come to his sister."

"Any harm?" I say incredulously. "So burning down Sir Vanderberg's hunting lodge, and killing Wilha—his *other* sister—was . . . what, exactly?"

"A grave mistake. And the guard who started the fire has been dealt with. But if you do not want to talk, I feel sure I could *make* you do so." His lips curve in a malicious grin.

His threats don't fill me with fear. They don't cause me to shake or tremble. Only tiredness, bone deep, descends over me. Months ago Lord Royce easily convinced me to give up Wilha's location, all because I didn't want to fall into Andrei's hands. Now that I'm here, will I betray her again?

As a small child I learned to tuck away my pain somewhere deep inside of me, where I wouldn't have to feel it. Could I do it again, one more time? Could I withstand whatever methods Lord Murcendor chooses to employ, and keep not only the pain hidden, but the words they want?

I think I'll try.

Whatever promise or *deal* Lord Murcendor offers me, I know he won't keep it. And for once, I'd like to believe I could be just a little bit more than my father ever thought I could be.

"I'm sure you could employ any number of vicious tactics to gain the answers you seek. I'm also sure you know there are enough ears in this palace to make certain that whatever you do to me will become known to the public." In truth, I am confident of no such thing. But it seems to give Lord Murcendor pause.

"Do you employ spies in the palace?" he says.

"I don't have to pay anyone. You and Andrei are hated enough on your own account. If you harm me, it will only fuel more people who are bent on seeing Andrei—and you—overthrown. But this is a pointless conversation." I lean back in my chair. "You can do whatever you like to me; I will still tell you nothing."

More than anything, I just want this to be over. Whatever Lord Murcendor says, whatever he promises, I know the end of this story.

I knew it the minute I walked into this room.

CHAPTER 59

WILHA

*I*t takes us nearly a week to backtrack and return to Lyrisia. Patric is concerned guards may be searching for us, so we travel only at night, staying off the forest paths and following the small stream until it connects to the Eleanor River. A group of children playing in a patch of wildflowers are the first to catch sight of us. A few of them sprint toward the village, shouting the news of our arrival.

One by one villagers swarm us, their faces etched in relief. The crowd parts for Lord Nichols. "Princess Wilhamina, thank Eleanor you are unharmed! When news of the fire reached us we feared you were dead."

"And my sister?" I ask. "Have you had any news of her?"

The villagers grow silent, and Lord Nichols stares at me sadly. "I think it's best if you go to Lord Royce. He's asked to speak to you immediately."

"Of course, Lord Nichols," I say, exchanging a frown with Patric. "I will go right now."

Inside his cottage, Lord Royce sits at the long wooden table poring over a stack of parchments. He looks up when I clear my throat.

"Lord Nichols said you wanted to see me."

"I have news, and I thought you should hear it from me

first." He picks up a bowl of blueberries and cream and offers it to me. I wave it away impatiently, although after so many days of traveling a part of me wants nothing more than a good meal, and a good sleep.

"What is it? What have you heard?"

"Your sister is under house arrest at the Opal Palace. Andrei—or Lord Murcendor, most likely—has decided to execute her."

Shock waves roll through me, chasing away the fogginess of traveling on the road for so many days, and I grab the table for support. I suppose I should have expected this news, but a week spent in the Weeping Forest walking next to Patric, speaking freely with him, made everything else seem far away, like a once vivid dream I was starting to forget.

"What are we to do in response?" I say, sinking into the chair opposite him.

"Nothing. Stefan Strassburg sent Sir Reinhold to the Opal Palace to beg for mercy. When that failed, he threatened to march a Kyrenican army right into the heart of Allegria—and Lord Murcendor has moved the date up in response. There is little else the crown prince—or anyone else—can do at this point to stop it."

"When?" I say, feeling light-headed. "When is the execution scheduled?"

"She is to be beheaded in four days' time."

"But surely there is something—"

"There's nothing," he replies in a clipped tone. "Elara is lost to us. We need to cut our losses and move on."

"*Move on*," I repeat, stunned. "Is my sister dead already to you?"

"We are lucky only Elara was captured, Your Highness. You could easily have been taken along with her. And your own safety is far from secure. Your sister has reportedly refused to disclose our location, but it has become too dangerous to stay in Lyrisia." He pulls out a parchment and quill. "I'm in the process of arranging for us to leave in a few days. So if you don't mind . . ." He dips his quill into an inkpot and begins writing, as though I'm nothing more than his bothersome child, and he's just dismissed me.

Yet this man is not my father. Nor is he my king.

"Yes, Lord Royce, I *do* mind. Quite a bit, actually."

"Excuse me?" he looks up, clearly annoyed that I'm not leaving.

"This conversation is far from finished." I lean forward. "*You* came to Elara with ideas about claiming the crown—it was not the other way around. *You* convinced her to become a queen . . . and now you're just going to let her die?"

"What would you have me do?" he says. "I no longer have any influence in the palace, or have you forgotten?"

"Surely there is something. Up until now, your resources have seemed unlimited."

"Even a man such as myself has his limitations—it will be

difficult enough finding another village to hide in. But once we are safely settled, we will begin spreading the news that you survived the fire, and still plan to pursue your claim to the throne."

"My claim?" I repeat vaguely. Are we already discussing life after Elara's death?

"Yes, I should think these recent turn of events will gain you much sympathy."

All at once, I read his intentions, and I think I understand. Lord Royce has never been comfortable with the idea of Elara and me ruling as joint queens. And as long as he thinks he can still get me on the throne, then he really has little use for Elara.

"Sympathy is no substitute for a sister," I say, standing. "And this isn't over." I whirl around and stalk from the cottage, where Patric is waiting for me.

"They're going to execute her," I say, a sob escaping my lips.

"Lord Nichols told me," he says as he enfolds me in a hug. "I'm so sorry, Wilha."

I lean my head against his shoulder, but my eyes are wide open. All around us, the villagers are husking corn, sorting blueberries, and weaving quilts, as though nothing is wrong. As though the earth itself hasn't just shifted.

"Does Lord Royce care at all for my sister and me?" I ask, pulling away from Patric.

"I think he genuinely believes the two of you are better suited to the throne than Andrei," he says carefully. "And I think he really wants to create a better kingdom for the people. But"—he sighs—"no—I don't think he carries any personal affection for either of you."

Behind the doors of the cottage, Lord Royce sits writing letters and plotting my ascension. Yet if it's me he wants on the throne, at some point, shouldn't *I* be the one making the decisions? It does not appear this is power he will cede to me.

I shall have to take it on my own.

"I will not see her executed, Patric."

"What do you mean?" he says warily.

"I mean, if I am truly queen among these men, will they follow me?"

"Wilha—*no*." A grim understanding dawns on his face. "I know what you're thinking, and it's too dangerous."

It *is* dangerous, and my heart twists with the choice before me. How easy it would be to sit back and do nothing. To let forces seemingly beyond my control determine the course of my sister's life. To claim there was nothing I could have done. Could I tell that lie to myself, day after day, year after year, and believe it?

Because if I am surrounded by men who claim me as their queen, the truth is, I am far from powerless.

"Assemble the men. Inform them I wish to send a rescue party after Elara. If there is a way we can get my sister out of the city, I intend to see it done."

CHAPTER 60

WILHA

*L*ord Royce does not oppose my plans so much as he tells me it cannot be done.

"Why can it not be done?" I say. I have never directly questioned Lord Royce before, and judging from the tension I suddenly read in the room, everyone is aware of it.

"Gone are the days when you could live anonymously," he says. "Your face is now known to most in the kingdom. Your guards' faces are also recognized, as well as those of my men, which means none of us can hope to get past the city gates. And even if we could, there is no way we could gain entrance to the Opal Palace. Every passageway will be watched."

"With all due respect, Lord Royce, that's not necessarily true." The men step aside to make way for Lord Nichols, who clutches a yellowed, flaking scroll in his hands. "Princess Wilhamina asked me to examine plans of the palace, and I have come across something that may prove quite useful." He spreads the scroll across the table. It is a map of Allegria and the surrounding area. "In the weeks following Queen Rowan's return to Galandria after being held prisoner in Kyrenica, she secretly commissioned her masons to begin a building project. A note in the accounts kept at the time indicates that whoever participated in the project was paid handsomely—and sworn to secrecy, under pain of death, should they ever speak of it to anyone, even their own family."

"And you think this building project was for another tunnel in the Opal Palace?" I ask.

"I do," says Lord Nichols.

"Another passageway doesn't help us," Lord Royce interrupts. "Queen Rowan would have passed that information on to her heir."

"I am not so sure. Queen Rowan died suddenly in her sleep while her heir was still young. With an unexpected death, and the tunnel not being completed until a few years after she died, it's possible the news was not properly passed on to the surviving Andewyn heirs."

Lord Nichols turns to me, as does everyone else.

"Show me the tunnel, and I will tell you if it is known to me," I say.

Lord Nichols reaches across the map with his index finger, landing on Gossamer Falls. "Do you see that mark, right there? Near as I can figure, an identical mark was made in every place where there is a passageway." He points to different locations on the map and I nod, noting there is indeed such a mark near all the passageways I'm aware of.

"I am not familiar with any tunnels leading to Gossamer Falls," I say. "Whenever my family traveled outside of Allegria we always left via the city gates."

"It's possible, then, that this tunnel is also unknown to Andrei and his men and will not be guarded," Lord Nichols says.

I look at the mark near Gossamer Falls, and consider Lord Nichols's words. Queen Rowan would have returned to Galandria under the full knowledge that the only reason she avoided execution in Kyrenica was because she either already knew of, or discovered the passageway leading from the castle to the cave near Rowan's Rock. If a passageway allowing quick escape from the Opal Palace to a location outside of Allegria didn't already exist, I have no doubt that is exactly what my great-great-grandmother would have commissioned.

"This is madness," Lord Royce says. "Even if you could get into the palace, there's no guarantee you will be able to get back out. We don't know exactly where Elara's being held, and Andrei still has a decent number of palace guards—"

"Many of whom secretly claim allegiance to Wilha and Elara," Patric says.

"We could draw many of the guards out of the palace," Lord Nichols says thoughtfully. "It would not be an overly difficult thing to do. The Lyrisians are planning on going to Allegria's market and they have sworn their allegiance to the girls. We could ask for their assistance."

"By doing what?" Patric asks.

"Use the rumors of Wilha's death. Tell them to say that on the road they encountered a band of armed men claiming they were coming to the city to avenge the Masked Princess's death. We know how quickly gossip spreads in the city. I would think if they repeated the lie enough, it would prompt a response from the palace. Andrei would be forced to send more men to the gates to defend against a possible attack."

Lord Royce shakes his head. "Even so, Elara would still be under heavy guard."

"Under your orders, Lord Royce, I watched Elara for years," Nicolai speaks up suddenly. "If there's even the slightest possibility of saving her, I will do all I can."

"As will I," Rolf says. "I once swore an oath to her, Uncle. I would not abandon her now." Many of Lord Royce's men nod heartily, and Rolf continues, "My face is not well-known to Allegria's elite, nor to any palace guards. But I know many who frequent the market. I volunteer to accompany the villagers to the city. I will carry the rumors."

The men turn to me. I grip the edge of the table, well aware of the import of this decision. This course of action, once undertaken, cannot be undone. If I send the Lyrisian villagers into Allegria carrying false rumors of an imminent attack, and the rest of us on a search for a passageway that may or may not still exist, so much could go wrong. So many could suffer.

A hundred years ago, an Andewyn daughter betrayed her twin, and Queen Rowan should have been executed. Now another Andewyn daughter faces death, and I cannot help but wonder if this is our chance to show the world that Elara and I will not be the rivals who betray each other. Rather, we will be the sisters who save each other.

Lord Royce is silent, his face impassive, yet I'm certain I read his thoughts: Elara's sacrifice is acceptable, so long as he gets me on the throne.

"Do you acknowledge me as your queen, Lord Royce? Do you acknowledge my sister as your queen?"

The men all turn to look at him. No matter how he answers this question, it will cost him something. And from the grudging resignation I read in his eyes, it is clear he understands this as well.

"I accept you as queen," he says finally. "And though I think it's folly, I will accept your decision."

"Good." I turn to Patric. "Organize the men and see that the villagers are ready to leave for Allegria in three days' time. The rest of us will make for Gossamer Falls."

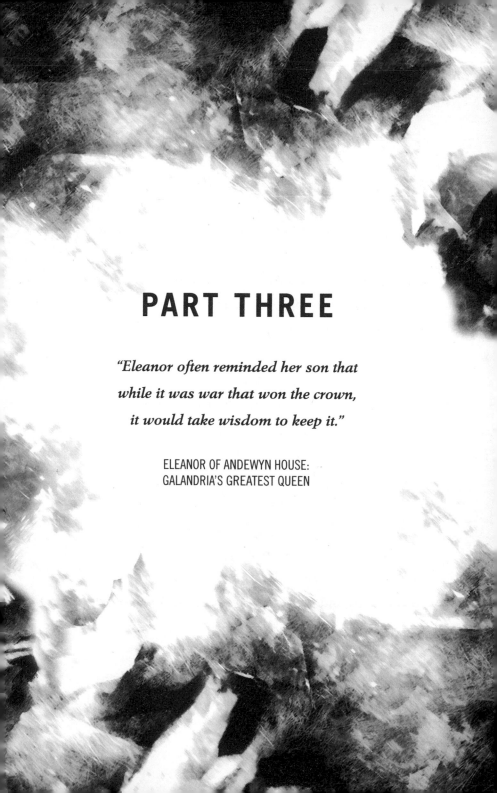

PART THREE

"Eleanor often reminded her son that while it was war that won the crown, it would take wisdom to keep it."

ELEANOR OF ANDEWYN HOUSE:
GALANDRIA'S GREATEST QUEEN

CHAPTER 61

ANDREI

Andrei Andewyn stands in the center of the Guardians' Chambers looking at the ten circular thrones. Sunlight pours through the high windows, bouncing off the crystal chandeliers and casting prisms on the wall. All ten thrones are empty. All ten are useless.

For what use is the Guardians' Chambers when there are no more Guardians to debate or disagree? When there is but only one Guardian now, whose voice silences all others?

For the young king is under no illusions now:

Lord Murcendor is slowly killing his family.

Elara is sentenced to execution. Wilhamina is dead, lost among a pile of ash. And his father . . .

But no, he will not think of Fennrick today. And just as autumn, the season of death, closes in, Andrei feels his own death nearing. He wonders if anyone will mourn him.

"You called for me, Your Highness?" Lord Murcendor doesn't look pleased at being summoned. He does, however, look healthy and robust, far from the black wraith who once used to slink through the palace corridors. Power would seem to agree with him.

Andrei studies the man who was once his friend. This is his Guardian. Has he ever known him? For he now knows the kindly advisor of his childhood was merely an illusion, conjured by his own longing and loneliness.

"I see no reason to execute Elara," Andrei says.

"No reason, Your Highness? The fact that she's a self-confessed traitor isn't enough?"

"I think she should be spared."

"*I* think you are too young to make such decisions."

Andrei and the man who was once his friend now eye each other as predator and prey. The new king feels the world spinning around him. Chandeliers, sunlight, and empty thrones; they are fixed things. Whereas he feels light and intangible, like dandelion seeds blown away by the breeze.

"I am still king, Your Lordship. I could walk into Eleanor Square and proclaim I was showing her mercy."

"You could, Your Highness. You could also have an unfortunate accident when you go riding tomorrow."

The threats are no longer veiled; and they come often now.

Andrei is tempted to command his guards to seize him. But he dares not, for he knows half of them are loyal to Lord Murcendor. And the other half won't spill their own blood. Not for him.

"Are we done now, Your Highness?"

"Yes, Your Lordship."

Andrei understands he will not win. Not today. But the new king is slowly growing his courage. He will not be beaten.

He will bide his time.

CHAPTER 62

ELARA

*I*n the end, they dispense with torture and decide to get straight to the business of killing me.

I suppose it was always going to end this way. The moment the life I had with the Ogdens—wretched and miserable though it was—was snatched away, this end was like a mark on a map that my life was slowly journeying toward.

No one comes to visit me as the days pass. I make a list of all the dead whose lips can say nothing to me now: Serena, Cordon, Mistress Ogden, Astrid, Fennrick. A deep frost blooms over my heart, and sleep comes often. My dreams are haunted by visions of small necks and blunt swords. Of executioners with unsteady hands, of chopping blocks with crimson stains.

Two days before my execution, my isolation ends and Sir Reinhold pays me a visit. He steps hesitantly into my chambers—as if my death sentence is a disease he might catch if he comes too close, and tells me he will soon be returning to Kyrenica.

"I have been recalled by the Strassburgs," he says. "Even if I were not, I am afraid I'm not of the mind to stay, not with things in Allegria as they currently are."

"I'm not of the mind to stay, either," I say with a braying

laugh. "Although as my mind shall soon be separated from my body, I don't think it matters much."

Sir Reinhold looks both flustered and horrified by my words and I laugh again. How much does this conversation matter? How much does *anything* matter, in comparison to the blade that's coming?

"I am truly sorry more couldn't be done for you," he says, sounding stricken. "On Stefan's orders I begged for your life to be spared." He sighs. "I fear it has merely ensured our two kingdoms will soon go to war."

"Well, take heart, Sir Reinhold. On that day, *neither* of us will be in Allegria to see it."

I laugh again, and from the way he shifts around awkwardly, I can tell Sir Reinhold thinks I've already lost my head.

"Yes, well . . . before I take my leave of you, I wanted you to know that the crown prince sent me a letter to give to you."

Hope breaks through my haze and I stop laughing. "Stefan wrote to me?"

"He did. But Lord Murcendor wouldn't let it pass through, and the guards confiscated it."

The haze reclaims me. Of course Lord Murcendor wouldn't let it through.

"But, if you'll forgive me, Your Highness. I had expected as much, and, well"—he grimaces—"I took the liberty of reading the letter." His cheeks redden. "The crown prince said many, er, *tender* things to you. And he said he forgives you."

"He did?"

"I believe his exact words were 'I forgive you without condition. And I treasure our time together, however short it was.'" Sir Reinhold looks supremely uncomfortable at having to recount the message.

Yet with those few words, a burden I didn't know I carried lifts from my shoulders. If Stefan were here right now, there is so much I would say in return. So many things I was too fearful to say before. And now the opportunity is lost to me.

Amid much shuffling and bumbling, Sir Reinhold takes his leave. After he's gone, I stare at the gold-leafed walls, filled with regret. I've always played a role, haven't I? I've always become who circumstances required me to be in order to survive, whether a servant, a princess, or a wannabe queen. But there's no surviving a death sentence. The blade will fall and my life will end.

And if I'm going to die, I decide suddenly, I'm going to die as *me*. I'm going to stop pretending.

I hurry over to the writing desk and find a quill and a piece of parchment. I dip the quill into the inkpot and begin a letter of my own:

Dear Stefan,

Your message has been carried and received. Your forgiveness means more than you will ever know. I will die at peace knowing that you have pardoned me for my crimes. I wish you were here and that I could see you one last time. There are so many things I wish I had done differently. Most importantly, I wish I had told you I loved you. I wish I had returned the words you once so freely offered to me. I wasn't sure what true love looked like; I have seen so little of it in my life, and I didn't want to say it before I knew for certain. I have told so many lies; I didn't wish to add another.

But knowing that your days run short has a way of whittling your thoughts and scraping away everything that doesn't matter. What I'm left with is, I love you.

I love you. And I wish you every happiness in this life. I hope, when death finally claims me, the last image that flits through my mind is of you, sitting by the fire, waiting to hear my stories.

I pause, not knowing how to end it. Do I sign it as Elara? Princess Elara?

With that thought, my eyes are drawn to the vase where I've stashed Astrid's letter. I've kept it hidden, figuring if Andrei or Lord Murcendor saw it, they'd just burn it and kill me faster.

But after I'm gone, I think I want at least one person to know who I really am. Was. I dip my quill into the inkpot and hastily add:

I want to die knowing that I have kept no secrets from you. Not too long ago, I discovered a letter written to me from my mother. I have told no one of its existence, and I'm enclosing it for you now. Once you read it, I think you shall understand I was not deceiving you nearly so much as either of us believed.

I scrawl *Elara* across the bottom, then fold the two letters up and seal them. Then I knock on the door.

"Yes?" comes a guard's voice.

"Could you please tell—no, *ask*—Madame Arianne if I could speak to her when she has a moment? Tell her it's important."

The guard responds noncommittally, but I hear footsteps striding away from my door. Soon afterward, the door unlocks, and Arianne enters. She steps hesitantly inside. "What do you want?" She doesn't look me in my eyes. Now that I think about it, neither do most of the guards who stand outside my door. Am I dead already to them?

"I wanted to ask you something." I hold out the letter. "Would you see that Stefan Strassburg receives this? There were several things I needed to say to him and it seems I won't get to do it in person." When Arianne hesitates, I add, "Please? You could consider it my dying wish if you choose."

Arianne's eyes flick to the closed door and she nods. "I will see that it's done."

CHAPTER 63

WILHA

*T*he day of our leaving dawns the color of blood. The Lyrisians have agreed to carry false rumors to Allegria, and they shoot me furtive looks while they load their carts with crates of corn, blueberries, and woven blankets to sell at the market. Once everything is packed, the men embrace their wives who whisper teary good-byes.

Patric and I and the rest of the men, nearly thirty in all, mount our horses and set off. The Lyrisians ride with us until we come to a fork in the road. With Rolf and Nicolai leading the way, they turn toward Allegria, and the rest of us continue on down the path. The trees on either side of the road are tipped with color, and the air smells crisp, like autumn leaves.

Just as the sun is dipping below the tree line and golden light filters through branches, we arrive at Gossamer Falls. The waterfall is large and thunderous; mist rises from it like moist incense. Hills lush with greenery surround the falls, and I'm dismayed to see that they also appear to play host to a number of shallow caves in the area.

"You would think Queen Rowan would have made the passageway easier to find," Patric grumbles.

I dismount my horse. While Patric has never openly opposed my plan, I can feel his disapproval nevertheless. "If it was easy to find it wouldn't be a secret," I say. "And I know you do not think this is the right course of action."

"I don't want any harm to come to Elara, and I would see her rescued if it can be done . . . but I defended the Opal Palace for years against outsiders. I know just how difficult our task will be—I also know it's highly unlikely we will all survive this night. If something happens to both Elara *and* you, there will be no one left to stand against Lord Murcendor. There are many men—many *good* men, Wilha— who would tell you the wisest course of action, and the best thing for the kingdom, is to turn back."

"And will you be one of those men?" I ask. "Patric, if it was *me* who was scheduled to die tomorrow, would you not come for me?"

"Of course I would. I would never abandon you."

"Neither can I abandon my own sister."

Our gazes hold until he nods. "Then I shall not abandon her, either. And I will do everything in my power to see you both safely out of the palace tonight."

He turns away and directs the men to spread out and search the area for a hidden opal. We look for hours, long after dusk has fallen and torches are lit, but discover nothing. I move to the top of the hill and watch as the mist rises to the stars above.

I wish I could see into the past. See the masons working away and glimpse the path they carved. I imagine Queen

Rowan standing at my side, cheering me on, willing me to find her secret.

My eyes are drawn to the rocks leading down the steep bank to the river. They seem to form a horizontal path skirting along the bank, where, to the casual eye, it looks like they dead-end at the veil of water cascading from above.

I begin edging down the bank, ignoring Patric's frantic calls for me to stop. The rocks are slippery and moss-covered and I tread carefully. Just as I suspected, the rock ledge is merely an illusion; it does not stop at the edge of the waterfall, but continues on around and behind it. I follow the path and step around the falls. The cave beyond is chilly and damp, and I quickly set my attention upon the rock walls.

"Wilha!" Patric's cries are but a distant echo, overshadowed by the roaring of the falls. By the time he and the rest of the men have followed me into the cave, my clothes are soaked.

The men join me in searching for the hidden opal, and with so many of us, it is not long before someone calls out that he's found it. Patric presses on the opal and hesitantly steps inside. After a moment, he reappears. "It's clear." He sends everyone on through, and then closes it behind them.

"What are you doing?" I ask. "Why did you close it?"

"I don't want you to go," he says, raising his voice to be heard over the waterfall. "We have no idea what awaits us on the other side of the passage. I promise you I will find Elara and bring her back to you, or I shall die trying."

"That is hardly an acceptable alternative, Patric." I move to sidestep him, but he blocks me.

"If you are caught, they could just execute both of you tomorrow morning. Please, please don't go."

I read the fear in his eyes, but I will not be swayed by his words. "Step aside, Patric. I have to do this."

"Someone has to, but not you."

"Yes, *me*," I say, my patience beginning to fray. "The only reason there wasn't a line of palace guards waiting for us when we returned to Lyrisia is because Elara refused to speak. That required an immense amount of bravery and loyalty, and she offered both to us freely—and it's time someone showed *her* some loyalty. I need her to know that I didn't just stand by and let her die. And I need to know for myself that I came for her, that I wasn't the weak girl everyone always believed me to be."

"But you have *never* been that girl. You are smart and kind and strong—though I think you often don't see yourself that way. You didn't let the horrors of the mask blacken your heart; it's one of the reasons why I love you—"

He breaks off suddenly. Mist rises around us. Rivulets of water stream from his black curls into his eyes and they look like tears. "I love you, Wilha." He reaches out and takes my hands. "I have loved you since our first training session, when you were so determined to prove to everyone you could fight. So I'm asking you, begging you, not to go."

He squeezes my hands, and I feel an electric thrill go through me. His words are a new song, one I have never heard before, but always hoped I would. They are bright and brilliant; beautiful enough to chase away nightmares, but I dare not linger on them too long.

"I love you, too," I say. "I love your valor and honor—but I think part of truly loving a person is trusting them. So trust me now, Patric. This is the right thing for me to do."

"What kind of a man would I be if I just stepped aside and let you do this, when I know how dangerous it is?"

"The kind who understands he does not get to tell the woman he loves what she can and cannot do. Particularly," I add, "if she is also your queen."

I read the anguish in his eyes; I can see him trying to swallow his doubts and summon his faith. "I trust you," he says finally. "And I will always go with you wherever you ask me to. But, if we survive this night, I want you to do something else for me." His face breaks into a wide smile. "I want you to marry me. I know I have not had enough time to properly win your hand. But these are not proper times. After this—after *all* of this is over—marry me. Whether you are a queen, or if we are both living in exile, marry me."

"Yes," I say, returning his smile. "I will marry you."

He draws me to him and cups my chin in his palm. His other hand tangles in my hair and he brings his lips to mine. While we kiss I forget the waterfall roaring beside us, the guards waiting for us, and even the threat that hangs over us all. I only know the sweetness of his lips and the knowledge that he has chosen me, and I have chosen him.

On the other side of the wall the men fan out and surround me, the light from their torches glinting off their drawn swords. Our footsteps echo as we silently journey down the tunnel. We travel for miles, and I imagine the city above us, sleeping peacefully, and hope that Rolf and the others have succeeded in drawing some of Andrei's men away from the palace. We encounter no one during the long walk, and the passageway dead-ends at a stone wall. I brace myself as Patric searches for the embedded opal, and hope we won't be walking into a room full of palace guards. The wall springs away with much creaking and moaning.

On the other side is panic and chaos.

CHAPTER 64

ELARA

*O*utside my chamber doors, a cacophony has steadily arisen, like an out-of-tune orchestra slowly warming up: rushing footsteps, strangled cries, shattering glass. What has the palace in such an uproar in the middle of the night? I pound on my door and call out to the guards, but receive no response. I pour myself a cup of tea and wait. Finally, there's a soft click and the door opens.

Arianne steps furtively inside. Her face is pale; her breathing is ragged. "Come with me. We need to get out of the palace."

"What's going on?" I follow after her, and we step out into the deserted corridor. "Where are the guards?"

"Gone. They're needed elsewhere right now. The city is in a frenzy, and there is a crowd at the gates demanding entrance to the palace."

"There have been people at the gates before, haven't there?" I say, struggling to keep up with her swift strides.

"Not like this, there haven't. Rumors have been swirling that the city was about to be attacked. A handful of men went to the gates, demanding shelter in the palace. I'm not sure what happened after that, but it seems the guards became nervous and attacked the crowd, which only added to the hysteria.

Now there's an armed mob outside the gates, and they're demanding to be let in." Arianne sucks in a breath. "Your ancestors built the Opal Palace during peacetime. It wasn't built to withstand a siege. If they breach the gates, the guards may not be able to keep them from entering the palace."

We turn a corner, and a maid carrying golden plates scurries up the hall.

"What is she doing?" I ask.

"Either she's taking those to lock them away in one of our storehouses—as she was ordered to do—or she's looting. Both are happening, and with the guards otherwise preoccupied, there's no one to stop it."

She pulls me into the old servants' quarters, the rank stench of the room coming back to me like an unpleasant memory from last year, and heads for the wall with the embedded opal. From the folds of her cloak she produces a small satchel filled with worthings. "Take the tunnel all the way to Eleanor Square. If you can find a way out of the city, this should be enough to get you across the border to Kyrenica."

I accept the sack slowly. "Why are you helping me now?"

She looks at me for a moment. "Because your brother asked me to."

"Andrei?" I ask, surprised.

Arianne nods. "This was his idea. I have served your family for years, and if this is the last night an Andewyn should rule, I want to end it serving my king."

"Where is Andrei now?"

"The last I saw him he was still in the Eleanor Throne Room." Arianne presses on the embedded opal, and the wall slides away.

"You mean he's not evacuating?"

Arianne shakes her head. "Lord Murcendor isn't allowing him to leave."

"Lord Murcendor isn't *allowing* him? But Andrei is the king."

A bit of the old scorn returns to Arianne's voice. "You really don't know anything at all, do you?" She gestures for me to step inside, but I hesitate.

I turn the sack of worthings over in my hands. Even if I'm not caught in the tunnels, my face is known to most in the kingdom. Exiting into a city on the brink of collapse doesn't seem like the wisest choice. And not far away sits Andrei. My brother.

My brother, who, it appears, can't save himself, but is trying to save me.

"I can't go," I say. "Not just yet."

"Then this is where I leave you." She steps inside the passageway. "But if you are recaptured," she says, fear haunting her eyes, "please tell everyone you escaped on your own. Otherwise, both your brother and I will die right alongside you."

CHAPTER 65

WILHA

*M*aids are ransacking a small storehouse in the southern wing. The women halt; their faces drain of color when they see me step in with the guards from the passageway.

"But, but they had you under house arrest?" one of them says vaguely. "And your hair—"

"Where?" I say, understanding her meaning at once. "Where in the palace?"

She continues staring at me strangely until Patric unsheathes his sword. "Tell us where," he commands.

"One of the smaller chambers in the northern wing—the one without windows."

The men start for the door, but I hang back. "What are you doing with the royal family's valuables?"

"We're not stealing them," she replies shrilly, exchanging panicked glances with the other maids. "We've been ordered to lock them away. A mob is at the gates—and if they get past them, Lord Murcendor fears they'll storm the palace."

"A mob?" A ribbon of dread coils around my chest. "Why? What's happened?"

"Rumors have been rampant that the city was about to be attacked, and it's stirred everyone up. Lord Murcendor has ordered all the palace guards to form a line in the courtyard to hold them back if they get past the gates." With that, she and the other maids hurry from the room.

But I am rooted to the spot. "Patric, this is my doing. *I* started those rumors."

"You did it to save your sister," he says immediately. "You had a hard decision to make, and—"

"And in the process, I've set the whole city aflame. I should have known. I should have realized. This city has been hanging by a thread, I should have—"

"You made the best decision you could."

"And if hundreds die tonight, will it have been a good one?"

"Let's just get to your sister's room. We can decide what to do after that."

I'm not sure what he means, but I follow him and we set off, surrounded by frightened cries echoing in the corridors. We come across a fallen candelabrum where dried wax puddles the floor. Next to it lies a leather bag swollen with jeweled items spilling across the hallway, as though someone planned to steal them, but was in too much of a hurry to come back after dropping the bag.

When we reach the appointed chamber, Elara is nowhere to be found. One of my masks, burnt and melted, rests on the mantel. I pick up a half-full cup of tea.

"She can't have left that long ago," I say, showing Patric the teacup. "It's still warm. Now where shall we look? Do you think it's possible she's left the palace?"

A heaviness seems to settle over the room, and the men exchange tentative looks with one another.

"What? What is it?" I say.

"Wilha . . . there are hundreds of rooms in the palace," Patric says. "It could take us hours to conduct a thorough search—hours we may not have." He pauses and glances at the men. "Many of us have been trained to protect not just your family, but this palace. I don't think any of us now want to just stand aside when all is being threatened."

"You want to join the soldiers in the courtyard?"

"You saw the terror on the maids' faces. If the gates are breached, many of the men and women who have spent their lives serving your family are going to face the wrath of an angry mob. Would you wish that upon them?"

"Of course not," I say. "But each one of you is considered a traitor."

"I daresay we will be welcomed back tonight."

Patric and the others look at me expectantly, waiting for my command. "Go," I say. "Go and save us from this mess I have created."

"I don't suppose it's too much to ask that you return to the waterfall?" Patric says softly.

"She's my sister. I have to keep looking for her."

He pulls a sword from his waist and holds it out to me. "Then take this with you. But promise me that if the gates are breached you'll evacuate."

Patric and the rest of the men make for the armory. If I strain my ears, I can hear the chanting of the people outside the gates. The sound brings back a lifetime of memories. My gaze is drawn to the blackened mask. Slowly, as if in a dream, I pick it up and tie it on, the metal cool against my cheeks. Then I leave the room, the path I'm set on well-known to me. For years I traveled it every Friday to appear before the crowds that came to see me. Now tonight, our positions are reversed. I am going to see them, and I hope their chanting has drawn Elara's attention as well.

I check every room as I make my way through the corridors, but I don't find her. When I arrive at the balcony, the doors are closed, though the screaming beyond the gates is clear as the people call down curses upon Andrei. Elara is nowhere to be found, yet I cannot help but pause to stare outside.

An ocean of torchlight trails like molten steel from the golden gates and down the hill to Eleanor Square. My stomach stitches itself into knots; I have never seen such a large crowd assembled in Allegria. It's only a matter of time before they gain entrance to the palace. Already I see the curling gold *A* at the top of the gates shaking against the pressure of the mob beyond. Below in the courtyard, every available palace guard stands at attention, armed and waiting to meet them.

"I had hoped you were still alive."

The sound of Lord Murcendor's voice startles me and I whirl around. I run my hand along the hilt of my sword, mostly to reassure myself that it's still there. Lord Murcendor also holds a sword; his fingers grip the hilt tightly as he gazes out onto the courtyard.

"Come away, Princess. This is no scene for a lady to be witnessing."

"You no longer command me, Lord Murcendor." I chance another look out the window. "Will the guards be able to hold the mob back if they breach the gates?" I say.

"We're not going to wait to find out."

"What do you mean?" I turn and read the look in Lord Murcendor's eyes; the way he strains forward—the way the entire contingent of soldiers in the courtyard strain forward.

And I come to a horrifying conclusion.

CHAPTER 66

ELARA

The screams of the mob outside the gates hurl through an open window as I make my way down a deserted corridor. The people are cursing, screaming, calling for Andrei's death. A shiver runs down my back. The voices are loud, louder than I've ever heard. Just how many are gathered outside the gates?

In the Eleanor Throne Room, I find Andrei alone, huddling on his throne. The opal crown sits askew on his forehead.

"I wondered if you would haunt me in death, Sister. Do you hear the people calling for me?" he says dreamily, and I realize he's mistaken me for Wilha. Before I can correct him he continues. "Do you know that when we were younger, I was quite jealous of you? Every Friday, for nearly all my life, it seemed the very walls of my room would shake as the people chanted, waiting for you, the famous Masked Princess, to make an appearance. Now it's *my* name they call. But I dare not meet them." He closes his eyes. "Wilha, I fear I have done a terrible thing."

I know I should correct him. But I feel frozen, unable to break the spell of the dreamlike haze that has descended over the room.

"What did you do?" I say.

"After Father got sick, he seemed to be getting better. Around this time Lord Murcendor had sent word through a servant loyal to me that he had returned to Allegria. We had been meeting secretly, and when he learned of Father's illness, he gave me some tea leaves and said it would cheer his spirits." The words rush from him, like a confession he's long wanted to make. "But shortly after I visited him, Father took a turn for the worse." Andrei opens his eyes. "And to this day, I don't know if the tea helped him or if it—or if *I*—" he breaks off, unable to continue speaking.

"Did you love Fen—our father?"

"I barely knew him. I don't think he particularly cared for children. Lord Murcendor said he only became a father because he needed to produce an heir." He swallows. "But I never would have purposely harmed him, Wilha. I swear to you, Lord Murcendor said the tea would help him."

It's hard to reconcile the monstrous image of Andrei I've held in my heart all these months with the pale, broken-hearted boy huddling on the throne. He doesn't look strong enough to plot the death of a king; he barely looks strong enough to stand.

"I'm not Wilha," I say. "And I'm not a ghost, either. I'm Elara."

"Elara?" He blinks, and his faraway expression disappears. "Arianne was supposed to come for you."

I hold up the sack of worthings. "She did."

"Then why haven't you left the palace?" He pauses, and in the silence the mob's screams push their way into the room. "Are you here to deliver the justice the people are calling for? Are you here to kill me? Lord Murcendor said you wanted me dead."

"Do you believe everything Lord Murcendor tells you?"

"I did," he says sadly. "I did not come to see him for who he truly is until it was too late." He leans back on his throne and continues. "When I was young Lord Murcendor often took me riding. He used to let me pretend he was a great knight, and I was his son, and we were setting off on a grand adventure. I understand now that everything he said and did was a lie, of course, but still, at the time those were my happiest days."

"Your happiest days?" I say. "Really?"

"Of course. Those were the days I had a friend."

I think of all the times Wilha tried to tell me of her loneliness in the palace, and how Lord Murcendor went out of his way to pay attention to her, and understanding suddenly blooms in my heart. If Mistress had shown me the slightest bit of kindness, how eager would I have been to do her bidding or believe her lies?

"It's a wonderful thing to have a friend," I say quietly. "It's almost as wonderful as having a family who loves you."

Andrei doesn't answer. He stares, unseeing, at the statue of Eleanor. He does not appear to have any intention of leaving the room. He seems resigned, as though he doesn't expect to leave the palace alive.

"Where are your guards?" I ask.

"They've fled. They didn't want the unhappy task of protecting me if the people breach the gates."

"Then what's preventing you from leaving the palace? I don't see Lord Murcendor anywhere."

"Where would I go? You hear the people screaming—who would harbor me? Do you know that I have never, not even once, been outside this palace without a line of guards and advisors telling me what to do? I know absolutely nothing about living life outside."

"But as it turns out, I know everything." Gently, I take him by the hand. "Come on, let's find a way out of here."

In some ways, Andrei and I aren't so different. Our father loved neither of us, and in the absence of parents who would protect us, others stepped in to fill their void. Mistress Ogden screamed her abuse, but Lord Murcendor had the most insidious tactic of them all: He cloaked his malice in the form of a friend. And while I learned early on to shut my ears and my heart to the poison blowing my way, Andrei never even suspected he needed to.

We step into the corridor; both of us freeze when we hear voices echoing in the distance.

Andrei turns to me, looking as if he's seen a ghost. "That sounded like Wilha."

CHAPTER 67

WILHA

"*F*or the love of Eleanor," I say, bringing a hand to my mask. "You're going to open the gates, aren't you? You're going to order the soldiers to attack the crowd."

Lord Murcendor's malicious grin is the only confirmation I need.

"No—call it off. The people are merely scared. They're angry—"

"They're traitors. And traitors need to be put down."

"*Put down?* It is our own people that you speak of, not a pack of injured horses."

"But they *are* injured," he says. "Gravely so. They're infected with revolutionary fever. And when one part of the body becomes infected, the only way to save the whole is to cut off the diseased parts."

"No, that is not the way. Tell the guards to *stand down!*"

Lord Murcendor's shoulders stiffen. "You are not in charge, Princess, no matter how much you would like to be. That power rests with your brother, my king."

"Then as your king, I'm ordering you to call them off."

I whirl around. Andrei and Elara stand behind us. Andrei looks pale but determined as he stares at me with wide eyes. "Thank Eleanor you live, Sister," he says.

Elara steps beside me, a joyous look on her face. "I *knew* you had escaped—" She stops short when she catches sight of the courtyard below.

"Your Majesty, you may be king," Lord Murcendor says, "but you are also still a boy. Leave matters that are above your head to your elders."

Andrei shoots a hesitant look at me. "Do you think we could calm the mob?"

"I think it's worth a try. We could appear at the gates and speak to them. We could *try*, Andrei, before we slaughter our own people."

Andrei nods. "Call your men off, Lord Murcendor. That is an order from your king."

"Of course, Your Majesty," Lord Murcendor replies, his dark eyes glimmering. He turns and opens the doors to the balcony. Then, before anyone can react, he turns back. . . .

And plunges his sword into Andrei's chest.

A scream rips from my throat. Elara rushes forward and grabs Andrei. They sink to the ground, blood from Andrei's wound spilling onto Elara's dress.

"Help Andrei!" I shout at Elara as Lord Murcendor slips through the doors and out onto the balcony. I follow him outside in time to hear him yell, "Open the gates!" to the guards waiting below.

I watch, horrified, as men spill into the courtyard. They see the soldiers waiting for them and are only deterred for a moment before running at them with their knives and pick-axes. The soldiers are only too eager to meet them. I draw my own sword and point it at Lord Murcendor.

"Call your men off!"

Lord Murcendor looks at me, a sour expression on his face, and flicks his sword generally in my direction, much in the same way a horse flicks his tail to rid himself of flies. "I believe we had this contest a year ago. You lost. And were it not for your sister, you would be dead."

I raise my sword and step forward. "I am not the same girl I was a year ago."

CHAPTER 68

ELARA

"*S*omebody help!" The only answer is my own echoing voice. "I'll find someone," I say to Andrei, getting ready to rise.

"No one will come. Not for me." Andrei's voice is hoarse and his face is pallid. The opal crown sits in a puddle of blood issuing from his wound. Even if I could somehow manage to find a physician amid the chaos, it wouldn't do any good. I take his hand and twine our fingers together.

"No one ever came for me, either." He nods, and I think he understands what I mean. He struggles to breathe, a rasping, painful sound, and sweat beads his brow.

"Do you know, Elara," he strains to form the words, "you are my sister, and yet I know nothing about you?"

A memory surfaces, and I waste no time telling him of it. "Once, a long time ago, a noblegirl was being mean to me. So I convinced her to stand in a swamp and bathe herself. I told her it would make her skin beautiful."

Andrei's laugh turns into a painful cough. "I once had a tutor who had the biggest jowls you can imagine. I used to make him recite the alphabet as fast as he could, just so I could watch his cheeks bounce."

I smile, imagining the scene, and Andrei says suddenly, "I would have helped you. With the noblegirl, I mean. I would have told her I rather liked girls with beautiful skin." He coughs again, and a crimson river escapes his lips. "I wish I could have known you. I suspect we might have got on nicely." He frowns, and adds, "I wish they would have *let* us know each other."

"I think I'll spend the rest of my life wishing that."

"I think I will, too." He gives a pained smile. "Though I suspect mine will be quite a bit shorter than yours."

An image in my head seems to rise up in front of me. It's so clear I wonder if Andrei sees it, too. Andrei, Wilha, and I are children, huddling in the Eleanor Throne Room. While Wilha looks on, a disapproving look on her face, Andrei and I are scheming, daring each other to get past the soldiers that guard Eleanor's statue. While I demand the guards listen to a story I've made up, Andrei slips behind them and climbs up the statue. His lips curl in victory when he touches one of the Split Opals in Eleanor's uplifted hands.

"I'm sorry," Andrei begins. "I'm sorry for—"

Before he can finish, he heaves a shuddering sigh. His eyes unfocus and his expression stills.

I reach out and close his eyes. With his death comes a dull ache of regret. Of all the things my parents' decision destroyed, chief among them was the ability of my siblings and I to know and love each other.

I look up, and am brought back to the madness swirling beyond the balcony doors. Wilha's sword is flying and flashing, as if she was born with a blade in her hand.

CHAPTER 69

WILHA

Vaguely, I've become aware that the screaming in the courtyard below has quieted down as Lord Murcendor and I fight. He lunges; I spin. I attack; he blocks. I step backward, and his blade slashes air. Moonlight dances on steel as our swords clash again and again. My lungs are burning; my arms are aching, and my breath comes in gasps. He lashes out—this time I am not fast enough—and his blade nicks the edge of my sleeve.

My skills have grown, but my strength still does not match his. I will tire before him, and when I do, I shall have to surrender. He sees this, too, and he smiles.

"I know you, Wilhamina Andewyn, even behind that mask," he says, stepping backward and pausing as if to give me a break. "Better than anyone else in this world, I know you."

You knew who I was. You do not know who I am now. I catch myself before the retort escapes my lips. I cannot beat him by strength alone.

But perhaps I can trick him.

"I suppose you do." I point my sword downward, just as Marko once taught me to do. "I have been dreaming again."

"You have?"

I nod and keep my eyes on his. I read his expression as his eyes slide to my blade, the nearly imperceptible twist of his lips. He believes I am giving up.

"What do you dream of this time?" At odds with his concerned tone of voice is the determined way he grips his sword and slightly shifts position.

"I dream—" He lunges forward to attack. Quickly, I bring my sword up and deliver a cut first to his arm, then to his thigh. He staggers backward and drops to the ground, cradling his injured arm. I kick his sword out of reach and lean over him. "I dream of a Galandria without you in it," I finish.

He stares back at me with dulled eyes, blood gushing from his wounds. It occurs to me that with one more slash, I could end everything.

But death is too easy. Let the people of the kingdom judge him.

That is, if come tomorrow morning, there still *is* a kingdom.

I glance back inside the palace. Elara cradles Andrei. Her eyes meet mine, and she shakes her head sadly.

The moon hangs like a scythe over the courtyard. Sculpted gardens have been hacked to shreds. One water fountain has been reduced to rubble. Peasants and soldiers alike lie on the ground, unmoving. Blood runs like a river from the steps of the palace, down to the golden gates. I can *feel* the hatred in the air, writhing and strong—strong enough to tear the palace down, stone by stone; strong enough to undo centuries of peace in one night.

My presence has been noted. The fighting has momentarily stopped; townspeople and soldiers stare up at me. I wonder at what they see. A girl wearing a deformed mask and a damp and dirty dress, wielding a sword dripping with blood. They wait silently for me, the girl who has never been able to find the right words, to speak truth and reason to the insanity that has descended over the city.

"Citizens of Galandria . . ." My voice is small, a single drop, in an entire ocean of rage. "I swear to you by the blood of my ancestors, the rumors are untrue. Allegria is in no danger of being attacked tonight by outside forces. Yet look at what we've done to our own brothers and sisters. How many of us are injured? How many of us have already died? My brother, your own king, is dead. How many more of us shall join him tonight? This city was built over a period of three hundred years. By my family. By your family. Will we tear it down in one night? Will we give in to our anger, but when the dawn comes, ask ourselves what madness descended over us that we should do such a thing?"

"You have been hungry, and my family has cared not. You have suffered, and we have turned our backs on you. But I promise you, that ends tonight. To the palace guards below holding the line: I command you as an Andewyn—as an heir to the centuries of wealth you guard, and as a descendant of

Eleanor the Great herself—open up the palace storehouses! Release the flour and grain inside. Let it flow until everyone has had their fill. To the rest of you I swear: A new day is dawning. A new time for us all is coming."

I do not know if I sound like a queen, or like a shrieking, foolish girl. I only know that someone has to stem the tide. Someone has to speak before we tear ourselves apart.

"I promise you also this: The excesses of the palace will stop. It will stop, and we will work with you to forge a brighter version of ourselves and our kingdom."

Before me, the courtyard lies silent.

Yet behind me, a sudden scream echoes.

CHAPTER 70

ELARA

Wilha speaks to the crowd, and from the silence below it seems everyone is listening. Yet there is one who is not enraptured by her words. Behind her, Lord Murcendor—deranged fool that he is—slowly inches along the ground, intent on reaching his sword. It's no great mystery what he plans to do with it, and my blood begins to boil. Doesn't he realize I'm *right here*, holding the king he's just murdered?

Lord Murcendor turns his head; his eyes meet mine. And in this instant I see it: This is the culmination of all our parents' fears. I could allow Wilha to take the blade. I could pick up the opal crown over Andrei and Wilha's fallen bodies, claim it for myself, and do what neither of them ever could: order Lord Murcendor's dismissal and death. And woe to any advisor or lord who dares stand in *my* way.

I could be queen. Unrivaled. Undisputed.

Or, I could surprise them all. Anyone who ever feared I would be Wilha's undoing. Anyone who ever thought I would harm her. I could become the person I have always wanted to be.

Lord Murcendor continues on, slithering like the serpent he truly is. He hauls himself to his feet, preparing to raise his blade. Quickly, I move away from Andrei's body and stand up.

I don't want a blood-soaked crown.

I want my sister.

I sprint through the doors and fling myself before Wilha. Lord Murcendor's sword rips into my shoulder, steel slicing flesh, and I sink to the ground, vaguely aware that I'm screaming. Uttering a cry of rage, Wilha knocks Lord Murcendor's sword away and delivers one cut after another to his good arm, forcing him backward, until he trips and falls over the balcony railing. Screams issue from the people below, followed quickly by a bone-shattering *thud*.

Silence. And then: "He's dead! Lord Murcendor is dead!"

My shoulder is a fire of agony. Wilha appears above me. She rips off her burnt mask, and she's crying underneath.

"You are a wonder," I say, though my voice sounds slurred and strange. "I wish I could be more like you."

"Don't talk," she says, sobbing. "Save your strength." She tears a strip of fabric from my dress and begins wrapping it around my wound.

I stare up at the sky. My vision is blurring, the stars are bleeding, and my breath frosts the night. The last thing I hear before the pain carries me away is a quavering, hesitant voice from below rising like a plea in the night, "*The king is dead . . . long live the queens?*"

PART FOUR

"Given her humble origins, few could have imagined the heights she would one day ascend. Yet centuries later, nearly all acknowledge she was one of the greatest rulers we have ever known. The world now patiently waits for the day when the next Eleanor will arise."

ELEANOR OF ANDEWYN HOUSE:
GALANDRIA'S GREATEST QUEEN

CHAPTER 71

ELARA

Wilha and I step forward. Behind us, our councillors stand in a line on the steps of the Opal Palace. The golden gates are opened. Palace guards welcome the Kyrenican carriages waiting beyond. My eyes meet Lord Royce's briefly and he nods. I return the gesture and arrange my features into a look of pleasant expectation, careful not to show the anxiety I feel twisting my gut. We're silent as we wait; the only sound is the pounding of hammers and the scrape and slap of mortar as our masons and statue sculptors continue repairing the damage done to the palace gardens last autumn.

Despite the early spring sunlight, the day is brisk. My shoulder aches from the chill—the only lasting damage I've suffered from the wound Lord Murcendor inflicted.

When the guards finally wave the Kyrenicans forward, Wilha turns to me. "When the carriages come to a halt, I think we should kneel."

"Absolutely not," I say through my pasted-on smile. "I refuse to kneel before Stefan." I glance quickly at Lord Royce, who looks at Wilha and me warily. No doubt our frequent disagreements are a disappointment to him.

Wilha's own smile becomes pained. "Ezebo didn't have to return the masks before we negotiate a new treaty; he would have been well within his rights to keep them. So if you could put aside your arrogance, a little gratitude could go a long way."

But it's not arrogance that stiffens my spine, even as our councillors, following Wilha's lead, all sink to their knees. It's something else altogether. With Ezebo unable to travel, Stefan was tasked with conducting new negotiations between Galandria and Kyrenica. As we have planned for the Kyrenicans' visit, Stefan's letters over the last several months have been addressed to both Wilha and myself. They have given no insight into his emotions. And he has made no mention of the letter I gave to Arianne, leaving me to question whether she ever sent it.

Something I cannot ask Arianne herself. Apparently, after deciding the darkness of the tunnels did not suit her, Arianne exited into Eleanor Square—right into the heart of a mob that recognized her as a palace official. Unfortunately, she received the full brunt of their anger.

But even if Stefan never received the letter, why the silence all these months? What happened to his declaration of forgiveness?

I wish I had not been so impulsive in enclosing my mother's letter with my own. I can only assume it, too, is lost. The absence of the letter has left me with no choice these past six months but to jointly rule with Wilha. My sister and I rarely see eye to eye, and oftentimes our councillors are more disposed to agree with Wilha's position. So many times while we have debated in the Guardian's Chambers I have wanted to scream, "I am the firstborn; you shall listen to what I say!"

But without the letter, I have no proof to back up my claim.

I give myself a small shake to clear my head. I bend my knees and kneel next to Wilha, just as the carriages come to a halt at the stone steps. I won't give our councillors yet another reason to favor my sister over me.

It's not Stefan who steps first from the Strassburgs' carriage. It's Ruby—she's grown several inches since I last saw her—and she comes bounding up the stone steps. She briefly stops at the sight of Wilha and me, before launching herself into my arms.

"I knew I would see you again!" she exclaims into my neck. I wrap my arms around her and hug her tightly. "I've missed you so much!" she continues. "We have so much to catch up on, Wil, I mean, Elar"—she pulls away to look up at me—"What should I call you?"

"Everyone calls me Elara." *At least for now*, I want to add, but don't.

Stefan emerges from the carriage and silently walks up the steps. His face is haggard and purple circles hang under his eyes. Gone is the playful prince I once knew in Kyrenica. Stefan now seems older, more careworn.

"Your Highness," he says, helping me to my feet. "I am most grateful to see you again."

I pause, unsure how to respond, but he is already holding out his hand to Wilha.

"He was so mad at you!" Ruby whispers to me as Stefan and Wilha exchange greetings.

"Is he mad now?" I whisper back.

"I don't know, he refuses to talk about you." Her lip puffs out. "He's not very fun to travel with."

"Your masks are in the carriages," Stefan says. "I believe your people will find them all accounted for."

Wilha murmurs her gratitude and the two of them turn and stroll into the palace. Our councillors and Stefan's men hurry behind after them, leaving Ruby and me alone. I hesitate, knowing I will be expected inside, but loathe to follow after Wilha and Stefan like I'm their servant.

"Will you give me a tour of the gardens, Wil—Elara?" Ruby asks.

"I'd love to," I say, grateful to remain outdoors.

We set off and wind our way through lavender-smelling paths that bloom with spring flowers. Ruby laughs when I point out the groundskeepers's shed and tell her how I once escaped out of the palace from a nearby underground tunnel.

We end up settling at a bench in front of a recently repaired water fountain and she tells me of the Strassburgs. Ezebo's weakened condition seems to be the new normal, and everyone is making the best of it. "Grandmother is just as nasty as ever," Ruby says. "But every time she opens her mouth, I just remember to—"

"Ruby!" comes Stefan's impatient voice, and the two of us look up. "I have been looking all over for you. I'd like you to go wash and rest up before dinner."

"But—"

"*Now*, Ruby. I need to speak to Elara alone."

"Oh, Stefan, you always know how to ruin a good time." She stands and curtsies. "See you later, Elara."

"I was just showing Ruby around," I say after she's gone. "I wasn't—"

"I don't fault you for loving my sister. She has missed you terribly, and insisted on accompanying me." He pauses and glances at my gown. "Royalty seems to suit you."

From the tone of his voice, it's impossible to tell if that's a dig or a compliment.

"It's my birthright," I say carefully.

"I suppose it is." He removes a parchment from his cloak and holds it up as though I should recognize it.

My breath catches when I do. It's the letter I wrote him.

Stefan seems in no rush to speak; he just continues to look at me. Behind us, the water fountain plays a musical, tinkling tune, and slowly my anticipation turns to annoyance.

"Stefan," I say when I've had my fill of his silence, "if you've got something to say, spit it out."

"Spit it out?" he repeats, color rising in his cheeks. "You don't think I deserve at least a small amount of your short supply of patience?"

"I sent you that letter months ago. I bared my heart and told you my deepest secret. And in response, you did nothing. So if you've got something to say, *now* would be a good time."

"And your timeline is the only one that matters, is that it? After all it was you who—" He stops. Takes a breath. "Tell me one thing. Did you mean what you wrote? Or were they merely the utterings of a woman condemned to die, who didn't think she'd ever be responsible for her words?" His voice softens when I hesitate. "I need to know, Elara. I need to know how you really feel. I need to hear you say it."

In his eyes I see a flash of old pain. I know what words he wants. Only three small ones. But I've never actually said them. Not together; not in that order. Not even once.

Stefan mistakes my silence, and turns to go. "That's what I thought."

My throat has turned to stone. Why it feels as though it costs me everything to voice a truth I've known for some time—a truth I've already admitted to once before—I don't completely understand. I think because in handing him my heart, it feels as though I'm willingly handing him a weapon, and trusting that he won't use it against me.

But I feel the girl I once was waking up again. I imagine her clawing her way out of the box I stuffed her in, screaming and yelling—demanding her own right to be happy. I hear her voice telling me not to be a fool. And finally, my lips become unstuck.

"Stefan—wait!"

He stops and turns around. His eyes are dead—so much like on that horrible day in the Kyrenican Castle. "What?"

I move toward him and close the distance. "I meant every word I wrote . . . I love you."

"You love me?" His features are carefully blank, as though he won't let himself believe. "These are the true feelings of your heart—and not some ploy to obtain more favorable terms in our negotiations?"

I flinch at his bluntness, but I know I deserve this.

"I don't care about the negotiations," I say, which is truer than it should be. "I care about you. I promised myself I'd never say it to you until I knew I meant it. I love you. Even"—a shadow passes over my heart—"even if you no longer return my love."

He pauses, before slowly breaking into a smile. "My love for you was sealed a long time ago. You are a puzzle to me, unlike any girl I have ever met."

"Really?" I say. "After everything I've done?"

"Yes, I love you. Really, and truly." Stefan cups my elbow and draws me close. "And I don't believe I have ever had the pleasure of kissing you without that wretched mask on your face." He feathers kisses along my cheeks until his lips land on mine.

As we kiss, a new emotion, golden and effervescent, bubbles up and floods me from the inside out.

I believe it might be joy.

"What now?" I say, a little breathless after we pull apart.

Stefan's smile vanishes and a grim look settles over his face. "Now we have many decisions to make, including . . . what to do with *this*." He removes another parchment from his cloak. My mother's letter.

I sit down heavily on the bench. "I have no idea what to do about that."

"Have you traveled much in the last few months?" he asks, joining me on the bench.

"No. We wanted to wait until it was warmer to gauge the mood of the kingdom."

"I have just journeyed through many of your northern villages and I can tell you exactly the mood of the kingdom: They're wondering."

"Wondering? Wondering what?"

Stefan eyes me warily. "How long it will be before you and Wilhamina go to war against each other."

I look away. "I think our councillors are wondering the same thing. They are in no rush to plan a joint coronation ceremony for Wilha and me. They never say it directly, but I'm certain none of them are happy with the prospect of two queens."

Stefan hands me the letter. "This secret has the power to change all our worlds. What do you plan to do?"

I rub my fingers against the parchment and try to conjure the image of my mother. When she wrote this, did she realize she was handing me the proof I would one day need to put aside my sister? *The firstborn shall rule.* . . . It has always been so. I open the letter and reread her words:

> *How I wish you could have seen me cry, still weak, still bleeding, the moment he told me of the decision he and the four Guardians reached. A mask for the first-born; an anonymous home for the second.*
>
> *It was, they said, the best they could do for the both of you. Your father insisted we not name our second daughter. "If she doesn't have a name, she cannot be hunted," he said. And although I did not then, and still do not agree with him, I went along with it.*

"I don't think I'll ever understand it," I say to Stefan when I finish reading. "How my father could have believed that sending me away was the best option, or how my mother could have silently stood by and let them take me."

"I don't understand it, either," Stefan says. "It seems unimaginably cruel."

"I guess sometimes, despite your best efforts, you *don't* receive the answers you seek." I fold up the letter and tuck it away. "Sometimes, I guess you just have to learn to live with the questions."

"But since you can never know for sure, you can *choose*

what to believe, Elara. You can choose to take your mother's words at face value, and believe that both she and your father were doing the best they could."

Stefan places his arm around me and I lean into him. Across the courtyard, I see the newly finished statues of Astrid and Fennrick. Wilha had them commissioned shortly after we assumed power. I've stood often before them in the last few weeks, wondering if their likeness could bring me comfort, as it seems to do for Wilha. But all I see when I look at them is dead, silent stone, and anger flares in my chest now.

"I know I can choose that—but if *I'd* had twin daughters, I never would have given one of them up. I would have valued the people in my life more than the power of a crown. I would have covered the cradle with my own body and dared them to cross me. I would have shouted the existence of my daughter until the entire kingdom heard me. Damn the crown; I would have *fought* for my family. I would have—"

I stop suddenly, visions of golden cradles and jewel-encrusted crowns vanishing in an instant. After all this time, I know how to finally cut the tie that has always bound my sister and me, but has never allowed us to truly become family.

CHAPTER 72

WILHA

The candles in my father's study burn low. The dinner with the Kyrenicans concluded hours ago, and I am sure everyone else has retired for the evening. Yet here I am stooping over my father's desk—for I cannot yet bear to think of it as anyone else's—working my way through a pile of official documents.

I rub my eyes, sign another document, and move it out of the way. How many times did my father sit in this same room, in this same chair, agonizing over the decisions facing him? Strange that now, over a year after his death, I feel a kinship with a man I was always so distant from while he lived.

My eyes fall on the pile of velvet boxes stacked near the desk. I pick one up and open it. The mask is painted white and filigreed with silver; milky lavender opals flower around the cheeks. Now that I am no longer condemned to wear the masks, I can appreciate their beauty—or, more accurately, their worth. I would love to sell many of them and give the proceeds to the royal treasury, but of course I will need to speak to Elara first. That is, if she can tear herself away from Stefan long enough to hear me out.

Tonight at the feast, Elara and Stefan spent the night sitting next to each other holding a private—and clearly intense—conversation that made the rest of the guests feel obviously uncomfortable. I think Elara was genuinely unaware of the effect her behavior was having upon the room. Far from appearing a gracious queen, ready to hear the concerns of the Kyrenicans and her own advisors, she came off as interested in speaking only to the handsome prince at her side.

I lean back in my father's chair. How do you tell your sister she's not qualified to rule? Particularly when it's because of our own parents' actions that Elara is so unacquainted with Galandrian court etiquette?

I blow out the candles and leave my father's study. The work will still be here in the morning.

I step into the Eleanor Throne Room; it's empty of all the nobles who stood queuing before Elara and me earlier this morning. Next to the gilded throne sits another throne, a wooden one that was hastily constructed soon after Elara and I assumed our place as queens. "*How ironic*," Elara had whispered when she saw the two sitting side by side. She seems to take a curious pleasure sitting in the wooden throne, and will not let us replace it with a more ornate one.

Elara sits there now, looking silently at the statue of Eleanor the Great. The Split Opals in Eleanor's stone hands glimmer in the flickering candlelight. Palace guards surround the statue, keeping watch, as always.

"Are you having trouble sleeping again?" I ask, sitting down in the golden throne next to her.

"Yes," she replies, not looking at me. "Are you working late again?"

"Not anymore."

"How do you think our kingdom's history—our family's history—would be different if Eleanor hadn't stumbled on her coronation day?" she asks.

"I don't know. Aislinn may still have betrayed Rowan. We may still have been separated. Who can say what would have been different? Maybe nothing."

"Or maybe everything."

I don't believe I've ever seen Elara so reflective and still. So often these days my sister seems like a complicated force of barely contained energy. I look at the statue, enjoying this moment of silence with her. Yet it feels like that one moment of true peace, just before the storm breaks.

"What's troubling you?" I ask her finally.

"While we both sit on these thrones, the kingdom will hold its breath, waiting for the day when we decide we can no longer rule together."

"I know," I admit. "I can feel it. I can *feel* them waiting."

"When I was younger," Elara says, still staring at the statue, "all I ever wanted was to find my name and my family." She turns to the guards standing watch and says, "Leave us, please." After they've gone she slides a letter from her pocket and offers it to me. "This is from our mother. . . . I'm so sorry, Wilha."

"Our mother?" Hastily, I open the letter. Reading my mother's words, hearing her voice through them, is like drinking from a cup of cool water, when I didn't realize I was parched. . . .

Until I reach the end, and the letter falls from my hand.

Did I read that correctly?

"You did," Elara says, and I realize I must have spoken the words aloud.

"Then we are sitting on the wrong thrones," I say. "We should switch." How many more lies have our parents told? How can they reach out, even from the grave, and haunt us still? "It's me," I murmur. "*I* am the one with no name."

"In Tulan there was once a woman whose husband wanted her to name their daughter Eleanor," Elara says. "But she refused. She said it was too much to live up to."

"It's a powerful name," I say, feeling as though I might be sick. I need time. I need to excuse myself, but I find I cannot move.

"But Eleanor wasn't always Eleanor. Once she was just a small village girl, the daughter of a family of miners. The name became great, because *she* became great. The name Elara was given to me in hatred, and for years I wanted nothing more than to shed it and claim another, one I thought would be a truer representation of who I am. But I wonder now if that isn't too much to ask of one small word." Elara turns, and finally she looks at me. "I've thought long and hard about this,

Wilha, and I no longer think it matters what name you carry. What really matters is what you do with it."

Her expression is fierce as she picks up the letter. Where did she find it? How long has she known?

"Why are you telling me all this?" I ask. "Are you saying you want me to claim another name?"

"What I want," she says, "is to find a way to keep the two of us from tearing this kingdom apart."

I recognize her words. They were once my own. "What do you mean?" I say.

Elara beckons me closer. And with Eleanor's statue watching over us, my sister whispers of new beginnings.

CHAPTER 73

THE QUEEN OF GALANDRIA

The opal crown sits heavy upon my head. I reach up to straighten it, and catch my sister looking at me. She smiles, and I offer her mine in return. Today we are dressed identically in gowns of lavender and powder blue, the colors of the Andewyn family crest. Our hair is tied back in ribbons. The only difference in our appearance is that I wear the crown, while she does not.

My sister and I, along with my new advisors, have all gathered here today for the unveiling in the Queen's Garden. The sheet falls from the statue and my sister and I step forward to make sure they have the inscription right. We smile when we see they did: *Wilhamina Andewyn, Queen of Galandria.* In the statue's hand she holds a mask, in remembrance of the years I covered my face. I suppose now if I come to the Queen's Garden looking for wisdom, it shall be my own face I look to.

Somewhere in a vault locked deep within the Opal Palace is my mother's letter. Elara wanted to burn it, but I could not bring myself to agree. The letter reminds me that even the smallest action, borne out of grief or madness, has the power to affect countless lives. I am certain it is a reminder I will need often in the years to come.

Elara's insistence that she no longer wished to rule came as a welcome surprise to our advisors. I do not believe I have ever seen them smile so widely as they did on the day she formally signed away any claims upon the Galandrian throne, a ceremony that paved the way for her betrothal to Stefan.

Next to my new statue is an altar, upon which sits the two Split Opals. Elara and I raise our hammers high above our heads and bring them down on the stones. Amid colorful shards, the two opals have been reduced to a pile of smaller—albeit still very valuable—jewels.

My sister and I begin handing a single small opal to each man who approaches and bows before me. Gone is the ten-member Guardian Council. In its place, I have appointed a General Assembly composed of a representative from each village in Galandria. The assembly shall instruct me and have far more power than the Guardian Council ever did.

No doubt one of their first orders of business will be to dangle princes from various kingdoms before me, in an effort to secure a betrothal that benefits Galandria. I glance over at Patric and smile. Little do they know, the question of my marriage has already been decided. And while I intend to serve my kingdom to my last dying breath, I will reserve for myself this one thing: The right to marry someone who has loved me, whether I am a masked curiosity, or a coronated queen.

Lord Royce—Allegria's representative—is the only member of the General Assembly who isn't smiling. He scrutinizes the small opal I hand him. His jewel is equal in size to the others; I have no doubt he wishes it was quite a bit larger.

Already there are those who say I am a weak queen to allow more power to pass to the people. *I* say it takes strength to recognize that change is coming, and yet even more strength to welcome it—to bridge the gap between who we are now as a kingdom, to whoever we shall become in the future. Eleanor Andewyn forged this kingdom three hundred years ago. But three hundred years from now, will a monarchy even exist in Galandria? Long after I am dead, how will people read of me? Will I be considered a great leader, like Eleanor Andewyn? Or a weak one, like my very own father?

History will be my judge.

I turn about the garden, meeting each of the statues' gazes without flinching and without shame. I no longer fear the eyes of my ancestors. For I am one of them. And with the help of the General Assembly, I will rule this kingdom with everything I am.

Three Years Later . . .

CHAPTER 74

ELARA STRASSBURG,
PRINCESS OF KYRENICA

I sleep well most nights, but tonight the pain in my back is too much to bear. I throw back my covers, heave myself from the bed, and walk to the place that has always been my refuge in the castle.

Well, these days I don't walk so much as I waddle.

I find Stefan in the kitchen lingering in front of the fire. Sleep still does not come easy for him, particularly now that the day-to-day tasks of running the kingdom fall solely on his shoulders.

"How is our little one?" he asks, pressing a hand to my stomach.

As if in answer, the child growing within me stirs and bumps against Stefan's palm. Normally the action brings a delighted smile to my husband's face, but tonight he merely turns back to the fire.

"What did the physician say?"

"He said we should prepare ourselves."

I wrap my arms around him and hug him silently. This is the news we've been dreading for months.

"Was your father lucid at all during the examination?" I say once I've settled next to Stefan.

"He was." His lips twist into a weak smile. "He said the physician was a fool, and that the only thing *he* was preparing for was the large mug of ale he planned to drink after his first grandchild was born." His face falls and he sighs. "But he also gave instructions for his burial—and for our coronation."

With a crown comes a price, and one day soon we will have to pay it. Stefan and I keep hoping for the daily miracles we so often take for granted. That Ezebo will continue to draw breath. That the peace in the region continues to hold. That there are many good days still to come. But it seems our time is running short.

I cup my hands over my swollen belly. My stomach is large and round; so much more so than any other of the ladies whom I've seen give birth, including Wilha. Yet in my womb I carry the future king or queen of Kyrenica, and in my frequent letters to Wilha I write the fears I dare not speak of to anyone save Stefan:

What if?

What if history repeats itself?

Wilha's own fears were laid to rest earlier this year when she gave birth to a single son whom she and Patric named Andrei. Stefan and I have already agreed that if twins are born we will announce the birth of both of our children. Immediately, and joyously.

And we will not be alone. In the years since she was crowned, my sister has become a wise queen. Galandria is slowly but surely recovering, driven by the strength of Wilha's dogged devotion to her kingdom. Already the people call her Wilhamina the Warrior.

Wilha has assured me that if my fears are proved true, she will join me in proclaiming the existence—the blessing— of two children. My sister and I will shout it from the depths of the Lonesome Sea, to the tallest peaks of the Opal Mountains.

And together, *we* will be heard.

ACKNOWLEDGMENTS

This book was written in the midst of an extremely busy season in my life, and I wouldn't have been able to do it without the love and support of my husband. Ryan, thank you for the camping trips you took the kids on so I could catch up on my word counts. Thank you for the meals you cooked, the nights you listened, and the support you always give. You are my biggest fan, my own personal knight in shining armor and prince charming, all rolled into one, and I know I am so lucky to have you.

To my friends and family who unceasingly support me, thank you for understanding when I have to hole up in my writer's cave sometimes. To Kerry Sparks, my agent, this book never would have been written if you hadn't believed in me and told me to just go for it and start writing Elara and Wilha's story. If I was a sculptor, I'd craft my own statue of you to commemorate your awesomeness!

To Marlo Scrimizzi, Teresa Bonaddio, Valerie Howlett, and the rest of the team at Running Press Teens, thank you for always taking such great care of me and my books.

To Elizabeth Thompson, Xochi Dixon, Chris Pedersen, and the rest of the lovely gang at Inspire Christian Writers, thank you for always being so quick to offer a prayer, a word of encouragement, or a meal when it's needed. I am thankful for you all.

To my two sons, Noah and Thomas: Thank you for waiting patiently so many nights and weekends while I finished my book. We made it!

Finally, thank you God, for that long ago day at the beach, when I told you I wanted a story to tell. I hope I have done this one justice.